THE LAST TIME
I SAW HER

Visit us at www.boldstrokesbooks.com

By the Author

Awake Unto Me

Forsaking All Others

A Spark of Heavenly Fire

Warm November

Two Souls

Taking Sides

The Last Time I Saw Her

THE LAST TIME I SAW HER

by

Kathleen Knowles

2018

THE LAST TIME I SAW HER

ISBN 13: 978-1-63555-067-2

This Trade Paperback Original Is Published By
Bold Strokes Books, Inc.
P.O. Box 249
Valley Falls, NY 12185

First Edition: June 2018

CREDITS
EDITOR: SHELLEY THRASHER
PRODUCTION DESIGN: SUSAN RAMUNDO
COVER DESIGN BY TAMMY SEIDICK

Acknowledgments

This story is partly autobiographical. I was a Girl Scout and I went to camp. I also volunteered at several women's music festivals.

I wish I could say I had the experience of this narrator but I didn't. Call this story novelistic wish fulfillment. I get to rewrite my own history.

Facebook, for all its flaws, is a powerful tool for connecting people. Through its magic, I found an old friend whom I hadn't seen or heard from for more than forty years: Nancy Dubois. Nancy not only supplied me with some priceless photographs and memories from our time at camp but also gave me a crucial anecdote from her own life. "Feel free to use it," she said. I'm so grateful we were able to communicate again. So a big thank you to Nancy.

As usual, my wife and sister were there for me. And this time, Jeanette's opinion on some aspects of my writing which correlated exactly with the ideas of my esteemed editor, Shelley Thrasher, caused me to rethink a lot of my work and change it for the better.

Dedication

To Jeanette, my honest and loving wife

CHAPTER ONE

February 1987

It wasn't long after Lois left before I got a call from Arden Weinberg. Lois had decamped with our tabby cat Whiskers, all the pictures we'd bought together, ditto the CDs, ditto the books, most of the dishes, and for some reason, all the light bulbs. I guess she was feeling extra vindictive. Since I'm often in the dark about what my girls are thinking or feeling, I suppose I wasn't surprised that she wanted me to be, literally, in the dark.

I've got no luck when it comes to women. One of my girlfriends once told me I excel at being a girlfriend for the first month, but after that I fall apart. As usual, though, I hang on to these relationships well after their expiration dates. In my defense, I do hate to give up; also, I don't do that serial-monogamy-overlap thing. I most definitely end the prior relationship before I begin the next, or rather they're ended for me. I've had lots of breakups, but at least they're clean. I'm not mean or cruel. I guess women think I'm just not there emotionally. My exes and I settle into friendships that are more like semi-distant acquaintanceships.

Anyway, back to Arden Weinberg. She isn't an old girlfriend but the producer of the Pacific Coast Women's Music and Cultural Festival. Arden lives in SoCal in that self-absorbed little pocket of gay known as West Hollywood. I'm from San Francisco, and we and Los Angeles have been rivals for years. We at least can agree to hold our gay-day parades on different weekends, but that's about it. Arden had been around Hollywood itself for years. She never made it to the big time since she wouldn't compromise to the required extent. "Once a dyke, always a dyke," she liked to say. Somewhere along the way she'd decided to channel her energies into the community by producing shows, fund-raisers, and in the early eighties, a music festival for the West Coast lesbians. There was Michigan, and there were East Coast and National Women's music festivals, but nothing past the Rocky Mountains. Arden saw the lack and decided to fill it. Some people think she's erratic and egotistical. She may be, but she sure knows what she's doing. She also knows a lot of performers, and they'll show up if she asks. Unlike most lesbian endeavors, her music festivals made money. That fact alone means a lot will be forgiven.

I had started volunteering to work at the PCWMCF around '82. By 1986, I was the security coordinator and actually got paid the princess-like sum of three hundred dollars. I was never going to get rich helping my community, but that didn't matter to me.

It may seem weird that someone who wasn't a cop would fulfill that type of role, but it's really not. Lesbians and gay men have no love for cops. We have a fraught history with law enforcement. It wasn't until the early eighties that the San Francisco gay parade even began to work with the SFPD. Community volunteers do the crowd control for big events, and that's how I started. I found I had a knack for it. I volunteered at every gay parade, street festival, and basically any kind of event.

That's how I ended up at the women's music festival. The first festival security coordinator was actually an ex Los Angeles police officer, and she designed the security program. In 1986, she decided she'd finally had had enough fun, and I took over. Arden liked me, a prerequisite for being given a coordinator slot. I didn't mind her occasional tantrums and abrupt changes of direction.

Arden said she was putting together a women's music festival for the southern states and asked if I would be interested in being security coordinator. Well, that was a no-brainer. At this point, being unencumbered by a lover was a blessing. One of the many subjects of discussion with my girlfriends was my love for spending ten days to two weeks away in the woods every year with a bunch of naked lesbians. If the given girlfriend was unable or unwilling to go along with me, I went on my own, leaving her at home to fret. But honestly, I never cheated on my girlfriends. I can't help it if women like to flirt with me. Probably a lot of them would want more, but I'm honorable. I tried to convince my girlfriends that I was faithful. Their anger probably had a lot to do with other things, and the music-festival fights were just distractions.

I told Arden I was absolutely a "yes," I would be happy to do it, and she sent me a contract.

I'm lucky to have the job I have. My managers are fairly laid-back, even though the work can be a little stressful. I'm a clinical research associate. I spend time on the phone coordinating with research sites on their patients and their schedules and their records. My company was working on a cancer treatment that was in Phase II clinical testing. Occasionally, I had to travel to visit one of our test sites, but not often. The new innovation that allowed us to correspond electronically, therefore called email, was a real help. The nurses who administered the experimental treatment at the test sites could copy and send their records electronically, which was much better than faxing. I asked for and got the days off for the music festival. It also helped that I asked far enough ahead of time.

On the twentieth of April, I received a letter from Arden with several pages of instructions, including the time frame to schedule my flight to Atlanta. She had recruited as many of her veteran volunteers as possible. We came from all over the West: Seattle, Los Angeles, Portland, and many places in between. A few people were from the Bay Area, but no one but me had signed up for the Dixie gig.

The festival site was at a church camp about two and a half hours north of Atlanta. I wondered if the church people who owned the camp knew the nature of the event they'd agreed to rent their space for. I doubted it, and even if some might object, money often trumps principle. The festival staff would arrive between ten days and two weeks prior to the opening of the festival, which would last four days, ending on Memorial Day A few people would stick around to break down and clean up. Arden had a core staff she depended on, and all of us were experienced at the work we'd be performing.

I scanned the list of staff and noted that a lot of the usual suspects would be showing up for parking, kitchen, box office, publicity, and to work as stage managers and carpenters. It would be really good to see them all. My second in command was Marty Anderson, a terrific woman from Colorado, and I knew a couple of other women who'd worked the Pacific festival. The kitchen honcho was Valencia Delgado, which made me smile. I loved and admired Valencia. I thought maybe this time we'd be able to consummate our two-years-long flirtation. I was finally between girlfriends, and if I could pry her away from her many admirers, I might have a shot. Besides Marty, I'd have to cull the rest of my security staff from volunteer festival-goers, always a hit-or-miss proposition. They could turn out to be great, indifferent, or terrible.

I scanned the list of staff, and when I got to medical personnel, I zeroed in on one name, Alison Bickford, and my hands started to shake.

Years before, when I was a Girl Scout camp counselor, I'd known an Alison. This was a different last name though. It seemed highly unlikely it would be the same person. Alison Livingstone had probably gotten married. That would be her likely fate, as she was surely very conventional. I suppose that was the reason, or one of them, why our connection ended so badly. I wracked my brain trying to remember where my Alison lived. She'd been from West Virginia but then had moved. The state of residence for this Alison Bickford was Georgia. I couldn't remember where I'd heard Alison Livingstone had moved or even who had told me. I hadn't had any contact with Alison after camp was over almost fifteen years earlier

I never read or heard the name Alison without enduring a painful stab of regret, and this time was no different. The name Alison called up images of my long-ago crush, from that last summer we were together, her as a twelve-year-old when we first met, and from all the years in between. She was an all-American blond, blue-eyed, clean-cut beauty with a gorgeous singing voice. It was her voice that first got me, even before her looks did, before I had any clue what it was about Alison I was so attracted to.

I didn't know for a long time what I was feeling about Alison. I had no frame of reference for it, nothing to call it. We were friends, really, really good friends in the manner of young girls, especially when they're at camp. I only found out later what was going on with me. But when I found out, I didn't know how to handle it, and I lost Alison

I traced my finger over the name, thinking about "my" Alison. My lovely Alison, who I'd last seen in 1972, and it hadn't been a happy occasion. My Alison, who I never thought to see again, and this couldn't possibly be the same girl because that would just be too coincidental, too far into the realm of fantasy. I tried to clear my head and talk myself back into the present.

I decided to call Marty, since there wasn't much of a time difference between San Francisco and Denver.

"Hey. It's Lane. How the hell are ya?"

"Oh my gosh, Lane, so good to hear from you. I think I know what you're calling about."

"I imagine you do, and you got the same instructions I got."

"Yep, you bet. You want me to plan on working nights, as usual?" Marty was a night owl, so she always coordinated the night Security. It was a blessing because I'm the opposite: I'm the morning person who falls asleep around nine p.m., which was another thing my exes often complained about. I wanted sex in the morning, and they didn't, except maybe one who did once in a while.

With Marty on board, I could take charge during the day and evening and know that the night shift would be covered.

"You got any friends who might want to trade a trip to the music festival for some volunteer time? They'll have to fly to Georgia though."

"The South? Geez. I doubt it. Aren't they like all homophobic rednecks?"

"Well, I don't know, but the festival is lesbians, remember?" Are we always going to stereotype people we don't even know? It was depressing to consider that possibility.

"I suppose so, but I don't know anyone. I guess we'll have to recruit locally. I will be bringing along my lover, Tina." This was news. Marty wasn't much for relationships.

"Whoa. Lover? Tell me."

She described where and how they met. If they were going to be like most lesbians who are coupled and attached at the hip, I was glad to hear Marty had induced her to volunteer.

"Well, this festival can't be that much different than the PC." We usually abbreviated the unwieldy name.

"I guess you're right. Dykes are dykes, no matter what part of the country they come from"

We chatted a few more minutes, then said good-bye, see you in a few months, etc.

I hung up wondering if I should have told Marty my speculations about Alison Bickford but glad I hadn't. I didn't want to jump to conclusions, and saying it out loud would raise my expectations of it being true. Which then caused me to question if I *wanted* it to be true. If it was *the* Alison, what would that mean? If it wasn't her, then how disappointed would I be? The answer, in spite of my apprehension, was very disappointed. As I sat there with the list in my hand, one very large chunk of my psyche wanted this Alison to be that Alison, never mind how we'd ended.

I kept thinking about Alison, even though I didn't want to. I had almost an entire month to fret about it, which was a real drag. I remembered the last time I saw her and shuddered. That had been a horrible day. But while I was drifting off to sleep, my memory oddly wanted to go all the way back to the summer we met, the summer of 1968, that horrible year in American history that seemed to be just one long string of violent events, one after the other. During all that, I spent two idyllic weeks in the northern panhandle of West Virginia. It was my second summer at Camp Triple Creek.

June 1968

At three thirty in the afternoon, the counselors gathered all us campers to meet each other and to tell us what to expect during our two weeks at camp. Our unit, Shawnee, was situated three quarters of the way up a big hill. The units went up in age, and we were the next-highest age level, eleven to thirteen years old. I was thirteen.

My parents had dropped me off a couple hours previously, and I had spent the time organizing my space in the four-person cabin where I would sleep. It was basically a tent with a wooden platform and four army cots with iron frames and thin, plastic-covered mattresses. I'd be sleeping in a sleeping bag, but that didn't bother me. I stowed my big army-style footlocker under one of the cots.

The unit kitchen was just a wooden shelter with a picnic bench, a storage box, and a fire pit/barbecue. It was open on all sides. We sat on the benches and listened to our two counselors.

"We need two volunteers for dinner to go half an hour early to set the tables and two for dishwashing after dinner. We'll post a chore schedule tomorrow." We all went around and introduced ourselves and where we were from. I was the odd girl out since I was from Pennsylvania. Everyone else was from West Virginia or eastern Ohio.

I raised my hand for the pre-dinner chore, and at five p.m., I found myself walking down the hill with a blond girl named Alison from the east side of Wheeling.

"This is my first time," she said shyly. "I've only been on campouts with my troop."

"I was here last year with my best friend, Olive, but she's going to band camp this summer. I wanted to come back here."

I looked over the fields stretching out on one side of the road and beyond at the hills. When I was much younger I had had a dream, and those hills were in my dream, and I recognized them when I saw them and knew I was in the right place.

Alison smiled slightly. "You must like it here."

"Oh yeah, I do. A lot. I think you will too."

She seemed a bit worried, because her brows knit. "I hope so."

The counselor in charge at what they called the camp house, where the kitchen and dining room were, put us to work setting tables for dinner and told us we had to sweep the floor after it was over. It was all familiar to me from the previous year. I showed Alison how it was done. She followed along easily, and we chatted about our families and Girl Scouts in our hometown. She had the most brilliant blue eyes I'd ever seen, and when she smiled, it was like the sunrise.

At dinner, I made sure I sat next to Alison, and we held hands for grace, and our elbows touched now and then.

For the next two weeks, I was never far from Alison if I could help it. Her shyness ebbed a bit, and she soon became the most popular girl in our unit.

❖

I couldn't even begin to imagine the amount of work it took to coordinate the number of flights and arrivals to ensure we all arrived at the Atlanta airport within a roughly two-hour window on the Saturday afternoon before the festival. Fortunately, Arden had an assistant, Becky, who was more than up to the task. If there was ever a woman who needed a level-headed organized, helper, it was Arden.

I had the entire six-hour plane flight to try to manage my mixture of anticipation and anxiety, which rose with each passing minute. I tried to do a little work on our security plan and managed to produce a rough outline, but my brain always went back to Alison, either the Alison of the past or the Alison of the present. If it was the same woman, what would I do? What would I say? What would she do or say? Would I even recognize her, or would she not know me or pretend not to, if, of course, it was even the same person, which I reminded myself it probably wasn't. It was all empty speculation, but I couldn't avoid it. Fifteen years before, she'd broken my heart, and our parting had left me with questions and regrets and a sense of incompleteness. I had managed to mostly forget about her and get on with my life, but I still thought about her off and on. Meeting some blond, blue-eyed woman or meeting anyone named Alison would immediately trigger my recollections as would hearing the Elvis Costello song, "Alison."

According to Arden's instructions, I would have to wait around another several hours before we'd arrive at the site, and who knows when I would meet Alison, whoever she was. I tried to concentrate on the fact that I'd soon be seeing several old friends and coworkers from the Pacific Music Festival.

As I walked into the Delta arrivals area, the first person I saw was Becky, carrying a clipboard as usual.

We hugged, and she checked me off her list. "When you get your bag, meet at the curb by the Delta gate. Arden's got a couple of vans to take us out to the land."

Ah, "the land." When a women's music festival took over a camp, or whatever property they'd rented, it became sacred space. Outright ownership of "the land" was rare, but nonetheless, once the festival operations began, it was automatically a colony of the Lesbian Nation.

I collected my duffel bag and my guitar and found my way out to the meeting spot. It wasn't hard to spot. The sidewalk in front of the Delta doors was already clogged with several dozen women, many I recognized. They were surrounded by piles of luggage as they greeted each other with hugs and shouts. It was a good thing we were outside. The sheer volume of that many lesbians chatting would have been overwhelming to any other airport customers. I spotted Valencia Delgado from San Jose, and we collided in a tight, body-melding hug. Valencia gave the best hugs. She was about my height, five seven, but she was round and curvy and had great breasts. She exuded sensuality. Between her cooking and organizing skills, outgoing personality and her buxom gorgeousness, she attracted a ton of attention. By the end of a festival, all her many helpers would be head over heels about her, as would most of the other volunteers. I'd have to take a number if I was going to get into her jeans. But that had never been a priority, until now.

"How are you, *chica*? You still breaking hearts all over SF?"

"Nah. They break my heart. I don't break theirs."

"You're a fraud, but you know I love you. I feel so *safe* now that you're here." She blinked. Boy, can Valencia ever put a ton of meaning into one blink.

"Oh, Magda, baby! Over here!" She waved wildly, and in a moment we were joined by the festival parking guru. She was a hundred percent Cherokee from Tacoma, Washington, and she'd come up with the system that allowed four thousand cars at the PC festival to be parked sensibly. She, like Valencia, commanded a loyal crew of helpers. I wish I could do that. I had Marty, but that was it. Now there was her girlfriend, who I fervently hoped had the "security" mindset.

As we stood talking and waiting for the rest of the group to assemble, a giant Delta Airlines porter was busy hefting and stowing our many pieces of luggage and equipment into the waiting vans. He looked around with a perplexed expression at the motley group of women. We were, of course, of multiple ethnicities, looks, ages, and demeanors. I don't know why people stereotype lesbians when we're all so different.

The porter asked of no one in particular, "Is this a girls' school?"

Valencia grinned and told him, "Something like that." We all giggled a bit. The porter looked even more mystified.

Someone tapped me on the shoulder, and I turned around, and there was Marty. We embraced, and then she introduced me to the woman at her side.

Marty was a fun-loving, devil-may-care professional auto-insurance adjuster, oddly enough. Security attracts two main types of people: one is my kind, the compulsive rule-followers and control freaks, or the ones like Marty, who just recognized the absurdity of human nature and tried to channel it away from self-destructive behaviors. I suppose I had a bit of that attitude as well. I started out way more uptight, but over a few years I had learned to be less controlling and anxious and much nicer. I liked to help people. I liked them to take care of themselves. They didn't always know how to do that. Good thing I was around to advise them.

Marty's girlfriend was wide-eyed at the scene. She had cute breasts, slightly outsized for her frame. I silently christened her Miss Tits. When we all finally got settled in the vans, Marty and I talked nonstop about the music festival, security, and essentially everything that had happened to both of us since the previous September at the Pacific Coast Festival.

Marty's lover, Miss Tits, finally got a chance to interrupt, and her question made my heart sink. Even worse, Marty's answer made my throat close.

"I hope I won't have to break up any fights, will I?"

"Uh," I said. Marty jumped in before I could gather my wits.

"Oh no, sweetheart. And if so, I'll come help you." She put her arm around Miss Tits and squeezed her shoulder. *Here we go.* Lovers, girlfriends, whatever you want to call them could seriously unscrew the most screwed-on head. I'd always considered Marty super reliable and on point, but now I wasn't so sure. If she had to go running off to rescue Miss Tits, she wasn't going to be my right-hand woman. Security people always have backup, but it's not always going to be the same person. I needed Marty to be on call for *me*, not for her beloved. That was another reason not to have a girlfriend, I reminded myself. They were too much work, and again, I was glad I was single.

Marty and Miss Tits went into an extended one-on-one discussion of just how much each appreciated and worshipped the other, and I excused myself and went to another part of the van and found Valencia surrounded by her usual coterie. I welcomed the distraction offered by Marty and Miss Tits, but once bereft of it, I went back to worrying on two tracks: Festival Security and Alison whoever-she-was.

"*Hola*, girl. Come over and sit by me." I obeyed, and Valencia threw a strong arm around me and hugged. She's femme, but she's wicked strong from throwing around giant pots and lifting fifty-pound bags of potatoes. I'm a semi-serious iron pumper and not a weakling, but I wouldn't ever try to arm-wrestle Valencia. My ego would never recover.

"Oo, baby, you are *hard*. Like a rock." She hummed her appreciation, and her gaggle of girls chuckled. Valencia's nonverbal vocals had tons of meanings, just like her blinks and her various grins. Not to mention her eyebrows. I got a tiny prick of arousal.

Maybe this festival, I'll finally get to fuck Val.

"Don't squeeze me so hard, Val. I'm fragile." A big chorus of groans greeted that lie.

'You don't look fragile," a girl named Tanya said, in a tone that suggested she might be someone who wanted to know more about my lack of fragility. As a matter of fact, I felt emotionally fragile from all the worry and anticipation about Alison.

"Hey, can we talk later—maybe before dinner after we get settled?" I caught Valencia's eye so she'd know I wasn't flirting.

"Sure. You got it." I moved to another seat and stared out the window. The urban sprawl of Atlanta and its ugly freeways was behind us. We were on a two-lane road, and I watched the green hills flying by. This was usually one of my favorite times: the ride to the festival. I was full of happy anticipation as I left the straight, uptight patriarchal society and the city behind to go to the woods, which would soon be full of women.

I suddenly recalled how it felt when I went to Girl Scout camp. It was the same sort of feeling. I was about to head into a place that was much more comfortable to me, away from civilization. I loved San Francisco. I loved its streets and its hills and the gay community. It was a special place, but I still loved being in the woods and the insular, tight-knit ambience of an all-woman environment. I told myself to cheer up; it was all going to be great, Alison or no Alison.

CHAPTER TWO

Y ou'll have a room in the infirmary building, so you won't have to share this time. Arden decided to put up all the coordinators in rooms, along with performers who don't have RVs. And there are still plenty of rooms left for the, ahem, patients." This was Becky again, showing us our quarters for the next ten days.

It was a long, low, nondescript building with a big waiting room at one end with a Dutch door where, obviously, the medical people would do intake on the casualties that inevitably result when you take a couple thousand women who are mostly city slickers and plunk them down in the semi-wilderness. Not much happens that's medically serious, but shit happens—sunburn, bug bites, hangovers, and the like.

Magda and Willa were standing next to me outside the infirmary as Becky made the room assignments. Willa was the head carpenter, and she was just about the femmiest carpenter I'd ever met, but she could direct a stage construction better than any old redneck foreman.

"Holy crap, this is like the Bates Motel," Magda said. She meant the motel in the infamous Alfred Hitchcock movie *Psycho*.

I laughed and agreed.

"Look out for Norman Bates's mother," Willa said. "Or maybe it's Norman himself in drag as his mom."

"Either one, you enter, and you may never be seen again," I said.

We riffed on the movie *Psycho*, and just like that, the infirmary/dormitory was christened Bates Motel or just Bates.

I went to my room and stowed my stuff. It was something having a room to myself, because that had never happened before. I didn't mind sharing tents or cabins with others; it was part of the fun. It was just like Girl Scout camp. Damn. There I was again back to that and, naturally, back to my fear/anticipation/wonder/dread about the identity of the mysterious Alison, who'd clearly not shown up yet.

I went to find Valencia, and she was, of course, in the kitchen, working already. She was like the Energizer bunny, nonstop.

"Can we chat while you cook?"

"Sure, but keep out of my way or I put you to work peeling corn on the cob for forty women."

I must have paled, because she laughed and patted my cheek.

"Don't worry, Lane. I know you are too important a person for that. I got many helping hands. What's on your mind?"

I had to sprint to keep up with her as she whirled around the huge industrial kitchen.

Valencia said, "Got to figure out where everything is. *Aiyiyi*. People cannot properly organize a kitchen." She was muttering to herself, but I knew she'd listen to me closely. Valencia was one of those crazy twelve-steppers who could sometimes sound like a really annoying oracle with her pronouncements. But once I stopped being grouchy about how she sounded and focused on what she said, I'd come to understand that what she said made sense, and invariably it was what I didn't want to hear but needed to.

I told her about the two Alisons who were maybe one and the same but probably not.

"Aha!" Valencia said, obviously pleased, and I was bewildered until she yanked what had to be a thirty-gallon soup pot from under the counter and flourished it in my face.

"So. What do you want to happen if it's the same girl?" Val asked me.

"I, uh, I don't know."

"Do you want her to apologize? Leave you alone, be your friend?" She cocked an eyebrow knowingly. "You want to pick up where you left off?"

"No! That was a long-ass time ago, and I'm still sort of pissed at her. She left me without a word."

"You're still pissed? What about her?" Valencia grimaced at me

"She's probably still mad at *me*. It was a terrible fight, and I haven't talked to her or seen her since. Not for the last fifteen years. Not a word. Not even a birthday card."

"Well. Whatever is going to happen will happen, but you might want to think about what you want and what you are going to say, but in the end, you'll let go of the results." The oracle had spoken.

"Hmph."

"All right, baby. Out of my way. I've got cooking to do."

I left the dining hall and went for a walk around the camp. It was blessed with a good-sized lake with a dock and a few rowboats and canoes scattered about. Then I thought about inattentive dykes falling in the lake and drowning. My mind always goes to the worst-case scenario. It's just my nature. I'm a worrier, and I care very much about other people, but I hide it under a stern, unemotional exterior. Also I'd seen too much foolish behavior in my years of doing safety both at festivals and at SF events. That's the way it goes, I guess. I just don't want people to get hurt, and I like to have things go smoothly. They never do, of course. The safety mindset is about managing chaos, but even I knew that was mostly an illusion. People, including lesbians, are just too damn unpredictable and headstrong.

A few feet from the entrance to the camp, two dirt roads met in a *Y* intersection. One wound past the dining hall and Bates Motel and up a slight grade, and cabins were situated along both sides, where the volunteers were staying. There was a small outdoor amphitheater that would be the day stage and workshop areas. Farther up the road was where the main stage would be. This was a beautiful area, surrounded by tall pine trees. The other road went past the kitchen and dining room and then up to the farther parking areas and camp sites.

The festival-goers, nicknamed festies, would be pitching their tents in designated areas up the hill. There would be clean and sober areas, family/children sites, S/M camp, and trans camp. Unlike the producers of other women's festivals, Arden was of the opinion if someone looked like a woman, acted like a woman, and called herself a woman, she was a woman, never mind her chromosomes. But all the subsets of the Lesbian Nation didn't necessarily get along. The festival tried to keep conflict to a minimum by separating the groups.

Near the top of the hill on the other road, I found the stage area where the stage builders were already at work, Willa among them. Those lucky gals had RVs to stay in.

All the way at the top of the second hill, where the camping would be, was the parking area and more camping space. I hoped the rowdier element would choose to reside up there. I would do a more thorough walk-around later but was happy to have something to do while my brain raced along, testing this scenario or that one in my mythical meeting with Alison. And I thought about Alison and me back in the day, during the good years before it got messy.

July 1969

In 1968, I got a guitar for Christmas. In Scouts, I learned to sing, and I worshipped the girls who could play, and I was crazy about folk music. By the summer of 1969, I had developed enough self-confidence to play in front of people, even if they were just my family or my Girl Scout friends.

In May, one of those friends sat me down in her family TV room in and said, "You have to hear this." She played the Joni Mitchell "Clouds" album, and I was entranced. I'm ready to admit it changed my life. Joyce and I played the record over and over, trying to figure out what chords she used, but we couldn't.

At camp that summer, I proudly showed off my musical skills, and Alison was very impressed. I told her I wished I could sing like Joni Mitchell. I could carry a tune well enough, but Alison was truly blessed with a crystal-clear mezzo soprano (as she described it), and I was happy enough to play while she sang. Like Joni, Alison had long blond hair, but she kept it tied back, and in my teenage mind, she got all mixed up with Joni. I worshipped both of them and longed for something that I didn't have a name for, only that it was tied up with Alison and Joni Mitchell.

We'd moved up to the unit for the oldest girls, the one at the top of the hill, called Alpine. Its isolation from the rest of the camp and the fact that we were the oldest helped us all bond. We were hotshots in those days, and Alison and I were tighter than ever. She'd grown out of her shyness, and she loved to sing. I got the reflected admiration because I was her best friend and a pretty good guitar player, if I do say so myself. We sang all the time at camp—camp songs and folk songs. We sang after lunch and at every campfire, and we just sang whenever. But nothing was better than when someone would say, "Ellie and Allie, please sing a song." That's who we were: Ellie and Allie, inseparable.

I stood on the dock looking out over the lake. It was a little humid and warm in the late afternoon but not uncomfortable. I could imagine how hot it could get in high summer. I lit a cigarette and contemplated the question that never truly was far from my mind. Just to know either way would be a relief. I stubbed out the cigarette on a rock and walked back to the dining hall.

A bunch of women were hanging out in front of the Camp Towanga dining hall when I arrived. It was five thirty in the afternoon, and I figured dinner would soon be served. An area in front was strewn with logs and tree stumps—handy for sitting. I said hello to a few more acquaintances from the West Coast group and saw a lot of women I didn't recognize. They had to be the Southerners. They looked like lesbians, dressed like lesbians, but as the sound of their voices drifted to me, I caught the Southern accents. Then I just plopped myself down on a log and waited.

Even at the age of thirty-two, I still hadn't totally outgrown my shyness, and I didn't want to go introduce myself to strangers. I think part of my initial attraction to Alison was how shy we both were with other people and how unshy we were with each other. One handy aspect of my volunteer work was it always gave me something to do with myself, a purpose, a function. When I was in a group and working as a volunteer, I could disguise my shyness. I could walk up to someone and tell her to do or not do something, and it wasn't like a social interaction.

In reality, I was, of course, looking for Alison, though I hoped I could recognize her. I was certain I would, as her face was one I'd spent plenty of time looking at and thinking about. Back in April I had dug out an old picture of us—the only one I had, and stared at it for a long time.

They called us in to eat, and I took my plate of chicken and corn on the cob and sat down with Marty and Miss Tits. They had the look of a couple who had just roused themselves out of bed. I didn't begrudge them that. They'd need to get their sex time in while they could, because once the festival started, their privacy and time would be limited.

Becky announced that we'd meet after dinner, and in due time, Arden arrived, and we got called to order. Arden sure had a way with public speaking—one I wished I possessed. I could, however, barely comprehend what was going on because I was still waiting for Alison to show up.

Arden said, "Welcome, everyone. This is the first Southern women's music and comedy festival." Everyone cheered.

"We're going to have a good time, but we have a lot to do over the next few days. We've got a fantastic lineup." We listened as she named half a dozen fairly famous musicians and comedians.

"So we're going to start by introducing all the coordinators who'll be in charge of executing all the tasks we've got to finish by Thursday. Y'all stand up please so we can see you. I'm working on my Southern speak." Dutiful laughter.

She started with herself and then ran down the list. When she got to me and Marty, I could swear the reaction was a little muted.

I might be paranoid, but sometimes the word security calls to mind "secret police." For that reason, in San Francisco, we called ourselves "safety." "Secret police" is not the image you want a bunch of free-spirited, lefty lesbians to have of you. I worked on keeping my persona mellow and approachable. I was not the secret police, not the enemy. I was just another worker with a specific function.

"Thanks, Lane and Marty. Medical? Do we have Medical here yet?" I waited, tensely, but heard no response. Becky whispered into Arden's ear, and she said, "They're due any minute. They called from the road. Becky is going to run through a list of announcements and requests for help. See you all later." Arden waved cheerily and turned the mike over to Becky, who looked at her clipboard and balanced the mike at the same time.

"There's a rumor that the kitchen staff will confiscate all beer stored in the kitchen." A few people chuckled. Alcohol was a necessity for pre-festival and post-festival. Not as much during festival, since who wanted to work sixteen hours a day with a hangover? Not me.

In spite of her officiousness, Becky didn't lack a sense of humor.

"Only premium beers will be taken. You can have the rest of it. I'm kidding. Just put your name on your stash. Now, parking for staff. Just so Magda doesn't start tearing her hair out, please park in the designated area at the north end of the lake and give your license number to her so we know who you are." After some laughter, a lot of side conversations started up.

"Focus, women. Let me get through my list."

Becky flipped a page over. "Stage is asking for four people tomorrow at seven a.m." Many groans greeted this request.

"I know, really? Seven a.m.? But anyone who can get up that early and possesses a few carpentry skills—and I know some of you in this crowd do—please come help them out. See Willa." Willa waved to the crowd, and Becky beamed as a few hands went into the air. "Thanks, women."

The pre-festival was graced with presence of not only experienced volunteers from years past but a sort of gypsy gang of itinerant lesbians who somehow had the means to spend months at a time on the road going from one event to the other, working for their room and board, basically. They were like deadheads and had almost the same sort of substance-imbibing habits, except they tended to stick to beer, wine, and pot instead of hallucinogens.

Becky went on and I got bored. I had my paper and pen and my sketchy security plan, but I was still too keyed up to concentrate. Restlessness made me leave the meeting. Outside, I thought maybe I would hit the PortaJane, take a walk, and try to calm myself.

Suddenly, I spotted three women walking toward the dining hall, and one of them was Alison Livingstone. I stood still, both because of shock and because I just wanted to wait and see if Alison would recognize me. She'd last seen me at age eighteen, when I was skinny and, in the fashion of the time, had long hair. Now I was muscular and my hair was cropped.

Alison still had lovely long blond hair, but she'd filled out some, and she looked good. She had more curves than I remembered, but in all other aspects she was the same. Still the same oval face and pointed chin and bright-blue eyes. The waves of memory crashed through me. At that moment, it wasn't that final fight that I thought of but all that we'd said and done before. It was like no time had passed: she was still Alison. Or at least she *looked* like Alison.

I watched and waited.

The three women came to a stop in front of me. The tallest of the three grinned and said with a thick Georgia drawl, "Have we got the right place? This where the music festival going to be?"

I said, "Yes. You have the right place." I made enough eye contact with the tall woman to be polite, but my gaze inevitably slid over and locked on Alison. I badly wanted to say something, but I used all my safety training to stay cool and ignore my pounding heart and dry mouth and just wait.

Alison looked at me closely, and her familiar face went through phases of generic friendliness, confusion, shock, and finally recognition.

"Ellie?" she asked in a tone of wonderment. I wasn't used to hearing someone call me that. I'd been Lane for so long, but somehow out of Alison's mouth, the name didn't sound foreign.

A zillion memories kaleidoscoped across my mind.

Her eyebrows went up. "Is it you? Are you...?

"Yup. Good to see you, Allie."

And at hearing her old nickname, Alison's face lit with a ghost of a smile, but it came and went quickly and was replaced by an expression of wariness. I sensed some sort of internal turmoil, though it was well disguised. She seemed to make a kind of emotional calculation as to what to say or do next.

She stepped forward and we embraced. Her body felt both the same and different. I let go first because my body was remembering back fifteen years, and it reminded me with a wave of muted but unmistakable arousal.

One of her companions said, "Alison, honey? Is this her?" The other one laughed and whistled.

Still in a partial embrace, Alison kept eye contact with me and said, "Yeah. It's her."

"Leah, let's leave them be for a minute."

"How come? We didn't introduce our—"

"Shush. Come on." I barely registered that the two women had walked away and Alison and I were left face-to-face, just staring at each other.

"I—" I stuttered.

"It *is* you. I couldn't tell for sure from the list 'cause the first name was wrong." Her West Virginia drawl had become richer, or maybe because she'd moved farther south and had grown more Southern.

"Oh," I said, light dawning, "You saw my name on the list." Dummy. Of course she'd seen the same list I had.

"Yes, I did, but I wasn't sure since it was a different name."

"It's not wrong, exactly. I changed it."

"So I see. You could be a Lane, I guess." She didn't sound sure.

"You haven't changed." This was true other than the slight effects of aging. I was entrapped in a sort of double vision. I saw the old teenage Alison and the new adult at the same time, and it was extraordinarily disorienting. I had been enamored of the younger version, but I wasn't sure how I felt about the current one. The final verdict would have to wait until I saw how she felt about *me.*

"Huh." Alison snorted. "You have no idea." She said this with such a bitter tone, it scared me.

"You're with the medical team?" I was so discomfited, I could only ask inane questions. The list of staff Becky had sent in April made that fact perfectly clear. And her two friends must be the other two medical coordinators.

"Sure am. Leah and Angie are the head honchos. I'm the assistant."

"Right. So…"

"You've been good?' It sounded as though she was seeing me after a couple weeks or a month instead of years

"Um. Yeah, I suppose. Mostly. You?"

"That's a matter of opinion, but I'm hanging in there."

How could this be anything but a hugely awkward conversation? We'd parted on the worst terms imaginable, and here we were face-to-face. The past had to come up in our minds and emotions, for sure, if not in our words. Yet…

I didn't know what I wanted from Alison. Though I'd done nothing but think about her for the better part of a month, I had no idea what to do now that she stood in front of me. What should I say in a situation like this? Should I just try to be casual, treat her like a distant acquaintance I'd just happened to run into? That was absurd. Should I just pretend like nothing happened? That didn't seem right either.

Her words so far didn't give me much of a clue about what was going on in her head.

We were still standing there in front of the dining hall in a cloud of uneasy silence, looking at each other.

Alison said, finally, "Well, I guess I better catch up with Leah and Angie. We just got here, and we need to find out what's what and all."

"Sure, yeah. See you around?"

She nodded, squeezed my arm in a perfunctory way, and walked off.

I stared after her.

THE LAST TIME I SAW HER

CHAPTER THREE

Having nothing better to do and feeling deflated, I walked back down the hill to the lake and the dock. It was getting toward sunset, usually my favorite time of day, but it didn't give me any peace. I took off my shoes, put my feet in the water, and lit a cigarette.

What did I expect? I guess I was prepared for hostility. I was hoping for a pleasant reunion, but I got apparent indifference. *That* hurt.

"I was looking for you." My head spun around. It was Marty and Miss Tits

"Here I am."

"What's wrong?" Marty asked. Shit, was my expression that bad?

"Nothing." I wasn't ready to talk about it.

Marty tilted her head, then said to her girlfriend, "Baby, I'll be along soon."

They kissed tenderly and she left.

She sat down next to me on the dock. "What's up?"

"Nothing. At least nothing I want to talk about at the moment. Let's meet at breakfast and start going over the security plan, and then we'll walk the entire site."

Marty looked as though she was about to say something, but she just said, "Sounds great." She stood up, dusted off her shorts, and left. She was good at knowing when to leave someone alone.

I sat for a few more minutes, then walked back to Bates and directly to my room and shut the door. It occurred to me that if I wanted to get laid, I wouldn't have any problem finding privacy. This setup was unique and should have energized me, but it didn't. If Alison was curiously indifferent to me, I was strangely unexcited by the prospect of finding a random willing girl at the festival to help me take advantage of my single room. I went to the bathroom to brush my teeth wondering if I would run into Alison, but I hadn't seen her since our meeting after dinner and didn't know where she was staying. She'd had no girlfriend with her, but that didn't mean one wouldn't show up later. I got into my sleeping bag, pulled it over my head, and tried to go to sleep. I was tired from the cross-country flight that I'd gotten up really early for. But the three-hour time difference between east and west was off-putting. I thought I could go right to sleep, but no way. I stood up and dragged some clothes on.

In the hall, I ran into Leah and Angie.

"Hi." I spoke as casually as I could. "Hey. Where's Alison staying?"

They looked me up and down as though I might be a potential threat, but finally Angie said, "She's up yonder with the rest of the workers. Cabin Three."

"Great. I can find her." I turned on my most affable grin. Leah glared at me and Angie merely nodded. What was the deal with them? I'd have to ask Alison later.

I walked over to the workers' cabins, and in a few minutes, I spotted Alison through the door of one of them, alone, thank goodness.

"Hi. I was hoping you might have a few minutes to talk."

"I guess so." She didn't seem either obviously happy or unhappy to be alone with me.

She looked around the room vaguely. "Not a lot of space. Reminds me of Triple Creek."

We had way more than a couple minutes of conversation, I thought, but I'd take what I could get.

"Well. First of all, it's great to see you. I mean that."

She was silent, those crystal-blue eyes of hers open and unblinking. The light was fading, but I could still see them.

My train of thought faltered, "I mean it's a surprise because I didn't know if the Alison on the list was you. Different name and all."

"Yeah. I got married."

"I see. Well, congrats,"

"And then divorced, a couple years ago."

"Oops, sorry. So how'd you end up coming here?" I wanted to ask her directly if she was a lesbian, but that would be too forward. There were women at music festival—though not many who weren't lesbians—who simply enjoyed the ambience of an all-women's space for a time. She could be a lesbian or she could not be. Or she could be undecided. She had to reveal that information on her own terms.

She eyed me, obviously calculating what and how much she wanted to say. She didn't use to be like this, not with me. In my memory, she was always either singing or laughing and surrounded by a crowd. I suppose over the years she'd become warier of revealing herself. The word divorce suggested some of her life hadn't been very happy

"Oh, uh. Lea and Angie recruited me. I work at the same hospital. I'm a nurse, but I guess that wasn't exactly clear."

"Oh. I got it." I still wanted to know a lot more about her, but I kept quiet.

"And you, Ellie. What about you?"

"First, I'm not Ellie. I'm Lane."

'Right. I'll try to remember that. Or maybe I ought to just call you Chipper."

Ah-hah, a glimmer of humor from her, and her use of my old camp nickname disarmed me.

"Please don't," I said with a little snicker to show I wasn't offended. "If you do, I might have to call you Willow."

"Ow. All right, I was just teasing anyhow. But what about you?"

I wanted to tell her so much but didn't know where to start.

"I live in San Francisco and work in biotech, but volunteering for things like this is sort of my hobby."

"What's that mean—Security?" She opened her suitcase and began to rummage in it. I wanted her complete attention but understood she had to unpack, though it couldn't amount to much.

"Oh, in SF we call it safety, but essentially my job is to make sure, or try to make sure, that no one gets in trouble, gets hurt, isn't bothered from the outside—oh, just a ton of different things."

'Like a cop?" She shook out a pastel-pink, sleeveless blouse and eyed it critically. Maybe she *wasn't* a dyke. The thought disappointed me.

"We don't act like cops, but sort of. Yeah. I can't arrest you, if that's what you're getting at."

She looked startled but then grinned.

"I've never been arrested and don't plan on being. But I like the idea of someone looking after all of us."

"I try to prevent the accidents, but you get to patch the women up when they happen."

She looked as though something just occurred to her.

"So that means we're going to work together."

Was she pleased or displeased? As the realization hit me, I wasn't sure how I felt. We were not going to be able to always avoid one another, and I didn't want to anyhow.

"That's almost certain. Is that okay?"

She paused and said, "Looks like it doesn't matter if it's *okay* with me or not. It's what is."

I made a snap decision.

"Alison. The past is past. I'm over it. You're here now. I'm here. Let's try to be friendly, if for no other reason than for the sake of a harmonious working relationship."

I sounded like an asshole, but so what?

"That's just fine with me," she said, easy-going Southern.

"'Cause, I sure don't want to upset you, and we really don't have to do that processing thing that dykes like to do. No point."

"Processing?" She said the word like it was some mystifying term she'd never heard. And she raised her eyebrows. Maybe they didn't call it that below the Mason-Dixon line.

"Talking something to death."

"Oh. Right. Around here, we just say that. Processing is something that happens to meat."

I laughed. Alison, it appeared, still had a sense of humor, even a slightly barbed one. I liked her stronger Southern accent. She dropped all the gs and sort of drew out her words.

"Whatever we call it, I don't want to do it," I said. Sincere and reassuring.

"Sure. Agreed. So, sorry, but I got to try and finish this up before I go to bed. Angie has all kinds of things she wants to do tomorrow." She rolled her eyes a little. I liked that. Maybe she found her two buddies slightly irritating. I hoped so, because I sure did.

And she gave me that winning grin I remembered. She seemed relieved. I was too, but I still wanted to process. I had lied to her to make sure she wouldn't be uncomfortable around me. The years in between then and now had certainly rubbed off the rough edges of my regrets, but seeing her again brought the whole sorry situation back to my consciousness, and I would think of what might have been, what happened, and what I had lost every single time I saw her, no matter what I told myself. And, I was itching to know about this marriage thing and what exactly her status was right now. Was she a lesbian? Did she have a lover? And I couldn't pretend that it didn't matter to me. Even though I intellectually knew I ought not even speculate, my heart had a different idea.

July 1969

"Sh. Don't wake everyone up." Alison admonished me to be quiet as I slipped onto the army cot next to her. We put one sleeping bag underneath us and one over us. We didn't discuss this; it just happened. There was something wonderful about being close to her in sleep, even squished together on the tiny cot.

I woke up early in the morning. The cabin was screened, but I could see the forest right outside, the trees faint against the gray sky. Somewhere a bird chirped. We'd be getting up soon, answering the toll of a bell from down the hill at the camp house. I slipped out of bed, leaving Alison and her warmth behind, and went to the outhouse. I stopped to sit by the fire circle for a moment. Our campfire from the night before was just gray ash. I loved being with everyone, especially Alison, but whenever I had a chance to be by myself, I would take it.

Summer would soon be over for us, and that filled me with sadness. I sometimes thought Girl Scout camp was my normal life instead of the one I lived back home with my parents and going to school. Alison and I could write to each other several times through the year, mostly about the summer to come. But it wasn't the same.

One night near the end of the summer, Alison and I were the last ones awake, along with one of our counselors, Buffy. We sat in dark in the unit house, which was a cabin with a front porch on stilts and a fireplace. It was the only structure like that in the camp and gave us the unique ability to gather even when it rained. It was clear that night, though. I went out on the porch with Alison, and we stood next to one another just looking out into the night. Buffy came up behind us and, without a word, put a hand on each of our shoulders. I moved closer to Alison until our arms touched, and the three of us stood there for a time, not saying a word, looking out at the forest.

Buffy wasn't like the usual young women who were our counselors and essentially just a few years older than us. Seventeen to twenty versus fourteen to sixteen. She was in her mid-twenties and married, which fascinated us. She wasn't afraid to answer the many questions of teenage girls. Not that I ever thought to ask her why I loved Alison so much and, as I was beginning to understand, in a much different and possibly dangerous way. Who knows what she would have said had I asked her that question, but I never did. Some innate caution kept me from ever saying anything.

Years later when I thought about that night, I wondered if that was Buffy's way of saying she knew and tacitly recognized what Alison and I meant to each other. Possibly it was just a kind, affectionate gesture for us both as individuals, but I'd like to think it was the former.

❖

The next morning, we stood in line to get eggs, oatmeal, and fruit, and sure enough, there was Alison with her two cronies. I caught her eye, smiled, and waved but didn't approach her. She didn't wave back but sort of nodded. I covertly watched her as we ate breakfast. She glanced over my way once, and I threw her a benign glance, but her expression was unreadable. If she wants arms' length, she'll get it, I thought grumpily. I had my clipboard with me and attempted to project an air of seriousness and busy-ness.

Marty, Miss Tits, and I set off on a walking tour of "the land." Becky had provided me with a map of the camp and its surroundings, which was a large space—about ten square miles. The northern outer perimeter ran up against a densely wooded area. One of the main camping areas was just inside these woods, and another side abutted a dairy farm, where cows placidly grazed. We circled around to the western end, where the parking lots would be. Magda was already there with a couple of her crew, starting to lay out the parking areas, and we stopped to chat.

She had a stranger with her she introduced as Sarajane.

Sarajane's "nice to meet you" dripped Southern charm.

"Are you from around here?" I asked, full of hope.

"Sure am. Live about forty miles down the road in Tentpole."

'What's that like?"

"It's okay. I like the out-of-doors, hunting and fishing. That's how I grew up. If I want excitement, I go to Atlanta." To Sarajane, excitement must mean other lesbians.

"What're the people like?" I sensed some disdain coming from Marty. She was a vegetarian, and if she didn't eat animal flesh, she sure wasn't going to approve the shooting or hooking of it for consumption purposes or otherwise.

"Oh, there's some good ole boys who can get a little rowdy, but mostly folks are fine. Since I'm from around here they don't mess with me. What you Yankees don't realize is that Southerners will tolerate some eccentricity as long as you don't make too big a deal about it. We're not all bigots. That's how they view me being a lesbian: I'm okay, just a tad eccentric. They just don't like people who shout it from rooftops and wave signs."

That sounded a bit like a knock against San Francisco, but I laughed a little to show I understood where she was coming from.

Marty, already put off by the hunting and fishing stuff, said in a colder voice than I'd ever heard from her, "By that, you mean as long as you don't talk about it and they can ignore the elephant in the room, you're okay?"

Sarajane dialed her down-home friendliness back a teeny bit. She paused, and her grin became set.

"Y'all might say we like to live and let live around here."

Before Marty could continue, I jumped in.

"Do you think we'll get any trouble from the locals? It's my job to be ready for that. Women like to feel safe when they're at the festival."

"Nah. I don't think so. Like I said, there's some rowdies, but I don't think they'll bother us."

Sarajane said her good-byes and left.

"Last night, one of my crew stayed up most of the night marking the rest of the parking lanes in the Artemis lot."

"Mags, are you sure you're not working your crew too hard? All night?"

She grinned, her black eyes sparkling.

"Nah. Evie's a night person, and she offered to sink posts in Artemis last night to help us get done quicker."

Magda had laid out five parking areas, each named for a Greek goddess. Which one would Alison most resemble, I wondered insanely. Magda knew to the inch how many spaces she needed and what sizes and how to make the access lanes. Artemis was the farthest out and likely the last one to be used.

"I see." I wondered what Magda needed from me.

"The thing is, Evie told me she got spooked."

"By what? The dark? Maybe a stray raccoon or fox? No bears in northern Georgia that I know of."

"Nope. She's not scared of the dark. She told me it was probably nothing, but you know me. I'm not going to let anything harm my girls." It was true. Magda was one big momma bear. Parking was a little like Security since her people were out there in the midst of virtually nowhere or dealing with the public in the form of excited and disoriented festies trying to park.

"Can I talk to her?"

"She doesn't want to make a big deal out of it. She said she thought something or someone was in the woods just past the west end of the lot."

I brought out the map, and Magda and I looked at it together. It showed that the western boundary of Camp Towanga abutted a hunting area. No one should be out hunting at night. It wasn't deer season either or turkey shooting. I didn't like hearing that something had spooked Evie, but her story was very sketchy and non-specific, nothing we could really pin down. Besides, Evie wasn't confronted with anything or anybody. She just had a feeling. Not that I discounted people's feelings. A primitive part of the human psyche senses danger or threat based on the subtlest signs. It's probably evolutionary, since our ancestors had to have well-developed senses if they were to stay alive. Here we were in nature, never mind that it wasn't exactly a wilderness. It would still call forth our ancient fears and unconscious knowledge. I took Evie's feelings very seriously.

"Well. We could go have a look tonight, if you want." I gestured at my two wide-eyed helpers, Marty and Miss Tits.

"Oh, could you? That would be fantastic. At least I could tell Evie I had Security check it out and they didn't find anything."

"Ah, yes. The all-powerful Security."

At least that got Magda to laugh. I sensed she was more worried than she let on.

I hoped Sarajane was right that no one would bother us, but I'd learned long ago that you have to be ready for anything. I would discuss the situation with Arden and Becky later.

❖

Marty, Miss Tits, and I finished our walkabout in the late morning. It was getting hot already, and I wanted to get indoors, or at least in the shade for the middle part of the day. Memorial Day Weekend was a good choice for the festival. Later in the summer the heat would be brutal. As a San Franciscan, I wilt when the thermometer reaches eighty-five.

I'd managed to not think about Alison for a couple of hours, though she was hovering just out of my consciousness. I wondered if I needed to talk to Valencia again or if I should just leave it be and wait for Alison to say something to me. It seemed stupid for us to act in such a distant way, but maybe she thought I was still angry at her and didn't want to get into anything with me. Honestly, I didn't know if I was still mad or not. Thirty-two sees things with a bit more clarity than eighteen. I decided I wasn't angry at her, but I wanted us to talk.

I took up my spot on the log in front of the kitchen, as I had the previous evening, to wait for lunch to be served and, truthfully, to watch for Alison. I wondered why I hadn't run into her in the bathroom at Bates, but I hadn't. She must have been hanging around the infirmary.

The three medical people appeared, and Alison favored me with a friendly nod, but that was all. Not knowing what else to do, I went to eat lunch with Marty and Miss Tits. I said to them, "Let's have a mini camp-out tonight. We'll get Val to give us coffee and hot chocolate and snacks, and we'll go out to Artemis lot and go snipe hunting."

They goggled at me.

"What's a snipe?" Miss Tits asked in a manner that suggested she thought a snipe might be a cross between a snake and cougar. Icky *and* dangerous

I laughed. "Well, let me tell you about snipes. They're unique."

They were unique, all right, as in they were imaginary. A snipe is really a sort of shorebird, but that's not what a snipe hunter is looking for.

July 1969
We were going to take the younger campers of Shawnee unit on a snipe hunt. This was a time-honored ritual at Triple Creek. It

was conducted the second week of camp, organized by Alpine for their amusement and to have a little joke on the younger girls. I had gone through it myself a few years before. We induced the second-year Shawnees to not give the joke away and promised we'd make them bearscares—those little woven friendship bracelets. I wore a couple myself, my favorite the one Alison had given me. It was made of green and purple interwoven string.

Anyhow, snipe hunts were too scary an activity to do with the youngest campers, but the twelve-year-olds were all excited to have us big shots include them in a special night-time activity.

Allie and Terry passed out a bunch of paper sacks. Then we put the younger kids in pairs so they wouldn't be too scared, and I gave the instructions.

"You're going into the Cathedral wood and fan out. You're looking for a small but vicious animal called a snipe. You'll know you've got one when you see its eyes glow in the flashlight beam like a cat. But this isn't like your pet kitty at home. This is a wild animal! You have to capture the snipe and put it in the bag and bring it back here. You've got an hour. The first team that finds the snipe wins."

They were squealing with that delighted sort of terror that grips young girls. Off they went with their flashlights and paper sacks into the dark woods. We'd round them up a little later, and maybe we'd let them know there was no such thing as a snipe in northern West Virginia.

"There you have it," I told Marty and Miss Tits, who rolled their eyes.

"You liked to scare little girls, didn't you? What a meanie," Miss Tits said.

I smirked. "They loved it. What do you say we meet at the kitchen at nine? Maybe we can use someone's car. I'm not staying out all night and hoofing it back here in the dark. I'll ask Magda."

"Right!" They scuttled off, likely to fit in some sex before our adventure.

I actually went back to Bates to lie down again. I'm not a night person, but I wanted to show my support for Marty and Miss

Tits. And I was curious. Was an intruder lurking up there beyond the parking area? If so, I wanted to know.

I lay on my cot and closed my eyes, but it wasn't snipes or mysterious intruders I thought of as I dozed. It was Alison as she'd looked at lunch today, calm and quite beautiful, chatting with her friends. She looked much like the Alison from our last summer before it all fell apart. I remembered suddenly that when we were younger, Alison always wore those sleeveless blouses. At lunch she had on one of a nice blue color.

I guess I had some lingering jet lag, because I fell asleep quite easily. I woke up with a snap, and my watch said it was three o'clock. Vaguely disquieted, I decided to search for Val. Valencia had her own room, but she would rarely be found in it unless it was the middle of the night. I think she slept, but I wasn't sure.

It was after lunch but before dinner prep would truly start, and I figured it would be okay.

"Val. Can I talk to you, when you can spare few moments?"

She snorted but motioned me to go out on the back porch of the dining hall with her. She wore jean shorts and an apron but no shirt. This was a typical get-up. Some of the carpenters basically wore tool belts and not much else.

I'm as fond of taking my clothes off as anyone at certain times, but when I was on duty, I didn't think I could project sufficient authority with my tits hanging out, so I kept my shirt on unless I was off duty, which was almost never once the festival started. I was used to seeing bare breasts all around me, though. When the festies started arriving, their shirts came off almost immediately the moment they handed in their tickets and passed through the gate onto the land.

Val and I sat down and lit cigarettes. That was another point of bonding for us.

It was getting rarer for lesbians to smoke. At the last West Coast festival, a lovely, dark-haired girl from the suburbs of LA had looked at me, shook her head, and said, "Why do all the cute butches smoke?" And I realized belatedly I had missed out on what would have surely been a pleasant interlude. Also I was still with Lois then, but that was beside the point. Still, it didn't make me quit smoking.

"What's on your mind, sweetie?" Val asked.

I took a drag before answering.

"It's Alison. Who else?" I sighed. "I can't figure out what's up with her."

"She got a girlfriend?"

"I don't know. Not as far as I can see. It's not that. I want to talk to her. I want to clear the air, and I want to be friends with her."

"So? Talk to her."

"I'm afraid to."

Val grinned sardonically. "The big, bad Security dyke is scared."

"Hey. This is different."

Val laughed. "Yes. It sure is. It means you might have to let someone see you be vulnerable."

I stared at her.

"I've known you a couple years, girlfriend. I've been watching you."

I started to snicker, but she cut me off.

"That's not what I mean, though the scenery is good." This time her grin was lascivious.

"I've watched you go about your business, and you're nice, and you're good at what you do. Everyone likes you. But you're guarded. Not any real emotion is getting through the façade. Right?"

"I suppose so. Some of my girlfriends say stuff like, 'I don't know you' or 'what are you thinking?'"

"And that's right before they leave you?"

I was looking away, but I snapped my head around. "Yeah. And they always do, eventually."

"You're not giving yourself to them, except sexually, I would guess."

"I *think* I am."

"This Alison…what happened to you with her, from what little you told me, was something else altogether?"

I nodded. "She was my first love."

Valencia pressed on. "But there's been no one since?"

I thought long and hard. "No. I thought there was, but I've never met a girl like her. We were just kids, though. It was a long time ago."

"Still, you obviously have unfinished business, or you wouldn't be obsessed about her."

"I'm not obsessed," I almost shouted, but what Val said was true.

"For your own peace of mind you should have a talk with her. Just tell her. She might just be holding back because she thinks you'd rather not open that particular can of worms."

"I told her I didn't want to process, but it wasn't true." I was glum having to admit this to Val.

"So?" Valencia stared at me, making me uncomfortable.

"Right. I have to be honest." I paused. "But what if she doesn't want to talk about it?"

"Then you have to accept that."

"There's that word again. Why are you so fucking fond of 'accept this,' 'accept that'?" I asked her, grumpy because I already knew the answer. When we first met, Valencia had explained to me about being an alcoholic and some of the things she had to do in order not to drink. "Acceptance" was one of them. I sort of got it, but I wasn't ready to admit that there were a lot of things I couldn't change.

"Yes. I practice acceptance because I want to be happy."

"Huh." What was happiness?

Val rubbed my arm and made it seem like she could be rubbing some other part of my body, but I didn't think she wanted to go there, and I sure didn't, not at that moment.

"Okay. Shoo. Talk to me any time you want. I'm here."

"Thanks, Val."

CHAPTER FOUR

Once Marty and I and Miss Tits settled ourselves out on the far boundary of Artemis in some folding chairs, we didn't have much left to do except talk. I realized I wanted company because I didn't want to have time to think about Alison and what might be going through her mind. I would have preferred that my only companion was Marty, but since she was part of a matched pair, I got Miss Tits too, whether I liked it or not. I thought I might leave them alone after a few hours since Marty was the one who liked to be up at night. I hoped I would become tired enough to sleep.

"Hey, Lane. A rumor's going around that your high school sweetheart is here and you haven't seen her in a really long time and you didn't know she was coming or anything." Marty was balancing Miss Tits on her lap and a thermos of coffee in her hand. To my cynical mind, it looked as though Miss Tits was smothering her since the breasts in question were right in front of Marty's nose. But what did I know? I was surely no relationship expert.

The pre-fest rumor mill was running along in its usual way: fast but not terribly accurate.

"Pretty much true but it wasn't high school. It was Girl Scout camp. And we weren't sweethearts. I wasn't officially out, and neither was she. We were 'best friends.'" I sounded sarcastic.

In her little squeaky voice, Miss Tits said, "Oh, I know how *that* is. How about now? Is she, like, you know, a lesbo?"

Miss Tits sounded like a Valley Girl dyke. Yikes, what a thought. Why would Denver have Valley Girls? And why would my usually clear-headed buddy Marty want to sleep with one? It was the tits, I guess.

"I have no idea, and I try not to make judgments about women without evidence."

"Well, you never know until you try," Miss Tits said in a sing-song voice.

Marty said, "Honey pie, leave Lane alone."

Marty knew enough about me to know I had become uncomfortable.

"Okay, baby," she said and squeezed Mary's neck tighter. Marty coughed, and there was the epitome of why I probably would never be great at relationships. Literal and figurative strangulation.

They began cooing at each other while I stared into the black woods. It wasn't just my unconscious, but my waking mind was also speculating about Alison.

Honestly, I didn't really want to seduce her, or at least I knew it wasn't the right way to go. I just wanted to know how she felt about the last summer we were together. Did she remember how we were? That summer we spent a good many weeks in that twilight zone between friends and lovers. At least that's what my memory said. Back then she was hard to read, mercurial and often distracted, though sometimes she acted like her usual affectionate self with me.

What would happen if I screwed up my courage and just asked her to talk about what happened to us when camp was over? Just to find out about what had gone on from her perspective? Would that make things easier for me? Would it would be a relief for her to hear from me that I no longer had any hard feelings? That I wanted to be her friend? Would she be friendlier if I just apologized?

'Shh!" Marty said in hissy whisper. This startled me out of my musings.

"Turn off your flashlights," I whispered, and they complied.

We sat in near-total darkness, though there was some light from a three-quarter moon.

The faint-gray sky filtering through the black trees reminded me of the nights I spent lying awake next to Alison in the cabin. I cleared my mind and concentrated on seeing or hearing what had made Marty raise the alarm.

The forest isn't totally quiet at night. There are animals, and breezes stir the trees. Almost anything could make a little noise; it didn't have to be of human origin. We sat, holding our breath for several seconds.

"I guess it was nothing," Marty said, sounding disappointed. I knew how she felt. I wanted there to be something real.

"Is it okay if I leave you two? Take me back to Bates, and you can keep the car. You don't have to stay here all night if you don't want to. Just spend a couple more hours. Call me on the radio for anything, anything at all."

Later I was still wakeful. Almost guaranteed daily interaction of some sort with Alison would make my feelings impossible to ignore, but I needed to be rested and ready for the festival later that week. I would talk to her, if for no other reason than to try to quiet my mind so I could get some sleep.

On Monday morning, Marty and Miss Tits didn't report any unusual activity, but I wanted to take a look around during the day. I have a pretty good sense of direction but was afraid of getting lost in unfamiliar woods, and I didn't have a compass. Then I remembered meeting the local lesbian, Sarajane, the day before. I found her and asked her to go along with me since she was an outdoors person and familiar with the area.

She agreed. Obviously, she liked being asked for help.

"I suppose some good ole boys might have strayed into the woods and got a little too close to the camp, but I bet they don't mean no harm and they'll leave us alone."

Her faith in her neighbors' good intentions touched me, but I wasn't convinced. I was still curious about whatever Evie had thought she'd heard or seen.

Sarajane and I bushwhacked a ways into the woods, maybe five hundred yards, then circled back. Fortunately, she had a compass.

I saw cigarette butts in a few spots, and I pointed them out to her. They didn't look old, but it was hard to tell. Butts, after all, aren't biodegradable. As far as I know, they hang around for years.

"Even a city slicker like me knows hunters won't smoke in the woods if they're actually trying to kill something."

Sarajane laughed. "That's true, but the butts still may not mean anything."

"Nope, but I have my doubts. What the heck would someone be doing out here if they weren't hunting?"

She shook her head.

I'd have to find a way to get women up at the Artemis parking lot to keep watch, and I had no idea if I would have enough volunteers to spare from other critical areas. Marty would be on duty and on the move. I would have to wait until the festival started. Then I'd try to get some women to sit up there at night. Maybe Magda would agree to contribute a couple of women to the task.

Sarajane said, "I'll try and keep my ears open and see if anyone around town's talking about the festival and what they're saying. But you know there might not be nothing said 'til it actually starts." Sarajane was staying off-site at home until the festival opened.

I thanked Sarajane and drove her back to the stage area, then thanked Willa for letting me borrow her for a while.

❖

Right after breakfast we met with the equipment mistress, Tanya. She was basically in charge of all material not directly related to the stage and sound set-ups. She was the person to go to for what you needed. She issued walkie-talkies to all the coordinators, and we worked out who was going to use what channel, and everyone learned basic radio-communication etiquette. I caught her eye a couple of times, and she still looked like she might be interested in me.

Arden had a surprise for us. She'd rented golf carts for some of the coordinators who had to be mobile, and that included me. We all received a lesson on how to drive a golf cart. The group included Angie from the medical team, who was the taller of the couple.

As we waited around for golf-cart driving lessons, she started talking to me. At festivals, in between the bouts of feverish activity, we wait and we chat. I wasn't sure I wanted to talk to her because Goddess knows what Alison had said about me, but at the same time, I could possibly get some insight into Alison from her.

Angie didn't waste any time jumping right into an intrusive conversation. The instant intimacy at music festival makes some women act like they can say anything to anyone for any reason. That usually irritated me, but not this time.

"Alison says y'all were at camp together."

"Yep. That's true. I think we met there when we were around twelve,"

"She told me you had kinda of a crush on her."

"I guess that's also true." I was starting to feel anxious. Where was this going? I didn't want to get into a discussion about Alison and me. I just wanted to know more about Alison, but I wasn't sure I could get one without the other.

"Alison's a good woman. She's not ticked off at you anymore."

Huh. If that was true, then why was she so standoffish? I kicked a pebble and rocked back on my heels.

Finally, I caught Angie's gaze. "Good to hear. I'm not mad at her either."

Angie nodded, looking at me thoughtfully.

"Good then. Maybe y'all can be friends."

"I'd like that very much," I told Angie with as much sincerity as I could muster. I hoped she'd convey the sentiment to Alison, and Alison would stop treating me like a stranger.

I finally received my golf cart and went to find Marty to show it off to her, if she wasn't busy with Miss Tits.

❖

I kept delaying my second approach to Alison because I was scared, and also I still wanted her to make the first move. The festival would open in a couple days, and I was afraid once that happened our chance to talk would be harder to engineer.

At breakfast, Marty and I refined my plan and figured out how many additional volunteers we would need. She, of course, still had Miss Tits hanging on her like a remora on a shark, and I had to let that go. I had enough to think about, and I had meetings with other coordinators to find out what their expectations were.

Of all the areas of the music festival, the ones that vexed me the most were the vendors and the main stage. I suppose it was because those areas had the most demanding customers. Every area needed some sort of security help, but those were the two that held the most potential for controversy. Personally, I was rather more concerned with people who drank too much, medical emergencies, or intruders in the remote areas, but vendors and performers had to be catered to because they were what made money for Arden. She had a difficult job as a producer, and I was sympathetic, but I had to work to keep my eyes from rolling when some prima-donna singer or overly tense jewelry artist waylaid me with her concerns. I didn't give a crap who got backstage passes, and if someone wanted to rob a vendor, I likely couldn't prevent it. As much as lesbians like to think of themselves as evolved, and we most certainly are way more advanced than the rest of humanity, we're still human. Sometimes we do antisocial or inappropriate things.

I was still, however, enamored of the novelty of tooling around in a golf cart. I saw Alison in passing a couple times on Sunday and Monday at meals, and every time I saw her, it was like getting whacked on the head with a mallet. She made no move to speak to me. She'd wave in a friendly fashion, and we'd go our separate ways. After the huge build-up in my head for this reunion, this was all very anti-climactic. It was clear that she didn't intend to approach me. If I wanted to talk to her, I would have to make the first move, and who knew if she'd even want to try to come to terms with our past

The temperature was rising. I was getting hot and wanted to change to a tank top. On Sunday, I'd avoided the infirmary end of Bates if I happened to be nearby, but I decided that was stupid and I wanted to see Alison if she was there.

When I walked up the steps, I could hear voices, and I stopped just outside the door to listen. I identified one as Alison's, and the others were likely her pals Angie and Leah. I carefully peeked in and there they were. They didn't appear to be the least bit busy. They were sitting around on folding chairs with sodas in hand. They didn't seem to notice me, so I stayed as quiet as I could.

Alison was fanning herself, though only a slight-pink tinge to her cheeks indicated she was feeling the heat. Her hair was neatly tied back, and she wore that sleeveless pink cotton shirt and blue Bermuda shorts. Her upper arms were evenly tan, as were her legs, which were razor smooth. I was suddenly self-conscious about my pallor. Like a lot of San Franciscans, I didn't wear shorts much because it never got hot, ergo, no suntan except on my face and arms. Alison looked wonderful, relaxed and very young. As a matter of fact, she looked almost exactly as she had at seventeen. My heart gave a little jump. It wasn't painful, but it was like a tug of reminder of why I had become obsessed with her in the first place. Now I understood why. I was in love with her, and that love included a huge component of sexual attraction. The years hadn't dimmed it. It had gone dormant, but being back with her, seeing her in the flesh brought that fire roaring back to life.

Alison's tall friend Angie was saying to her shorter lover, Leah, "Honey, am I going to have to put tape on your mouth? Stop pestering Alison, even though she looks as good as an ice cream sundae at a softball game."

"Oh, you know we're just fooling, honey. Alison loves me best, don't you, girl? Now don't get jealous, Angie."

Angie gave a sardonic little snort. "Huh."

Leah sounded like one of those women who just liked to tease until you wanted to slap her.

She obviously was talking to Alison, who had been silent since I began my eavesdropping.

"If you don't watch out, one a' these no-account, wild-ass West Coast types is going to catch you."

"I don't think so," Alison said.

"Maybe that Security gal. Your old camp buddy. Hmm?"

I was amused that they were ragging Alison about me. That was interesting, if juvenile. I kept myself out of sight, hoping to hear more.

Alison said, "Leah, honey, give it a rest. That's ancient history."

Leah said, "Oh, but you never know about them old flames. They can flare right up again."

"And then you get burned. Angie, tell your girl to stop bugging me."

"Leah, honey. I told you to stop messing with Alison."

"Oh, all right."

They started talking about something else, and I felt safe to reveal myself. I waited a few more moments.

"Hi, women," I said breezily, but I fixed my gaze on Alison and gave her a big hundred-watt grin. "Everyone behaving herself? Have you had any customers today?"

Leah said, "The word's 'y'all,' and if we weren't behaving ourselves, what would you do about it?"

She was sitting with one leg crossed and bouncing her foot up and down, staring me down like we were in a gunfight at the OK corral.

"Um, let me see. It would depend on what you were doing. I'd consult my rule book and come up with a suitable punishment."

This caused a chorus of "oohs" from Leah and Angie, but Alison just looked at me.

"Nope," she said. "No one's been around."

"Well, let me just go and see if I can find something for you to do." This time I beamed at all three of them.

'You don't have to do that. We're just fine," Angie said. "Are you bored?"

"No. I'm never bored. I can always find something to do."

I don't know why I made that remark sound salacious, but I was trying to keep talking so I could stick around and look at and talk to Alison. I didn't mind her cohorts. Too much.

"Just what is it you do exactly?" Leah asked.

"I keep people safe. Or I try to. I can't be everywhere at once. And well, whatever people ask me to do. For instance, I'll have a couple people stationed backstage when the festival starts, just to keep the chaos sort of manageable. Someone always says she's so-and-so's friend and so-and-so's expecting her."

"Sounds hard."

"Sometimes. Well, I just stopped to say 'hi.' Have a good day."

I waved good-bye and went back outside. Then I paused for a microsecond and went back to stand by the door out of sight. I felt silly, but I still couldn't stop myself.

"What's up with Lane?" It was Leah talking. "That was kinda random." She drew out my name into two syllables in a very obnoxious way.

Alison said, "She's just being friendly. You said the West Coast people are sort of abrupt and standoffish. Now here's one being nice, and you think she's up to something."

Hmm. Alison sounded impatient.

Leah said, "She might be. Up to someone, not something."

Alison said, "Now don't you start in on me again. She's an old friend. There's nothing going on."

Leah cackled. "You told us y'all were hot and heavy back in the day. Or at least she was. But you were little Miss Priss. You held out on her."

Angie said, "Honey, if Alison doesn't want to talk about it, let it go. Though I'm kinda curious how you're doing now that Ellie or Lane or whatever the heck her name is has actually shown up."

I froze. What in the world had Alison told them? What did it mean I'd 'shown up'? At the music festival or just now?

"It wasn't like that then, and nothing's up now. Leave me be, you two. I'm fine with Lane. Geez. Y'all are like a couple of magpies."

Then I heard more laughter, but I suspected Alison wasn't laughing. She could be humorless sometimes, especially if she didn't want to talk about something. But I was intrigued that she didn't find their teasing funny and wouldn't engage. I snuck in the back door of Bates, changed my shirt, and went off to look for the stage manager. My chat with the three musketeers reminded me she was one coordinator I'd not talked with.

Cruising in the golf cart, I made my way up the road, enjoying the ambience. Things were coming together. The festival was less than two days away, and more women were around, but nothing like what would occur once we opened for business Thursday noon.

Across the road from the kitchen was a small amphitheater with about a hundred seats. This was going to be a workshop area. By force of habit, I parked the golf cart and walked toward the stage just to take a look around the back area to make sure all was well.

I passed a couple with a little girl of about seven. She was between them, holding on to both their hands and jumping and skipping. As I walked past the family, I grinned and said hello, and they chorused hello back to me. I strode ahead a few paces, scanning right and left. I couldn't have been more than fifteen feet in front of them when I heard a slight scream and some scraping and shuffling sounds. I turned around and saw the child on the ground thrashing and twitching and the two women bending over her, their faces registering shock and fear.

I sprinted over them, and when I was able to see the little girl, I knew what was going on. *Seizure.*

I knelt next to one of the women and took a moment to settle my own jolt of adrenaline and shock.

"It's okay. I'm calling the medical team." I put a hand on her arm, and she nodded her assent. I pulled my radio mike to my mouth and clicked it on.

"This is Lane. Over."

The radio crackled. "Angie here."

I gave her the details of what happened and my location.

Then I turned back to the couple.

"They'll be here really quick. Don't worry." I used my best reassuring smile, knowing that my calm voice and my official-looking walkie-talkie would signal helpful authority figure. I hoped they wouldn't spin off into hysteria. Sometimes that happened, especially with parents of kids. Something going wrong with a child will send the parents into orbit. I'd dealt with a few lost children at gay events back in San Francisco.

Within five minutes, a golf cart pulled up, and Angie and Alison jumped out.

"We're nurses. Try to stay calm, and we'll take care of her." The couple retreated and let Angie and Alison tend to their daughter.

I backed off too and just watched as they took the child's vital signs and looked her over. She was awake but obviously disoriented.

I watched Alison, her facial expression and the movements of her hands. She and Angie spoke in the clipped shorthand of medical people exchanging information. She was calm, compassionate, and very, very self-confident. She put a stethoscope on the child's chest as Angie examined her pupils with a pen light.

Something shifted in my mind. I was looking at the new Alison, the adult Alison, not the teenage crush who broke my heart. To my mental list of what I loved about Alison, I added "good nurse."

They finished their exam and looped their stethoscopes over their necks as one. Alison spoke to the two moms.

"We think she's all right. You say it was a brief seizure?" The mothers nodded, still looking worried.

"We'd like to take her back to medical for observation for a little while."

The two moms looked at each other, and some nonverbal exchange occurred between them. Then one answered, "Yes, please."

Angie and the mothers got themselves arranged in the golf cart with the girl on her mother's lap.

Alison said to Angie, "I'll be along in a minute."

Alison turned to look at me. "It was good you were here."

"Is she going to be all right?" I asked.

"I think so. It's likely just a case of missing her medication dose or too much excitement. It was a mild seizure, not a bad one."

"Okay. Great."

"So this is what you do?" Alison asked.

I was confused and it must have shown on my face.

"What…?

"When there's some medical problem, you know what to do. You don't freak out."

"Oh, no. I've seen a lot of stuff. I know some first aid. But I always call Medical. I work more on making sure nothing *else* goes wrong. If we were in the middle of a crowd, I'd keep the gawkers back."

"That's really good." She smiled that familiar Alison smile at me, and it gave me a spike of pleasure. And because I had Alison's attention, I couldn't help but boast a little.

"It's strange. I often seem to be in the right place at the right time. When something happens, I seem to be there so I can jump right in and try to stabilize the situation and call you guys, of course. With my radio." I held up the microphone. I was truly being dopey, but I couldn't help myself. I wanted Alison to really understand how seriously I take what I do.

Alison nodded. "Well. That's wonderful. Those women would have been panicky and might not have known what to do or where to go. Your being here made it much easier for them."

"I'm glad to help. That's what I'm here to do."

Alison stared at me as though she was coming to a realization.

"What?" I asked her, with a touch of humor.

"Nothing. I don't know. My impression of you was that you're kind of a hard-ass. No nonsense, no fooling around. You kind of stride around with your sunglasses and your radio like you're the boss of the world."

I was both amused and irked.

"Really? That's how you see me?"

"I remember you were pretty bossy when we were kids. And impatient."

I laughed. "Well, I'm still impatient sometimes, but I've mellowed a bit. Also being bossy's kind of a part of my job."

Alison kept that same look on her face as she gazed at me.

"Well, I guess it's your boots and your shades. And your haircut and the, um, fact that you're sort of muscled. Makes you seem tough."

I couldn't help smiling. It sounded as though she was flirting with me.

"Yes, it's true. I'm butch."

She winced slightly. She didn't like the word butch?

"But it doesn't seem like you're insensitive or even that masculine. Quite the opposite." She said this like it was a big surprise to her. I didn't know whether to be touched or irritated. It seemed like Alison hadn't been around too many varieties of lesbians. Well, she was going to get a crash course on all species belonging to genus *dyke* at the festival.

We were both at a loss, it seemed, for what to say next.

"Well, I've got to get back to Medical. See you later, okay?"

"Yeah. Sure. See you." She walked off, and I went back to the golf cart and just sat for moment.

My mind churned. What was that? Did something happen? Was I imagining things?

Her voice had taken on a tender tone, with an undercurrent of laughter. Since our meeting the evening before, she'd gone from totally standoffish, to neutral, to mildly friendly, to…flirting? Nah. I was imagining it. I was just glad she no longer treated me like I was about to throw a fit and rip her a new bodily orifice. I noticed she'd sounded Southern but less so than in the conversation I'd overheard at Bates.

Huh.

I shook my head and recalled I'd been on my way to the stage to talk to the stage manager before I got waylaid. I drove up to the main stage area, dismissing my fruitless speculation about the state of Alison's psyche.

The stage construction was progressing well. The workers had already built a sturdy wooden frame, and bare-breasted lovelies wielded hammers as they nailed the boards in place.

The stage manager, Nadia, was a pleasant woman with a multi-pierced ear and a butterfly tattoo on her wrist, but I knew from experience that you didn't want to mess with her.

"Hey, Lane. I'm glad you're here. Let's go talk in the RV."

After being in the hot sun for a while, it was a nice change to be indoors in a relatively cool place.

We sat at the little midget RV kitchen table, and I took notes.

Nadia said, "Once the festival opens, I need six women for Security full-time."

I stopped myself from saying, "No way."

"I would love to be able to promise you that, but I can't. I'll have at least four volunteers for every evening performance, and I'll have two people sleeping overnight on the stage every night, plus there's a night supervisor. Marty? You know who she is? And her girlfriend, Tina."

Nadia nodded, but she said, "You know what it's like, Lane. That's not enough."

I *did* know. We were about to be overrun by an invading horde of Visigoths, otherwise known as lesbians. They'd end up all over the place and would even wander into areas posted as no access.

"I understand your concern. I'll do the best I can."

"We need two backstage, two in front, two for wherever."

I loved it when women tried to tell me how to do my job, and I tamped down my irritation. I couldn't decide anything anyhow until I gathered my volunteers once the festival started.

CHAPTER FIVE

At Arden's request, I kept my radio turned on twenty-four hours a day. The number of women on site had doubled since our arrival three days before. I didn't mind since I was used to being on call basically the whole time the festival was actively going on. As more women arrived, the chance for something to go awry kept increasing. So far, it had been quiet except for the little girl with the seizure. On Monday, however, the crafts women started showing up, along with workshop facilitators, and then performers would begin arriving Tuesday and Wednesday. Tuesday was a good day to go shopping, in case you didn't have enough labyrises or cunt coloring books in your life. That's when I would buy jewelry for whatever girl I'd left behind. It helped mollify them a little. No girl at home this time and I could save my money.

Just after lunch, Becky radioed me, "Lane, can you come over to the house? Now? The county sheriff is here."

What the hell? Didn't these guys believe in calling ahead? They likely didn't care about the inconvenience and wanted to put us off-balance. That was a power move. I'd dealt with law-enforcement people before, but this would be the first time I had ever interacted with cops of the Southern species. I admit I had a preconceived image of what they were like, probably formed from watching too many movies like *The Heat of the Night* and learning the history of the civil-rights movement and police brutality. I had the lefty lesbo's distrust and dislike of police, but I knew how to disguise it under a veneer of cooperation.

I needed to keep an open mind and turn on my most cooperative and amiable persona. We didn't want to raise any alarms with the local law, and we certainly didn't want any sheriff's deputies showing up unannounced during the festival, because that would surely freak everyone out.

Arden and Becky were occupying the little house that belonged to the camp director. It was way back behind the kitchen, out of the main festival area.

When I walked into the living room, they were sitting with two tan-clad men with guns. They were all drinking coffee, and it appeared to be a friendly visit. Maybe. I made sure I had on my best calm and professional expression.

Arden said, "Sheriff, Deputy, this is my head of Security, Lane Hudson."

I shook hands with both men and sat down. Becky brought me a coffee.

Arden looked pleasant and relaxed. She was an expert schmoozer, and she didn't need me to support her, but she knew it best to have the cops meet me. If there was a critical situation where we have to summon the cops, that's not the best moment to meet for the very first time. I knew the drill because I'd been through this before. We needed to be human beings to one another first. We didn't have time to establish relationships, I was happy to meet with them, just uneasy that they hadn't made an appointment.

After the usual pleased-to-meet-you chitchat and random compliments of the beauty of the northern Georgia countryside, we got down to business.

The sheriff, Tanner, was above middle age, balding, with a deep voice and avuncular manner of slightly uptight but basically okay guy, like an uncle. The deputy, who was younger, was obviously much less at ease and had a tight, uncomfortable smirk—all teeth and no real humor.

Arden took the lead and told the two sheriffs about the size of and the nature of the music festival. She, of course, didn't use the word lesbian. No use in waving any red flags. While she talked, they nodded gravely.

Sheriff Tanner said, "We've checked your permits and with the owners, and that's all in order." Another subtle message— we're watching you.

Arden asked me to describe my function.

I gave a practiced speech about our process of self-policing, making my persona as inoffensive as possible. No police types like to have their authority challenged, even subtly, so I turn on what charm I possess when talking with them. I sort of turn down the butch factor. There's no use in antagonizing these guys, who were already a little freaked out about dealing with women in power. If this was true of cops in San Francisco, bastion of liberal politics, then it would be even more true in northern Georgia.

"We don't expect that we'll have any sort of trouble from any of our attendees, but please feel free to call us right away, if necessary, for anything," I said.

It was rare, but once in a while one or more of the girls got into a situation with a local, and I had to help resolve it. Rural Northern California wasn't the same environment as cities like San Francisco, Seattle, or Los Angeles. In fact, its ambience had more in common with northern Georgia, just without the Southern accents. The starry-eyed, exuberant festies sometimes forgot that fact and ran afoul of an easily offended local, and I had to smooth things over. Here in the South, I was more worried about locals causing trouble for *us*, but I needed to find a diplomatic way of bringing that concern up.

I was thinking of what Sarajane had said the day before. Her assurances were all well and good, but what might we expect if the locals hassled us and we needed to summon the sheriff?

I asked the sheriff that question in a diplomatic manner.

"Well, you've got a hunting area on the west side of here, but the boundary of the camp is clearly marked, and no one would have any reason to trespass, though I guess some people who ought to mind their own business could get a little nosy. We don't want any trouble for anyone, including your people, but you best make sure no one goes wandering out of bounds. Could be a little messy." And I heard the meaning behind his words. *Keep within your boundaries, and you won't have any trouble. Out of bounds, and we may not be on your side so much.*

I sure hoped that no one at the festival started wandering around and left the safety of the land. That wasn't typical, because we were trying to get away from the outside world, so it was counterintuitive to think anyone would leave. Once the festies arrived, they basically couldn't drive anywhere. They were stuck for the entire four days except for an emergency. That was how Magda designed the parking, and there was no other way to manage it. We didn't need constant coming and going. The festies knew to bring everything they needed because they wouldn't have any in-and-out privileges.

I explained our policy to the sheriff, and he seemed to relax a little. Deputy Trent never changed his expression during the conversation.

"That's good to know. Well, Dwayne," he said to his uptight deputy, "that 'bout wraps this little confab up. Ladies?" Neither Arden nor I made a peep of protest at this condescending manner of address. We didn't have anything to gain.

We all shook hands, and we murmured polite thanks for their visit.

"Here's my card," Sheriff Tanner said. "Y'all go right ahead and call if you need anything."

I went back out to my golf cart to visit the crafts area.

The work crew at music festivals spends ten days of hard work preparing for the event, and when it finally arrives and the thousands of women descend upon us, we're almost disappointed, as though the festies have invaded our space and spoiled all our fun.

But this time, I wanted the festival opening to come faster so I would have a lot more to do and not too much time to think. If I could share a normal friendship with Alison, that would suffice. I didn't know where she was about her sexuality when we were teenagers, and I didn't know now, and essentially it wasn't any of my business.

After another circuit of the land, I was at loose ends that afternoon so I went to the kitchen to hang out with Valencia and her crew. The stage-construction people were busy all the time and didn't appreciate any distraction. The kitchen staff worked like crazy around meals but had a lull after lunch and before dinner. If Valencia thought I was being a nuisance, she'd tell me to leave. Otherwise I was her friend who was welcome in the kitchen.

"Hey, girl!" Valencia waved me over. She was sitting amongst a crowd, but I noticed the younger woman with a ring in her nose who was sitting next to her had a hand on Val's leg, dangerously close to her crotch.

Ah-ha. The empress had chosen a favorite. She might not last, but she was obviously the girl of the moment. Some of the women were clutching beers, which wasn't unusual for the breakfast and lunch cooks. They were off duty, and even if someone was needed for dinner, drinking a beer or two wasn't considered bad form. All the functional areas had their own rules about alcohol consumption during work periods, and the kitchen was the loosest in spite of Val's clean-and-sober status. She could be merciless, however, if someone screwed up.

Val was raucous enough without alcohol. She had a loud guffaw that just made me smile whenever I heard it.

When I pulled up a chair in their little circle, she gave me a nice hug.

"Are we safe today, Boss?" she asked me. "For those of you who don't know, this our Security coordinator, Lane. She's the best and the butchest and the baddest. You want her on your side."

"Depends on what you consider safe," I said after the laughter died down. I flicked a glance at the wandering hand of her little girlfriend.

The kitchen helpers chose to take this as a sexual innuendo, which was pretty much routine at the music festival, and let loose a chorus of "Ooos."

"If you want to know if we're safe from storms, yeah, the weather report is good. No intruders reported. No injuries reported except for a carpenter with a splinter. Someone from Medical kissed her finger and made it all better. If you want to know if I've busted anyone for carnal activity or drinking, no. I'd never have a moment of rest if I paid attention to all that." I got a good, hearty laugh for that small joke. Humor is always the best way to get people on your side.

"So what about around here in the land of pots and pans? What's going on? Are you sure you got enough garlic on hand? I didn't smell any in the pasta yesterday."

They giggled, because garlic liberally laced just about everything we ate. I'm not sure why this was. I guess because it's a good spice for most anything and it's cheap, Valencia added huge amounts of garlic to everything but our granola. I think I stopped tasting it by the second day.

"We're good, we're good. I just have to keep cracking the whip because, with all this estrogen running rampant, it's hard to keep our minds on cooking." I didn't want to ruin Val's joke by saying that it was actually testosterone that gave women their sex drives, so I only laughed.

"Hey, Lane. What are the four major food groups at festival?" This was from one of the gypsy volunteers. She'd clearly been working on the answer for some time and was very proud of it.

"I give up. What?"

"Sugar, fat, alcohol, and body parts." This sent the whole group into waves of laughter.

"Y'all are so bad."

I didn't know the woman who was speaking, but her accent clearly marked her as being from the land of Dixie.

Val snuggled closer to her companion and took a big gulp of Pepsi. That was her poison of choice rather than beer or vodka or red wine.

"Why's that, Marla?" someone asked, and her tone suggested she knew the answer already.

"Well, first of all, it's like all y'all ever talk about is sex. And if y'all aren't talking about it, y'all are thinking about it. If y'all aren't thinking about it, you're doing it, and if you're not doing it, y'all are about to do it or just done it."

Sardonic laughter greeted this rant.

"Gosh almighty, y'all are obsessed."

"Don't Southern women have sex?" one of Val's people asked.

Marla favored her with a sarcastic grimace.

"Well, of course. We're not crazy. We just tend to be a tad more discreet."

"Yeah, well, wait 'til all the festies get here. You're going to trip over the gals getting it on," one woman said.

I said, "That's when I get involved. If anyone complains, you understand."

They chortled.

Another one said, "Yeah. You won't believe what lesbians are like out in the woods surrounded by nothing but other lesbians. They go crazy, and I predict the Southerners will too."

"I really doubt that," Marla said. "You won't be seeing them all yanking all their clothes off and walking around buck naked, I bet. We're just way too conservative for that stuff."

Marla looked as though she could use some loosening up. I predicted she'd be shirtless and shagging every girl who crossed her path in a short while. Festivals tended to have that effect on women. I knew some of the most copious sex occurred between the festival volunteers. If I happened to have a girlfriend with me or if I was between girlfriends, which was not generally the case, I had my share. But this time, other than maybe Tanya, I just hadn't spotted any likely prospects besides Val. Yet.

Val took another gulp of Pepsi. "I see."

"So now that you've been around all the West Coast women for a few days, what else is different besides the nudity part?" She grinned at Marla.

"My goodness, let me see. Y'all talk too fast, move too fast. Y'all are exhausting. We like to take our ti-ime." The group crowed and giggled.

Marla wrinkled her nose in exasperation. "Not just *that* but with everything. And another thing, this whole vegetarian deal y'all are so into is not going to be popular. We're meat eaters. Barbecue, fried chicken. Y'all aren't right."

The festival staff dinners did include animal protein, mostly chicken, but the festies were fed strictly vegetarian food, for budgetary reasons. If they wanted meat, they'd have to bring it with them. I already envisioned barbecues full of burning coals tipping over and starting fires. I estimated about half of the West Coast volunteers were vegetarians. Evidently none of the Southerners were.

Marla was on a roll, and she kept going on about the various odd characteristics of non-Southern lesbians: multiple piercings, goddess worship, S/M sex, too much cursing, etc.

Finally, Val called a halt to the discussion. The kitchen staff had to get to work, and hangers-on were to leave unless they intended to help with dinner. One of the kitchen crew came around the building and said, "Hey Val. The Sysco delivery is here."

"Roger. Well. I have to get busy. Say, Lane. If you're not in a hurry, come help unload the truck."

It was the least I could do since I was the recipient of so much kindness from Val. I abhor physical labor most of the time, but I could help out just a little.

The gigantic truck held all sorts of large restaurant-style quantities of oatmeal, syrup, flour, canned vegetables, and other dry goods and produce. In two days, Val was going to need it all to prepare breakfast, lunch, and dinner for two thousand festies, plus a hundred or so workers.

In short order, a line of women was transferring boxes and bags from one to another, like a line of ants. I'd seen versions of this type of cooperation many times. We could do anything, given enough warm bodies. I took a spot near the kitchen back entrance. It's a nice feeling, really, the camaraderie. This was what I meant when I compared the music festival to Girl Scout camp to Alison.

I decided that moving food crates was an acceptable substitute for the weight-lifting I was missing.

A crate came down the line that required two women to lift it.

When it arrived to me, one of the women said, "You'll need another set of hands."

Nonsense. I'm plenty strong.

"I got it." They handed it to me, and it was much heavier than I thought it would be and appeared to be full of cabbages. I fumbled and staggered, and one end of the crate fell directly onto my left foot. My eyes watered with pain, but I clenched my teeth. Several women rushed over and grabbed the crate, which I was foolishly still trying to muscle.

"Come sit down here," one of them ordered. Nope. This wasn't the drill. I give orders. I don't take them unless from Arden.

"Nope, I'm okay. Don't wor—"

They ignored me and made me sit on the steps by the kitchen's back porch.

My foot throbbed horribly, but I was more embarrassed than anything else. I was hoping not too many girls had noticed that I was obviously not as butch as I seemed.

"Just sit," one of the kitchen crew said. "Can we use your radio to call Medical?"

"No! I said I was okay." I tried to stand, but the pressure on my foot made it hurt more. I staggered on one leg.

Valencia appeared and looked at me critically. She motioned someone over, who didn't say a word but looped my arm over her shoulder

"Lane. Behave. Sit down. Now."

I was seeing little black things in my vision and felt dizzy. This was crazy. I was also feeling nauseous, so I sat down without more prompting.

"Take off her boot," Valencia ordered one of her girls. Someone unlaced my hiking shoe and made me turn and rest my heel on the step above where I sat. I knew enough first aid to realize this was the correct thing to do. I was angry with myself for allowing this to happen and already fretting about the consequences to my work. Not that much was going on at the moment, but in less than three days, a lot would be going on, and I couldn't afford to be laid up.

Val stared at my foot and said, "I'm getting Medical."

And with that, she grabbed my radio mike and spoke into it. Next thing I heard was Angie's voice affirming they'd be there ASAP.

A few minutes passed as I got myself under control by breathing through the nausea and not attempting to move again.

"Well. What have we here?"

To my combined relief and consternation, Alison and Angie were standing in front of me. Alison was staring at me with some sort of look that could be either concern or disapproval. I told them what had happened.

"Let's get your sock off," Angie said. Alison did the honors, and the three of us observed the bruise on my instep. Bruises I could handle, but I prayed nothing was broken. Alison touched my foot gently, moving my toes.

"How does that feel?" she asked.

"It's okay."

"How about this?" She pressed on the top of my foot, and I nearly screamed.

"Ow."

"We better take you back to Bates," Alison said with finality.

I could only nod weakly. The excruciating pain was really coming on now, as what I assumed was mild shock dissipated. I was in no space to argue anymore with anyone about anything.

Angie and Alison each took one of my arms and pulled them over their shoulders.

I went instantly tense as the right side of my body connected with Alison's. I was hyper-aware of how warm she was and that our breasts were millimeters away from one another and actually touched as we jostled slightly. Only the terrible pain I was in kept me from losing it altogether.

Before I could fully absorb the impact of being close to Alison, they set me in the backseat of the golf cart, and we drove to the infirmary. To get me inside, they had to repeat the process. My feelings about Angie touching me were purely indifferent, but not so with Alison. I was nervous that something would show in my face, but I think I was hurting too much to register anything but a grimace.

"Let's put you on one of the cots." And with that I was soon lying down with a pillow under my foot. I endured more prodding and movement of my injury by Angie as Alison disappeared, only to return a few minutes later with some ice and some aspirin.

Finally, Angie said, "I don't think anything's broken. Just a bad bruise."

Alison nodded. "I think so too." She turned to me and grinned. "Well, hotshot. You're going to have to be still for a few days. Can you manage? Or do we need to knock you out?"

"I'll be good. I have to get better by Wednesday. Or earlier."

"We'll see about that," Angie said severely. I was optimistic. I'm a good and fast healer. I'd gotten little bumps and owies before, when I was pumping iron.

"We're going to give you some anti-inflammatories and ice and elevate this foot, and you're going to stay put. Okay?"

"Sure," I said, "But I would love to have something to read. There's a book by my bed."

They agreed and left me in the little room feeling foolish and trying to act cool while I contemplated how much this development would disrupt my work and my routine and how much my goddamn foot hurt. Then I wondered if it meant I'd see more of Alison. I hoped she'd be my caregiver. If someone was going to have to help me get around, I wanted that to be Alison. I guess you could say I enjoy torture, or just maybe if we could get a little time together, maybe we could talk some more.

July 1970

"Well. I guess we'll just have to write. You promise you will?" I asked Alison. *We would be too old to be campers the next year but not old enough to be counselors.*

"Oh yeah. I'll write you every week."

"And then we'll be counselors the next year. You promise?"

"I promise, Ellie. We'll come back just like we talked about."

The summer of 1971 was the first we'd spent apart since we met, and it almost killed me. I went to Camp Henry Kaufmann in Pennsylvania as a junior counselor that summer, and Alison went to church camp.

At CHK I acquired a lot more Girl Scout skills, but I also learned that what I felt about Alison had a name—lesbian. It was a big joke, something girls would make fun of and accuse each other of being. "Les-be friends," one would say and put her arm around another, and everyone would laugh. It made me nervous. I would try to laugh but it always made me feel anxious.

Meanwhile, our letters kept up, and in the spring of 1972, we were both hired as camp counselors for the summer at Triple Creek.

CHAPTER SIX

I must have fallen asleep. I woke up to a hand on my shoulder, and when I rolled over, Alison was peering at me in the gloom.

I turned on my back and struggled to wake up. I was sticky from the afternoon heat and groggy, but I was overjoyed Alison was waking me up, not someone else.

"Hi," I said, a bit hoarse. Alison gazed down at me with what I chose to interpret as tenderness.

"Hi there. How do you feel?" Her hand, surprisingly cool, touched my forearm.

"Not bad. Foot hurts less."

"Can I take a look at it?"

"Help yourself."

Peering through the gloom, I watched Alison as she moved a chair next to me. She was so neat and graceful, it made my heart ache. Her hair was tied back, and she wore a femmy little gold wristwatch on her right arm. In the semi-dark, her tanned face and arms made a startling contrast to her white sleeveless shirt.

She moved the now-room-temperature ice pack and tugged my toes and ran her fingers all over my foot, including the bottom, and I jumped and giggled.

"Ticklish?" she asked, smiling. "Sorry."

She absolutely didn't sound sorry. If this was the only way I could get Alison to touch me, I'd take it. I wanted to say something, but I didn't know what. She made me tongue-tied. In the grayish light of the little room, we looked at each other.

"The swelling isn't that bad. I think you'll live to walk again."

"I hope so."

"You will need to stay off it for a while—twenty-four hours at least."

"I promise I will. Say, is it dinnertime yet? I'm hungry."

"Oh yeah. It's suppertime."

She grinned, but judging by her body language, she was unaccountably tense or uncertain. Could touching me have unnerved her? That was a fascinating thought.

"Uh, could you bring me something to eat?"

"Sure." She stood up and turned as if to leave.

"Uh, before you go, could you help to the bathroom?"

She helped me stand. I was nervous but also happy to have Alison holding onto me.

"Do you want crutches?" she asked.

"Not really." I hated the thought of that. "I can hobble if you help me." *Oh, you conniver. You just want to prolong the time she has to spend touching you.*

She wobbled a bit while trying to keep me from putting weight on my bad foot. We staggered our way down the hall to the toilet. And with much careful maneuvering, I was able to accomplish my mission without her help until it was time to walk back to my room.

Back on my cot, I felt a bit done in with the effort.

"Oh. What do you want to eat?" Her voice was neutral, but I could detect a bit of tension underneath. Interesting.

"Everything, but just water to drink."

"You got it."

She left me alone with myself and my sore foot and my futile longings, confusion, and jumbled thoughts about how and when to ask my questions. Would I ever get the answers? And if I got them, would that even satisfy me when I wanted so much more from Alison. Now I didn't just need to put the past to rest. I wanted a present, and I wanted a future with a woman whom I once knew so well but understood so little. If there was a chance for us, I wanted to not pass it up. If there wasn't, well, I wanted to know that too.

Meanwhile, I was dying for a cigarette and was ashamed to ask Alison to help me get outside so I could smoke. With some effort, I pulled myself upright and hopped on one foot to the door and sat on the steps smoking, waiting for Alison to return. At least I was a little bit hopeful. Even though she could just be acting kindly toward me as a patient, it seemed like it could be more. I finished smoking and struggled back to my room.

About forty-five minutes later, Alison returned with not one but two covered plates of chicken cacciatore, garlic bread, and salad. I could smell the garlic fumes when she walked in the door.

I swung my legs gingerly over the edge of the bed.

"You must think I'm a pig if you brought me two dinners."

She gave me an irritated look. "One of these is for me."

"Oh. Okay. Sure."

This took me aback. She was going to have dinner with me? Just us? Was I detecting a subtle shift in her attitude—a thawing? She seemed to be going out of her way to take care of me like I'd hoped, and maybe she was smiling a little more often, and she seemed a little softer and less wary around me. I hoped so. I thought about the situation around the little girl's seizure.

"I know I hate eating by myself. It makes me feel like I have some kind of social disease. So I thought I'd join you. Hope that's okay with you," Alison said calmly.

Whoa. Not only was it okay. It was terrific. She wanted one-on-one time with me, and I hadn't had to ask for it. This was progress. I felt much better. Bruised foot? Bah. Insignificant.

She'd even brought a little cup of parmesan cheese, and she went and found a little table from the treatment area and put it between us. She sat on the chair and I sat on the bed. If we were in a fancy restaurant in downtown San Francisco on a romantic date, I couldn't have been happier than I was at the moment. For the first time, I felt that we were behaving more like the old Allie and Ellie but as our adult selves. This was deeply gratifying. Were we closing the emotional gap? I hoped so. If I couldn't have my fantasies about the future come true, I would settle for just not being distant and weird together.

"Have you had to eat by yourself a lot?" I asked her, trying to make conversation.

"A bit. After I got a divorce, for sure. But before that too. He drank a lot, and I came to prefer eating alone to the sound of yelling and dishes breaking."

"Oh, wow." I swallowed, thinking how that must have frightened her. Then I thought about how loudly I'd yelled at her the last time I saw her. I felt terrible all over again, even though I'd apologized.

I said, "I'd rather eat alone, too, under some circumstances. I don't like the sound of deafening silence when I'm actually sitting across from someone to whom I've got nothing to say. And vice versa."

"That happen to you a lot?" Alison asked. Was she wondering about my relationship history? I'm not sure I wanted to go into detail about that. I noticed also how deftly she kept the conversation away from herself and directed it back to me.

I lied a bit. "Sometimes, but no, not that much. Just hard when it does. How long were you married?"

"About three years."

"No kids?"

"No, thank the Lord. He wanted one, but I didn't. I'm the opposite of most girls I grew up with. They usually got pregnant to get their guys to marry them. They'd lie that they took birth control and it had failed." She laughed then, in a mocking way.

"Me? I lied to Tom that I had not a clue why we couldn't get pregnant, when I was taking the pill the whole damn time, and he never figured it out. I was so glad I did, considering how it ended."

She shivered. Before I could think too much about it, I blurted out my main question.

"Alison?" I took a breath. "Are you straight? Or what?"

She picked at her chicken cacciatore and snorted a little and shook her head.

"Not straight. Maybe 'or what.' Honest to God, I don't know quite what I am. Angie and Leah just think I haven't met the right woman. I'm not taking on any more men, that's for sure. I've had enough of their nonsense. Sex-wise mainly, but their selfishness and crappy attitudes and holier-than-thou ways with women really burn me up."

My heart lightened a little. Indecision was good. What I could do with this information was the issue.

It also reminded me that I had a question for Alison about Angie and Leah. I just needed to ask it without revealing that I'd eavesdropped on their conversation.

"That's part of the reason lesbians prefer women, sure, but there's a lot more to it."

Alison poked a piece of chicken cacciatore with her fork. "If y'all are so hot for women, then why do you look like a guy?"

Then she stuck the chicken in her mouth and chewed, her expression challenging as she waited for me to answer.

Ouch. This wasn't a tough question, but I thought carefully. I tried to figure out what Alison was thinking and why she'd asked that question. She looked curious but not hostile.

"Well, if you look at it from another perspective, I'm just a woman in a different way."

"Huh. I didn't recognize you at first because you didn't look at all like the Ellie I know and..." Was she going to say "love"?

"I'm still her inside," I said, and I fastened my attention on Alison's face, willing her to meet my gaze and understand what I meant.

Her expression softened and she smiled.

"I know that. And I have to admit you're pretty darn cute with your shades and your boots and your attitude. But I can see how much of a softie you really are. That was obvious when you called us about the little girl who had a seizure. You're not that tough."

"I'm only tough when I need to be." I had grown so tense I could barely get that sentence out. She sounded flirtatious again. We hadn't broken eye contact since she'd asked her pointed question. We'd stopped eating our chicken cacciatore as we stared at one another.

"Alison, I wanted to—" There was a clatter on the steps outside and then some footfalls in the corridor. We both turned, and Angie and Leah appeared in the doorframe. *Great.*

"Hi, y'all. How's the patient doing?" Angie asked.

"Pretty well," I said.

Leah winked. "With all this TLC from Alison here, you look like a dead pig in shit."

What the hell did that weird simile mean? And what was with Leah's attitude? She was really beginning to annoy me.

Alison and I glanced at one another. She seemed a tad uneasy, and that sparked my curiosity.

"She's accepted that she's gotta just sit her ass down and not be running all over the place for a couple of days," Alison said.

I grinned genially. "Guess I've resigned myself to my fate."

Angie continued to simply look at us, smiling vaguely, but Leah rolled her eyes.

"A fate worse than death, I bet," she said.

I really wondered how much they knew about me beyond what I'd overheard the day before.

"Need anything from me, girls?" Alison asked, and I could swear she had an impatient edge to her tone.

"Nothing at all," Angie said. "We're going to take a walk. See y'all later."

After I was positive they were out of earshot, I asked Alison boldly, "Have you told them about me? And you?"

She looked uncomfortable. "Not a lot."

"Okay. Well, I get vibes from them. Especially Leah."

"Vibes? Is that some kind of San Francisco term? What the heck does that mean?"

"You know, like they know something they're not saying."

"There's nothing." Alison spoke with finality but I didn't believe her.

"Right. And what's that crap about a dead pig in shit? What's that mean?"

Alison laughed. "That's Southern for grinning from ear to ear. When a pig's dead, its lips pull back and show its teeth like it's smiling."

"Yuck. Alison, I wanted to ask you something else."

She stood up and grabbed our trash. "Sorry. I better clean this up before I get to work."

"Work? What work?"

"I have to staff the infirmary when Angie and Leah aren't around. We agreed someone would be here every day, starting after breakfast and all the way till ten. Then..." She stood up and grinned. "Well, see you later, okay?"

"Alison, wait."

She stopped in the doorway but didn't turn around.

"Could you stay and talk for a few more minutes? Just now I started to ask you a question, and then Angie and Leah came in."

Once I decide something, I'm real stubborn, so I was determined to get her to tell me the truth about what I'd been wondering about since the last time I saw her.

She turned around and faced me and crossed her arms. "Yes?"

"Well. I know you said you didn't want to get into stuff from the past, but I'm having a hard time. I've thought about you and me for years. I've got a lot of questions. As long as we never had to see each other again, I could let it go, but now, we're here. Together. I see you every day, and it's really hard. I just want to talk, honest. I want to know some things from you for my own peace of mind. I swear, I'll never ask you for anything else."

July 1972

"Oh my God, Ellie. Will you just relax for one second? We need a rest, even you."

She was referring to my nonstop plans for activity. I think I was trying to make sure we were always busy so I could distract myself from my incomprehensible, overwhelming feelings about her. And the thought that she was bothered about something and I could be the cause disturbed me. But she never said anything. She was just moody—sometimes happy and affectionate, other times distant and quiet.

It was after lunch and it was hot. Usually we'd rest for a while before getting the kids together for an afternoon activity.

"You relax if you want. I'm going to go chop some wood for tonight," I said.

"Good grief. Come here and lie down." She was motioning for me to get on the mattresses with her. We'd put our beds on the floor, which was far more supportive than the rickety, noisy steel cots. Also we could push the mattresses together. Neither of us discussed this arrangement, just as we never mentioned the times a few years before, when at night, I'd climb into her sleeping bag with her.

From behind, she wrapped an arm around me. I tried to relax, but it was impossible. I didn't move, however, since I adored the way it felt to lie next to her in this way.

Alison looked at me with sadness, regret, compassion, and something else I couldn't interpret. She came to sit by me and then gave me the tiniest of grins.

"I'm having a hard time seeing you every day too. It always reminds me of that summer. That was a tough period in my life."

"I sort of understand that, but I want to know more. Maybe telling me about it would help? It would help me feel better, and I bet it would help you too."

I put my hand on her arm. She looked at it but didn't pull away.

I said, "My friend Val always tells me that speaking what's on our minds, what bothers us, helps us get through it."

Alison blinked, and some sort of emotional pain flitted across her features. I badly wanted to know what it was. Could I heal it? Doubtful, but I still wanted to sate my curiosity.

"Ellie, I'm not much good at talking about my feelings. I'm not used to it, and it scares me. I've started to learn, but it doesn't come easy to me."

I gave her my most convincing smile.

"I don't want to make you feel bad about yourself. I, uh. It would make me feel better if I could hear a few things from you."

She looked at me for a long minute. "All right. Ask your questions."

I took a deep breath and nodded.

"Did you know that I was a lesbian and that I was in love with you? Back then?"

She sighed and looked away.

"Yes," she said in a pained voice. "I didn't know what to call it, but I knew you were in love with me."

"What did you think of that?"

She scrunched up her forehead. "I don't know. What is there to think? It was you."

"Did you love me?"

"Yes. Of course, Ellie. I did love you."

"But I mean, in the same way. Did you really love me?"

"I don't know exactly how to describe it, but yes, I loved you."

Her answer was unsatisfactory.

"What did you think when I kissed you that night?"

"I don't remember. I guess I liked it. But…"

"But you didn't want to go further?"

"Well, I was scared. I don't know. I was very young. *We* were very young."

This explanation was even more uninformative and maddening than her not saying anything at all. I worked hard to keep my temper under control.

"Come on. It's safe to tell me now. I'll be okay. I'm not going to lose it."

She got up and walked to the window, looking very uncomfortable and uneasy. I was sympathetic, but I still wanted her to answer me.

"I was just too young and confused to really respond to you."

"Yes, but you did respond, and what you said and what you did really hurt me."

"I'm sorry. I really am."

"Well, thanks for that, but I sort of would like to know a little more."

"Look, Ellie. I know you would, but that's about all I can say. I've apologized, you've apologized. Can we just drop it?"

My shoulders, which were right up around my earlobes because I was so tense, dropped back down. I felt like I'd run into a brick wall.

"Right. Sure. No problem. Thanks for talking with me."

She came back to sit next to me.

"Ellie, er, Lane. I truly am sorry we ended so horribly. We can put it behind us and just go on. I still love you as a friend, and I want you to be okay with me, with us. Is that possible?"

I wouldn't look at her. I spoke to the floor in front of me. "Sure. It's fine. I'm fine. You're probably right. I should let it go." Then I turned and caught her gaze and held it.

She said, "I have to go. Do you want me to help you go to the bathroom?"

That didn't sound especially romantic, but I'd take it.

"Yes, please, if you'll let me smoke first."

She rolled her eyes but didn't say anything.

Finally, after all that was done, she helped me to my little bedroom and plopped me down on the cot.

"Are you okay. Need anything else?"

"Nope. Thanks."

"Okay. See you later." She left me alone with my thoughts, which were all over the place. She didn't want to talk, yet she'd gone out of her way to have dinner with me. She could have insisted I use crutches, but she'd just helped me walk.

Marty appeared a little later and interrupted my musings. She had actually come by in person, and for some reason, Miss Tits wasn't with her. Was there trouble in their little paradise of two?

I sat there, propped up on pillows holding a glass of juice, which I'd used to take three more OTC painkillers before I went to sleep. The thudding ache in my foot had dulled, and I was attempting to calm down after my talk with Alison and, as Val would say, accept my situation. The foot situation I was cool with. Mostly. The Alison situation was something else.

Marty pulled up a chair next to my cot and appeared to be a bit concerned. Whether it was about me and my injury or about assuming responsibility for Security, I couldn't tell.

"Are you all right? No ambulance? No broken bones?"

"Nah," I said, attempting to be nonchalant. "It's just a little banged up. Bruised, they tell me. Fifty pounds of cabbages. Boom."

Marty laughed. "Ouch. But you're tough. Don't worry. I got it covered. I hope you're better soon, though. Before you-know-what starts."

"Oh, believe me," I said with my usual confidence. "I'll be ready. My foot will heal. I promise. If I have to get around exclusively by golf cart, then we'll deal. Meanwhile, you'll be fine. We're still in touch by radio. Call me any time. I can still talk and I can still think."

Marty looked relieved. She would handle things. I truly wasn't that worried.

"Yeah. Totally."

On Tuesday morning I wasn't feeling too bad. My trip to the bathroom was awkward but not horrible. I got a zing of pain when I put my foot down, but I could handle it. And I felt even better when Alison showed up with some breakfast for two. She was back to being cheerful and companionable, and as we consumed our bran muffins and yogurt and granola, I summoned the courage to try again to induce her to talk about our past.

"Will you ever feel like discussing what happened between us? I maybe didn't make it clear that I don't want anything from you, but I'd like us to be friends, and I would feel a lot better if *I* could tell you what I want to say. You don't have to do anything but listen. Just let me say some things to you that I've held onto for fifteen years. Would you do me the courtesy?"

She looked at me silently for what felt like a long time.

"You just won't quit, will you? All right, but we need to go somewhere private. Not Bates."

"Yup. Absolutely. I've got wheels. And they work, too!" I was happy to see her grin slightly.

"You just need to go up the hill and get the golf cart from Marty. She said she'd leave the keys in the box under the seat."

A short time later, we were tooling up the other fork of the road toward the camping area. Alison insisted on driving, and since I wanted her to talk, I didn't argue.

"Where is it you're taking me exactly?" Alison asked me as we chugged around the lake on the way to the farthest distant point from the central camp area as one could go, excluding the Artemis parking lot or the S/M camping area. This camp site was only a grove of willows with a sign nailed to one tree, indicating what it was. I didn't want our talk to take place in a blank field marked with a colored rubber-tape grid, in the hot sun, in a golf cart. And we needed somewhere to sit. Alison's tone seemed to imply I was kidnapping her. I had thought about that but...no.

The cluster of little cabins and tents would be the disabled area, but no one was there yet. It had been chosen for its accessibility, privacy, and the fact that it boasted its own charming little fire circle. We could sit on rustic tree stumps, similar to the logs that we had once rested our butts on at Camp Triple Creek. I thought that was appropriate.

"Remind you of anything?" I asked as we sat down.

She grinned. "You know it does."

"Good. That was the general idea. Actually, I think the whole music festival, at least the pre-fest part, reminds me of Girl Scout camp."

Her brow wrinkled in what seemed like consternation and skepticism. "How so?"

"Well, think about it. It's an all-female environment, out in nature. We care for each other, help each other, work together to construct a great venue and a great experience for the music festival. We espouse the same values as Girl Scouts: cooperation, good work ethic, honesty, and integrity. I think it works."

Alison tilted her head. "To a point. It kinda breaks down when you throw in the use of controlled substances, as well as drinking, as well as sex of who knows what kind."

I assume she was referring to some of the work crew, who were quite openly leather dykes. There were just a few—some from Portland and a couple of SoCal gals. They sported chains, piercings, tattoos, and an air of knowing something the rest of us didn't. I didn't care, but I understood that, to a lot of women, this was out of the lesbian mainstream, if such a term could be used.

"Point taken. But think how much healthier it is for us to not repress our sexuality the way we did at camp."

Alison squirmed a little bit. *Ah.* Maybe this was part of her standoffish attitude toward me. Well, we were going to talk it out. Process, if you like. I didn't want to feel odd around Alison. I didn't want her to judge me. I wanted to be myself.

"So," she said.

"So?" I said.

We both laughed. I looked at her clean-cut profile. Her features were so regular they could belong to a model. She clearly had no idea that she was beautiful. She had apparently suffered some psychic damage along the way that had convinced her she was worthless. It was different from the shyness I remembered. If I ever found out who had emotionally beaten her down, I was prepared to commit murder. My money was on the ex-husband.

"That night?" I started to say.

"Yes. *That* night."

"No, wait. It wasn't just that one night. You know that. That didn't come out of nowhere.'

"No. I suppose not."

The look in her eye told me she was thinking about us, about back then. I was still staring at her profile because she wasn't making eye contact with me.

"I was in love with you. Profoundly, thoroughly, deeply in love with you. It started when we met, when we were kids. By '72 we weren't kids. We were nearly adults. I loved you. I was in love with you."

"Yes. What, you were eighteen as of May third? I was going to turn eighteen in October?"

"Yup. You remembered." That touched me.

"Old enough to…"

"Let me explain a little bit about me." Then I told her about Camp Henry Kaufmann and all the rest of it.

"Why didn't you let me know about that then, El?" she asked. I didn't even care that she didn't use my correct name.

"I was scared. I was terrified."

"And your solution was to attack me?"

"That's what I want to apologize for, Allie. I thought maybe…I don't know. Maybe if I could show you how I felt, you'd understand. I couldn't verbalize it. I couldn't explain."

"But then I rejected you and you got mad," she said sadly. I shivered, remembering how angry I'd become. "Well. I did. I shouldn't have, but I did. I'm sorry."

I wanted to say she was making me crazy by being so all over the place, just like she'd been in the summer of '72. She was incomprehensible, and I wanted to know why. I'd wanted her to tell me back in '72, and she didn't. I wanted her to tell me now, but that wasn't really the purpose of this conversation.

I was there to make my apology explicitly and honestly and with no excuses and no equivocation.

"I accept your apology. It's good to hear this. I feel better about you. Honestly, El, you were so angry, I had to leave. I was afraid of you. First the…then the anger."

"I know. I can control my temper better now." I was still miffed that she couldn't say out loud what I'd done. I'd kissed her. I'd tried, well, I'd tried very clumsily to seduce her. She'd started to respond, and then she stopped cold. I wanted to know why. But I wanted her tell me of her own accord.

"That's really good to hear." She smiled slightly.

"I'm not going to apologize for loving you."

Her eyes clouded. "You don't need to. I know you loved me."

"I still love you in a way. I never got over you." This sudden realization had been hovering just out of my conscious mind the entire time since I had read her name on that list. And now it hit me.

She looked at me cautiously.

"Do you know that song by Elvis Costello? 'Alison'?" I sang a couple of lines for her.

I'd heard that stupid song when it was released in '77 and almost lost my mind when it played on the radio. My life had gone on after Alison and I parted ways in August of 1972, but that song instantly brought everything back to me. I would hear it on radio multiple times a day for weeks and start to cry. That was my first year of grad school, a year when I drank a great deal and smoked a lot of dope and screwed a lot of girls. I was kind of a mess. Maybe I still was when it came to Alison. Evidence said yes.

She stared at me. "That was a pretty famous song. I'd been married to Tom for about a year when it came out. He'd sing it to me, too."

I scrutinized her face, trying to discern how she felt about it. I was also ticked off because that was *my* song for Alison and no one else's.

"Yeah, well, that's your song." I wondered how she felt about the rest of the lyrics. Alison might look like a Greek goddess, but she was actually a sphinx, and her secrets were locked inside her.

And it seemed like she would never tell me the whole story. Maybe I could torture Angie or Leah and get the truth? I could get the leather dykes to advise me on methods. Yikes. I really was losing my mind. Not only was I not into S/M, but that wasn't the way it worked anyhow. Torturing Alison's friends? God. I needed a reality check.

She said, "I ought to get back to work."

"Yeah, I suppose." That was the end of our heart-to-heart, and I didn't feel much better. When one friend makes a confession, etiquette dictates that the other friend confesses and apologizes too. That's supposed to be the way it works.

Also, I'd said I still loved her, but I got no response.

We went back to Bates, and she helped me walk to my room and sat me down on my cot. She didn't say anything, just patted my leg gently. Little shots of electricity passed from her fingers to my nerve endings.

"I'll check in on you later today. Don't walk anywhere unless you have to. I'm serious."

Her order irritated me, but it was also endearing. She gave me a funny little wistful look over her shoulder as she left my room.

CHAPTER SEVEN

E ven with regular updates over the radio from Marty, it was a boring day. I even had a visit from Tanya, who brought me a fresh battery and stayed to chat. I was sure I was getting the signal she was interested. She arrived with my new battery and sat on the end of the bed fidgeting with it, looking adorably at a loss. But she could have sent Marty over with a new battery for my walkie-talkie; no reason she had to come herself. She was cute in a nondescript way. I no longer knew if I wanted to try to find a sex partner even for a night, let alone the entire festival. My soul was one big Alison-sized empty space. Tanya grinned at me, and I formed a generic noncommittal smile back at her, but we had little to say to one another, and she finally left.

I pulled out my guitar, which I hadn't played once since I'd gotten to the festival. I settled it on my lap and strummed once. It needed tuning.

June 1972

At the campfire, I sat across the circle from Allie. I would've wanted to sit next to her so parts of us could touch, but I also loved to just look at her. She looked especially good in the orange fire glow.

Our unit was having a fire circle, and Alison led the singing. We ran through "Kumbaya," then "Piney Wood Hills" and "Five Hundred Miles." The campers were as mesmerized by Allie as I was.

"Oh, Chipper, let's sing that one you learned at Henry Kaufman—the sad one?"

" 'The Water is Wide'?" I asked.

"Yeah, that's the one!" She came over to sit next me on the log.

I played the intro chords: C, F, Am, G.

Alison sang. She was very fast at learning words. She'd had them memorized the second time we sang it. This was only the third time.

"The water is wide, I cannot cross over.

"Neither have I wings to fly.

"Give me a boat that can carry two and both shall roam,

"My love and I."

This song really got to me. I kept putting Alison and me in that boat. The ending was problematical because that's not what I wanted to happen, though, not what I thought would happen. I was going to love Alison forever. Of that I was convinced.

As I played the last chord, the kids were silent, too silent.

This wasn't a song where I felt like joining in. It was better with just Alison's clear, soaring soprano. I watched her as she sang, since I could play my guitar without having to look at my fingers. I'd gotten that proficient. The plaintive melody and minor key saddened me.

A long beat of silence followed after I played the last chord, and Alison and I stared at one another for what I realized was probably too long.

Then one of the girls called out, "Let's do 'The Lion Sleeps Tonight.'"

And that broke the spell. It was a good song to involve everyone, since it was sung in parts.

After lights out, we laid on our mattresses on the floor.

Les-be friends. *It gave me a name for what I was thinking, for what I was. But what that meant for Alison and me, I hadn't a clue. Was she the same? I thought so and I hoped so. I was happy when we reunited at Triple Creek, but I was full of secret knowledge and speculation. I was less innocent and much more emotional but not much more articulate. Being around Alison gave me both joy and pain.*

A knock on my open door startled me out of my reverie, and there stood Alison.

"Hi," I said, trying to sound casual. I was in a sort of double time frame. I was remembering us in 1972, but her appearance kicked me into the present. Those teenage girls we'd been were still inside us, still present. I knew that was true of me, and it seemed to be true of Alison too. Something about her shyness was familiar. *She* was approaching *me.* I was enchanted that she'd heard me and decided to appear.

"I heard the chords of that song. Whatchamacallit? That one we played all the time that last summer."

"Yeah. I played, you sang."

"Right. Oh, can I come in?" she asked, hesitantly. Charming

"Certainly."

There was no place to sit but on the bed. My nerve endings zinged as she sat next to me, jouncing the cheap mattress. *Oh shit.* Just like the day before when she had to help me get around, I responded in a raw, sexual way. I got tense and a little warm, and my emotions were shooting all over the place: pleasure, longing, nervousness.

"So play it."

I stared at her, dumbfounded, but I obeyed. She started to sing, just like she always had, like an angel. Like Joni Mitchell. After fifteen freaking years, Alison still got to me. Neither the trauma of our parting nor the passage of time mattered. Here she was in front of me, in the flesh, and my feelings were identical to those of my eighteen-year-old self. This time-traveling was overwhelming. I tried to focus on my guitar playing, and that helped somewhat. The song came to an end, and we fell silent. Alison stared at the floor, her foot jostling. She wouldn't look at me.

"You still sing beautifully. Just like you always did," I said, as calmly as I could.

"Do I? I think I'm out of practice." She was looking down, and she slowly turned her face up and over toward me until we made eye contact.

From a far distance, I heard myself say, "Nope, not at all. Still perfect pitch."

I'd meant my remark to be lighthearted and teasing, but my tone was low and serious. Her face was still, almost somber. I knew, like me, she was thinking about the summer of 1972.

"Alison, I—"

"Al? There you are."

At the doorway stood Angie, who looked at us like we were busted. For what? We were sitting up, fully clothed and not touching. What the heck? I still felt guilty for some reason. The barest glimmer of a thought was there. *Maybe Alison's gotten over what stopped her in 1972. If she is really a lesbian, then maybe we can recapture what we had and what we were, the love we shared.* I was really losing my grip on reality if I was entertaining that notion.

"Hi, Ange. What's up?"

Alison's voice was neutral, but a hint of a strain lurked underneath, maybe.

"It's time to go meet Arden."

"Oh. I thought you didn't need me for that."

"You better come, too. So's you get the same info."

"Sure." She stood up and favored me with a smile as she walked out the door.

Alison had clearly picked up on my badly disguised feelings, and Angie might have as well. I was going to be in big trouble if this spun as out of control as it had back in the summer of 1972. I sat still, my guitar in my lap. I stroked a loud, jangly chord, then put it away and lay back down with my hands behind my head and closed my eyes.

I was heading out on a road with Alison that could only lead to heartache. If I could share a normal friendship with Alison, that would suffice. Even if we never fully discussed our past, maybe we didn't need to. I surely didn't want to lose my heart again. Another ending like that one would kill me for certain. I had never loved any woman the way I loved Alison, and maybe I never would. There was absolutely no reason to think Alison and I could pick up where we left off, forget the pain we caused each other and march off together into the sunset.

The rest of the afternoon was a big bore. I talked to Marty on the radio a couple of times, and Alison stopped by only once to tell me I could get up and go to dinner in the golf cart. She stayed close to Angie and Leah while I ate with Marty and Miss Tits, who took me back to Bates and hung out with me for a little while. I was happy with their company but kept thinking about Alison. I hoped my foot would be healed enough by the next day that I could get up and about and keep busy, or at least in motion. Around sunset, Marty and Miss Tits left, and I fell into an uneasy sleep.

Then I was abruptly awakened.

It wasn't the crackle of a voice on the walkie-talkie; it was someone shaking my shoulder. I turned over and found Marty bent over me.

"Sorry to have to wake you, Lane, but I need your help."

I was disoriented and loopy. I shook my head and tried to get my mind in gear. I'd lain awake for who knows how long thinking about Alison. Again. I was going to be a zombie if this kept happening.

"What's going on? Hand me that water bottle, please, and speak slowly and in complete sentences."

She obeyed, and I took a long drink of water and switched on the dim light next to my bed. I could finally see Marty, and she looked unhappy. She wouldn't have awakened me unless it was important.

"Okay. What's up? What time is it?"

"About twelve thirty. One of the groupies and Miss Tits came into our cabin and got me up. I think she was scared to come find you." She referred to the festival gypsies by their other nickname.

"Oh, God. What happened?"

"They got the bright idea to see if they could float a golf cart on a raft."

"What the fuck?" I was aghast. This was so brainless. The golf carts were rented equipment. If we messed them up, we'd get charged.

"Yeah. So they've got it stuck in the mud in the marshy area over to the right of the dock."

"Well, I guess we should be grateful they didn't sink it in the lake."

"Yeah. What do we do? Tina's down there to make sure nothing else happens."

Hmph. I wasn't sure Miss Tits was up to being left alone, but I had to hope Marty hadn't made a wrong decision. It was just me not trusting Miss Tits to handle things.

"Some dyke here has got to have a good heavy-duty truck and some chains. We're going to have to pull it out. I hope those silly girls haven't gotten the thing waterlogged."

"I don't think so. Just stuck."

I pulled on some shorts and shoes and my jean jacket. I didn't want to wake up Becky, and I certainly didn't want to wake up Arden. I would tell them later when it was all resolved. Then Arden might not have as big a meltdown. Not that I would blame her, but I just didn't want to be subjected to it tonight. Who had the right equipment to save the day?

Marty and I jumped into our golf cart and drove down to the lake, where Miss Tits stood guard. Sure enough, a few feet off the shore was a sad golf cart sitting in a blue raft full of mud.

Lesbians. I made a mental note to tell Marty she had to guard the key to our golf cart with her life and never let it out of her possession.

I called Val on the radio. She knew everyone the best and would know who had a truck.

"You better be waking me up for a good reason, *chica*. I have to be up at four."

"I swear, Val, I would never do this unless it was really important." I wasn't flirting at all. I was desperate. "Who's here that has nice big truck with a V8 engine and some chains?"

"Lane, baby, what the heck are you proposing to do?" At least her sense of humor had awakened too.

"Just find me the dyke and the truck, and I'll explain everything."

Even at one in the morning, we drew a little crowd to witness the great golf-cart rescue. The gypsies stood by looking chastened.

They naturally had been drinking, and all sorts of dumb shit sounds like a great idea when you're drunk.

As one of the carpenters gently pulled the unfortunate golf cart to safety chained to her Ford F150 with the women's-music bumper sticker, Alison appeared.

"Hey. What's happening?" she asked me.

Hmm. Couldn't she sleep either?

"Hi, Allie. Just some Boone's Farm-induced shenanigans with a golf cart." Yes, the gypsies had pretty poor taste in booze, but they didn't have much money. "No one hurt, if that's what you're wondering."

She yawned. "That's good. Well, I better go back to bed." She turned around and started to walk away.

"Alison?"

Without turning around, she said, "Yeah?"

"Would you like to come by for a little while tomorrow and, eh, maybe sing some songs, reminisce a bit?"

She turned around. I couldn't see her face, and I didn't want to blind her with my flashlight, so I kept it pointed at the ground.

"Sure. I'd love that."

"I guess you still want me off my foot, and, well, I've got time. If you do."

There I was being silly and inarticulate again. Sheesh. I better just shut up.

"Okay...good." She paused. "Good night, then."

I wasn't imagining her nervousness. I could hear it in her voice. *But she said yes. Hallelujah.*

"'Night, Al." I shined the flashlight on her as she walked away. And I'm ashamed to say I checked out her ass. She'd seemed as awkward as I felt, and that perversely gave me reason to hope. Hope for what, I couldn't say. Hope for us to truly become friends again? More than that was simply out of reach, I sternly told myself.

❖

I watched and attempted to keep my inconveniently warm feelings under control as Alison tested my toes and pressed my instep with her delicate-looking but strong fingers.

"How about here?" she asked. "And here?"

I winced.

She made a compassionate face. "The bruise looks bad, but you're okay."

"I'll live to walk again?"

She gave me skeptical look. "You're being dramatic, but sure. You can walk today. To dinner. That's it."

"I promise I'll go everywhere in the golf cart." I raised my hand in the Girl Scout salute, which made her laugh.

"Allie, do you still have some time today to hang out?"

She paused for only a moment. "Sure, this afternoon. I have to staff the infirmary for a while, but after two is okay."

I just nodded and went back to my book, but I was actually thrilled.

A bit later, after lunch, I went to my room and tuned my guitar and was about to go find Alison when I heard a light knock. I looked up, and there she stood in the door in a bathing suit, smiling sheepishly.

"I thought since it was warm, we might go for a swim, or at least down to the lake for a while, instead of staying inside."

I gaped at her. She wore a lime-green, modest but very fetching, two-piece suit. She must have spent a good deal of time out of doors already that spring because the even tan from her arms and legs extended to all the rest of her skin that I could see.

"Oh, uh. Yeah. Sure. That'd be fine." This abrupt change of plans threw me.

I took up my beach towel and put on some flip-flops. "Okay. Let's go."

"You're not going to change?" she asked, wide-eyed. "You're swimming in your clothes?"

"No." I laughed. "The festival is bathing-suit optional, and most of us opt for the other option." I sounded much more confident and blasé than I felt. I was worried Alison would judge my pasty-white SF body. And again I was furious at myself for even worrying about it.

"Oh." She looked alarmed.

"Don't worry. You don't have to. That's why it's optional." I didn't want to tease her too much, so I spoke gently and casually.

"I'm not comfortable, uh, with no bathing suit."

Ah, Southern modesty, just as Marla had described. It was actually cute and more than a little arousing, though I didn't want it to be.

"It's fine, Allie. Really. I heard Southerners are a bit on the conservative side."

Alison had gone silent. In social situations, when people do that, I sometimes get nervous and try to fill the empty space with chatter. Alison was still making me a tad nervous. I hoped that would stop soon.

"Do you remember that time we took the kids down to the swimming pool at nine at night and had them go skinny-dipping?"

She looked at me, "Yes, but this is in the middle of the day."

"I know, silly, but my point is, after we all got in the water and started splashing around, everyone was fine."

"I remember," she said, somewhat reluctantly.

Late July 1972

I guess it was my idea. I knew it was probably against the rules to go swimming at night, but I managed to convince Allie we should go ahead. I figured it would be fine, since we both had water-safety training. Also our campers were teenagers, not little ones, and were all good swimmers

"Come on!" I said wheedling tone. "It'll be fun, the campers will love it, and so will you and me." She finally assented, and we waited until after lights-out was called at nine thirty. As I predicted, our charges were supremely excited at getting away with something "bad," especially with our instigation. Allie and I spent a good amount of time trying to instill Girl Scout values like honesty, service, responsibility, etc. into the girls we worked with. This was a chance to loosen up a bit with something harmlessly

out of bounds. All of us found it hard to contain our giggles as we hopped the fence to the pool area and took off our clothes in the pool house. Somehow, the veil of night made it easier for the shy ones. Within a couple of minutes, everyone was splashing around and having a great time.

The swimming-pool water felt warmer at night, thanks to the cooler air temperature. I especially enjoyed the sensation of swimming with every inch of my body in contact with water. Under the night sky, skinny-dipping is absolutely magical. I swam up next to Alison and grinned at her.

"Good idea?"

She had a dreamy expression, and her wet hair hung about her face, making her look like a mermaid.

That was the moment my confused feelings crystallized into a coherent thought. I was in love with her, and I wanted her. Up to that point, I'd had inchoate longing, indescribable, headlong emotions. That night in the swimming pool, surrounded by our playful campers and armed with some facts, I had a name for what I was and what I wanted. Alison was my true love. Where we would go next, I hadn't a clue. I wasn't very clear on the mechanics. All the teasing and chaff I'd heard from the Camp Henry Kaufmann Girl Scouts didn't contain anything concrete about what "les-be" friends really meant.

The refraction of moonlight on the water slightly distorted my view of her body, but I could see well enough. She was a fascinating pattern of tan versus white from her bathing suit. She slid through the water gracefully, a much better swimmer than me. I wanted to embrace her right there in the pool, but I didn't. I wanted to wait until another time and place to tell her. And show her. Truly, I had no idea what she would say, or do.

I was pulled back to the present, and there stood Allie looking at me doubtfully. We took Medical's golf cart, and a short while later we stood on the dock amidst a dozen women, all of them nude.

"I'm going swimming, and I'd love it if you joined me." With that I stripped off my clothes and jumped into the lake. I had spoken very quickly, trying to run away from my unease.

The familiar shock of cold water hit me, and I swam away from the dock, catching my breath. I turned around and saw her taking off her bathing suit.

I had to watch, but I didn't want to obviously stare. I didn't want to unnerve her, but I couldn't stop myself from looking. Alison was still a beauty. She looked different than she had at seventeen, but then don't we all? I was far more muscular than I'd been when I was younger. She used to be thin, a little gangly, and now she was curvier, softer. She'd been slight and delicate looking. Now she was a mature woman, and her proportions were amazing. I've seen a lot of naked women, and I appreciate the charms of all body types, at least aesthetically. But Alison existed on a rare plane of Greek-goddess-statue perfection. The *Winged Victory of Samothrace* had nothing on her, and unlike the famous statue, Alison possessed a head but no wings. She dove into the water in correct form, like she was starting a race.

She stroked toward me and we faced each other, treading water.

"Feel good?" I asked, breathless, and not just from the shock of the cold water.

She spit out a little water and looked at me, her expression inscrutable.

"Yep. Once I get used to it." We said nothing more, but turned at the same time and began to swim side by side. The sounds of laughter and splashing faded into the background as we swam. There was nothing but cool water, sunlight, some soft green hills in the distance, and Alison.

We made it out to a rubber buoy and hung onto it, panting.

She mesmerized me, and I was mesmerized by the drops of water beaded on her brown face and forearm. The sky made her eyes glow bluer. That old Shondells song, "Crystal Blue Persuasion," floated through my head. I kept reminding myself to keep my grip on reality. I created a fantasy around Alison that she was my lover with whom I was enjoying a sensual swimming experience. And a little later, we could slip into a sleeping bag, our bodies cool and fresh and relaxed from swimming. We'd make love, then take a nap. Being close and asleep, we'd warm up, and half-awake, I'd stroke her hip.

But we were not as we were when we were young. We were practically strangers. She was really just like another random woman at the music festival. No matter how nostalgic I became, I would never be able to recreate the past, and anyhow—I only longed for the good parts. I didn't want to relive all of it. I'd tried to forget the pain of our last meeting and my guilt around my behavior and my fury at hers. These thoughts and a thousand others raced through my consciousness as we hung onto that stupid buoy staring at one another.

"You ready to swim back?" I asked.

And she simply nodded. I would have given anything to know what was going on in her head, but I didn't think I could ask. We weren't girlfriends; we weren't even best friends. We were sort of friends, and such a question would be impertinent. This was just a friendly swim. That was all.

Back on the dock, we sat drying in the sun. I struggled to keep my gaze trained everywhere but on her. I was impressed she kept her clothes off as she sat on her towel next to me.

There was plenty else to look at. This was the last afternoon for just the workers before the festival opened, and a lot of women were at the lake. I glanced around so I didn't have to look at Alison.

Like any dyke, I'm a connoisseur of breasts. The large, the small, the round, the flat, big nipples, small nipples, pink nipples, brown nipples. And I saw everything else that makes up the female form in all its glory, including cellulite and varicose veins, muscles and curves, boniness and pulchritude. What a feast for the soul *and* the eyes. I was struck, as I often was at a festival, by the essential innocence of the scene. To us, it *is* paradise found. The women at the lake, in all their variety, enjoyed themselves, each other, and their environment without fear.

We must have some ancestral memory of the times when women were often left to themselves. They spent all their time together communally, helped each other with children and many other tasks. Their men were off hunting or making war, and they would return some time, but until then, the women had only each other for company. Surely some of them must have found out, if only by chance, how much sexual pleasure was possible without their hulking, hairy male mates. Who knows, but I'd like to think so.

Four adventurous gals climbed onto a surfboard. (Who had thought to bring such an object?) Squished together, pussy to ass, they paddled around to the cheers of the onlookers.

I stole a look at Alison while her attention was on the surfboarders. Of course, her breasts were perfect: medium-sized, nipples pink and proportional to her breasts, not too big. They showed stark white against her tan shoulders and arms. She had shaved her armpits, which made her an outlier in that crowd. I swallowed a little, uncomfortable and entranced at the same time. I had to wrench my gaze away, hoping she hadn't noticed my intrusive stare.

Once, just once, a long time ago, I had put my hands on those perfect breasts. I tried to remember what they felt like, but my memory was hazy. I had my imagination, though. If I put my palms on her breasts, I knew those rosy nipples would become hard and engorged with blood, so I had to force myself to stop my fantasy. I was becoming unhinged and decided I needed to get away from her.

"Well. Going to go lie down for a bit until dinner." I pulled my gym shorts on and stood up. She looked up at me, and I couldn't read her expression. She wasn't smiling, but she looked thoughtful.

"Okay," I said. "See you at dinner. Okay if I take the cart?'

"Sure," she said, seeming oddly bereft of emotion.

"Bye." I nonchalantly tossed my shirt and towel over my shoulder, thrust my feet into my flip-flops, and limped away without a backward look. I wasn't nearly as together as I looked. My head was spinning, and I was in my double time zone again: past and present.

In the golf cart on the way back to Bates, I stewed. I did want to go take a nap, but I wanted it to be with Alison. My fantasy continued. We lowered the shade to make the room dark We got into bed and pressed our damp, cool bodies together until they warmed up. I could smell the lake in Alison's wet hair as it fell over me when she kissed my chest and neck. This was maddening, and I was thoroughly unnerved as my thighs tingled and my clit throbbed.

I gave up trying to take a nap and went in search of Val, even though it was getting close to dinner prep time. I told her about Alison and me and our interactions of the past two days, except for the sexual-fantasy part.

Val sat leaning back against the post that held up the roof of the back porch of the kitchen. She had her hands behind her head and her eyes closed. I waited for her words of wisdom.

"I'd say she's definitely holding back. I agree that's kind of awful for someone with whom you were supposedly so close. It must hurt a lot."

"It does. I keep trying to let it go, but I can't."

"There isn't anything you can do, baby, if she won't talk to you."

"That's not what I want to hear, Val."

"Yep. But you need to figure out how to take care of yourself. You need some distraction, I think."

"I suppose."

"Tomorrow I'll have two thousand plus distractions."

"Right."

"You're visible, you're out there. You know what to do. You need a festival fling. I don't believe that would be impossible for you to accomplish."

I wanted to whine "I don't wanna," but Val was right.

"What about you?" I lowered my eyelids, then arched my eyebrows.

She patted my cheek. "We've missed our window of opportunity. I'm sort of fond of Libby. She's a love. I think I'll keep her for the time being. You and I wouldn't work anyhow."

"Why not?" I *was* really feeling pouty. Libby must be the girl from the other day with her hand practically buried in Val's crotch.

"We're too much alike."

She must have meant we were emotionally similar, because we looked nothing alike. We could be poster girls for butch vs. femme, which contributed to the sexual energy that flowed between us.

"You're a power femme. I like that."

"Sure, you'd like it, until we started butting heads, along with other body parts. Not that I wouldn't mind taking you for a spin, but I'm a one-at-a-time kind of girl."

"Okay. I tried." I shrugged.

She gave me a kiss on the cheek. "I'm here for you if you need to talk. Any time. Now off with you. I got to get to work."

I limped to the golf cart and decided to take a ride out to the Artemis lot, find Magda, and ask her if she had any other reports of suspicious sounds at night. I needed some activity, and I probably needed more friends so I wouldn't bother Val all the time. There was no one though. Not even Marty. I was actually thinking I might go ahead and get a little tipsy at the workers' party the night before the festival opening. I deserved it. I had no girlfriend, after all.

I should have told Val I was in love with Alison, but what good would that do? She'd just roll her eyes and say the same thing again. "Let it go."

Distraction. That's what I needed, and I could start with the available pool of festival volunteers and then go on to the bigger pool of festies, if I didn't find any likely fish to snag amongst the volunteer workers. It should be easy enough. Getting laid was a prime objective of pretty much everyone at festival. Sure, there would be a lot of couples. But not everyone was half of a couple. I started to feel somewhat better as I drove out to the Artemis lot. My volunteer work and recreational sex were what I needed to help me get over Alison.

CHAPTER EIGHT

Since it was the day before the opening of the festival, after dinner (which the Southern girls called "supper") we were going to have a little ceremony. The Wiccan priestesses would perform a ritual to bless us and bring us good fortune and a peaceful festival. I'm not a believer in any religion, but I was all for creating whatever aura we needed from the universe to ensure *I* didn't have any major issues to deal with. We would also receive our bright-blue wristbands signifying we were festival workers. Once the festies arrived, we all needed to be able to tell the difference between the staff and the guests, so to speak.

We met in the dining hall. I had been avoiding Alison as much as possible, and after our little afternoon swim, she'd made no move to talk to or see me either.

Becky stood at the front of the dining hall, and we lined up to get banded. Then we trooped outside.

It was near sunset, and because we were on a slight grade we could see the sun clearly as it moved toward the horizon.

As the priestess came forward with her helper, we all grew very quiet.

She wore a lot of colored scarves and feathers and had a fist full of sage. She said, presumably for the uninformed, "We are about to perform a ceremony of consecration. We will ask Mother Goddess to bless our festival and keep us safe and give us strength and inspiration." I saw some of the Southern girls nudging and smirking at each other.

I lost track of what was going on, because my thoughts somehow wanted to go back in time to Camp Triple Creek. This apparently had been a perpetual go-to for my psyche ever since I'd arrived. Being around Alison triggered too many memories—some of them hard and bitter but some quite lovely. I thought of a twilight with a campfire on the hill with the big view where we had gathered the whole camp. For the Girl Scouts, ritual is as essential as it is to the Wiccans, although it's a lot different. I understand the necessity of ritual to bind people together as a group, and I like it even if I had no interest in religion.

We finished the consecration with a chant honoring the Mother Goddess, and then it was time for the party.

Back inside the dining hall, the stage people rigged up a DJ booth and speakers, and the kitchen staff and others cleared out the tables and benches to make a dance floor. I took a seat near the back wall, as far away from the speakers as I could get. I liked dancing as much as the next gal, but the volume near the speakers was hard to take. I wanted to be able to talk to someone, if possible, prior to seduction.

Among the items I'd brought were a green button-down shirt and leather vest, and with tight, faded jeans and my hiking boots, I was decked out to be reasonably attractive to any girl who went for soft butch types. I decided to break into my bottle of scotch in honor of the occasion. I don't like to indulge in much drinking until the festival is over, but tonight, I was in the mood to get a little loose and to party. If Alison was there, and I presumed she would be, I wanted to be happy and act happy and like I didn't care. Did this attitude bear a strong resemblance to what my eighteen-year-old self might have indulged in? Oh, yes, but I didn't care.

Outside, night fell, and inside the party was going strong. It was our last chance to be together until the festival was over in five days, and in between we'd have too much to do and time for only short breaks.

It's such a cliché, but I spotted Alison from across the big dining hall. I won't admit I was looking for her.

She was by herself—no sign of her two buddies. I couldn't help it. I enjoyed watching her from afar. That is, I enjoyed the idea of her. If I could pretend we were strangers and she was just some pretty woman I spotted in a club or at a party, then it was fun. I tried, but it wasn't that easy. I was still me, and she was still Alison, and we had a world of memories and regrets between us and around us. Damn, she looked good though. If I could only concentrate on my fantasy Alison and forget the real version.

I sipped the water bottle I'd filled with scotch and shamelessly ogled her. She was wearing jeans, for once, instead of Bermuda shorts, and her tight, yellow knit top showed off her breasts. She might be on the hunt for a sex partner too. That possibility both intrigued and profoundly disturbed me. She'd not definitively identified herself as a lesbian, but she was presenting as one. Her outfit shouted, "I'd love to get laid." Or so it seemed to me. But of course, my next thought was this: If that's the case, here I am, baby!

I took another gulp of scotch and willed myself to look away from Alison and scan the crowd. About a hundred women were there. Surely there was one for me who wasn't Alison Livingstone Bickford.

After an hour or so, I guess, I'd lost track of time, and the room was almost dark except for a few lights from the kitchen and the amplifier lights. The dance music was pounding out of the speakers, and the party had heated up considerably, temperature and otherwise. Finally, I spotted Tanya standing by herself near the door to the kitchen. She'd do.

I'd drunk enough scotch to be feeling pretty damn good. The DJ was spinning Aretha's *Freeway of Love*. Yes, I wanted to get on that freeway.

Tanya brightened as she nodded her assent when I asked her to dance. I took her hand and led her into the middle of the floor. The DJ played "I'm Looking For a New Love" by Jody Watley. Ah, perfect. I put my hands on Tanya's waist and moved into her. She met me in the middle, and we gyrated and dry-humped.

I let the gestalt sweep me up. A little buzzed? Check. A little hot and sweaty? Check. Getting way turned on by Tanya? Absolutely. That tune ended and faded right into Cindy Lauper's "Girls Just Wanna Have Fun." They sure did, I thought fuzzily.

We danced through a few more, and I whispered to Tanya that I needed some air. She stuck right to my side. I'd acquired my own remora apparently. We staggered outside and leaned against the building around the side, away from the crowd.

Tanya's fingers stroked down my arm and my hand, and when I lit a cigarette, she took it from my lips, took a drag, and then returned it to my mouth. Very sexy.

"You're cute. I don't know why I haven't noticed you before." I did know why, but I wasn't going to share that with Tanya.

"Oh, I saw *you*. You're always driving around in the golf cart with your radio, looking all official and shit."

"That's me," I said dreamily. I put the cigarette out carefully, then stuck it in my pocket. Tanya stared at me.

"Can't litter," I said apologetically.

"Guess you're a rule follower." She was winding herself around me, and my crotch was starting to melt.

"Mostly," I said weakly. She was a little shorter than me and raised her mouth and closed her eyes. I kissed her, thinking I tasted like scotch and cigarettes and hoping she was just drunk enough but not too drunk. I certainly was drunk enough not to care about anything except getting my hand down Tanya's pants.

I went for it. No surprise, she didn't object. I stuck my index finger between her wet labia and explored her gently. She almost collapsed and I had to prop her up. I backed her against the wall, and we kissed and groped each other. The pleasures of making out under the stars were mainly unavailable in San Francisco, because the fog and wind made the nights too cold almost every day of the year. The northern Georgia night was an absolutely perfect temperature, even pleasantly cool. I enjoyed the roof of the night sky sheltering Tanya and me and our growing desire.

"I'm in a cabin with three other people," she said against my mouth.

"We're in luck, kid. I've got a private room." She wiggled against me, almost making *my* knees buckle.

"Let's go," she said, raggedly.

I picked up my water bottle full of scotch that I'd remembered to bring outside with me, and with my arm wrapped around Tanya, we walked back to Bates. It was a bit of a hike, and my foot ached some, but I didn't care. I zeroed in on getting my hands back on Tanya's wet pussy and plush breasts.

There was a light on in the infirmary, but I wasn't really paying attention. We went in the back door, and I took Tanya to my room and plopped her down on the bed.

"Gotta pee. How about you get ready and I'll be right back."

"Hurry." She tore her shirt off and gave me a quick look at her breasts. *Nice.* I stared for a half second and then stumbled out the door and down the hall.

Just as I reached the toilet, the door opened and there stood Alison, in shadow, backlit by the bathroom light.

"Oh. Hi." I sounded idiotic to myself. Or maybe I just felt stupid. Or guilty.

"Hi, yourself. Are you drunk?" She spun out that question in an oozy Southern drawl.

"Hmm. Well. Yeah, I guess I am." I was so flummoxed by Alison, I'd forgotten all about my need to hurry back to Tanya and start fucking our brains out. I was embarrassed but insanely happy to see Alison. I knew I should get on with my business, but I couldn't move. God damn it.

"You look drunk," Alison said, clear censure in her tone. "Maybe you ought to get to bed. We've got a big day tomorrow."

"Yes, we certainly do, and yes, you're right. We have a majorly big day tomorrow." I'm certain I was grinning foolishly, and I didn't move. I just stood there in front of Alison.

Then I heard Tanya's voice behind me.

"Hey, I thought I better go too before we—oh." She must have spotted Alison.

I turned, and she was shirtless.

"Hi, there. It's Alison, right?" Tanya said with surprising calm.

"Yes, it is. You're Tanya, the equipment mistress, aren't you?" I could swear Alison's voice was a bit clipped, its smooth Southern cadence absent. Also, she made "equipment mistress" sound dirty.

It was clear what Tanya was doing at Bates, and she hadn't come for medical treatment or to fix some piece of equipment that needed repair.

"Sure am." There was an enormously long and, to my mind, uneasy pause. All traces of arousal had drained from my body, chased away by an inexplicable sense of shame. I was feeling like I'd betrayed Alison, which was nuts. Anyway, I was sobering up and realizing I didn't want to sleep with Tanya.

"Well, nice to meet you," Tanya said to Alison, and she winked at me. "See you in a minute." She slipped into the bathroom.

I was left facing Alison in the dim light of the hallway with no idea what to say.

"Okay. Have a nice evening. See you tomorrow, bright and early."

She might have rolled her eyes, I'm not sure, but I chose to interpret her words as evidence she was pissed at me, which was ridiculous.

"Good night," I said to her back as she walked away.

I went back to my room and flopped down on my cot without taking my clothes off.

A fragment of the Elvis Costello tune drifted into my mind. My aim was way off the mark when it came to my Alison. I tried to shoo both the thoughts of Alison and the song lyrics away, but the name and the reality of Alison were never going to let me alone again.

Tanya came back, shutting the door behind her, and had climbed on me before I could say a thing. The cot gave an ominous creak. She busily licked my neck and murmured, "Why didn't you take your clothes off, baby? You want me to help you?" She started unbuttoning my shirt.

"Tanya, Tanya? Let's sit up for a second." A corner of my mind issued an observation—*both of us smell like garlic, along with booze. Yuck.*

She rolled off me and almost fell on the floor. It was only a single bed, and a very narrow one at that. Not made for two people who intended to engage in vigorous sex.

When I swung my legs over and sat next her, she wrapped her arms around me and whispered in my ear, "Let's get our clothes off. I can't wait—"

"Tanya. I can't. I'm sorry. Very sorry. I don't want to hurt your feelings."

She leaned back and stared at me, eyes narrowed. "What the fuck? What's the matter?"

Oops. She was pissed, and I didn't blame her. I was about to leave her hanging, pants on fire, and I wasn't going to be the one to douse the flames. I was a first-class heel, clit tease, and all-around jackass.

"It's not you. I just can't do this. Please accept my apology, and please go."

She must have looked at me for a full minute before she stood up. "Fine."

She walked out the door, putting her shirt back on.

I lay still for a moment. Then I rose and walked down the hall toward the front of the building and the infirmary rooms.

The light was on and Alison was there, reading what looked like a brochure, I thought. It was hard to focus. Guess I was still drunk.

"Hi. What in the hell are you doing here at this time of night?"

"Where's your little friend?"

She couldn't sound more contemptuous if she tried. I didn't know if her disdain was directed toward me or toward Tanya. Or both?

"She's gone. Alison, I—"

She looked at me, the pamphlet in her hand, seeming neither angry nor especially happy. I couldn't gauge her exact emotion, and I still couldn't figure out why she was in the infirmary at what had to be one thirty in the morning.

"You don't need to explain yourself. It's none of my business." Cold tone.

"Uh. No. It's not that. It's just that I—" I had no idea what I wanted to say.

"Never mind," I finally said. "See you tomorrow." I turned before she noticed I was tearing up.

Back in my dark, cramped little room on my rickety cot, I couldn't sleep.

I was in such deep shit. I could neither let Alison go nor assuage my feelings with meaningless sex. The Elvis Costello song reverberated through my brain again. I pulled the bottle of scotch out from under my bed and sipped it until I passed out.

Of course, I'd not set any sort of alarm. I had an alarm clock with me but had forgotten all about it. My walkie-talkie squawking finally woke me up. And it was the sound of Becky's voice that finally penetrated my scotch fog, but that was all I could grasp. I couldn't fully comprehend what she was saying.

I fumbled on the floor until my hand touched the radio, and I keyed the mike. "Lane here." My voice was a rusty croak. "Oh, hey, Lane. Didn't see you at breakfast. Arden wanted me to find you and ask you where you were going to be this morning."

Breakfast? Where would I be? I was in bed. What? What the heck was going on? There was a lot of sunlight in my room.

"I don't know. Where—"

"She's just checking in. Maybe you ought to start out at the gate." *The gate?* My memory began to function ever so slowly. Holy shit. I was royally hung over. I scrabbled for my watch. Gah, it was nine thirty.

"Oh, sure. But it likely won't be long until I have to go somewhere else." I was slowly coming to, and the experience was not pleasant. I was being forced to think, and it was making my head hurt and my stomach do flips. I wouldn't have time to take a shower.

"Oh, sure, but we already have a line up, and you know how anxious the girls can get." What the fuck was she going on about? Then it finally penetrated my woozy brain: it was opening day of festival. *Shit.*

"Sure. Let me pull myself together and get out there." I sounded almost like my normal self.

"Thanks, Lane. You're the best." God, she was overly cheerful, or maybe it was to mask her panic. Nah. Becky didn't panic. *Arden* panicked and then started yelling, and Becky took care of it. Whatever *it* was.

I slowly got out of my sleeping bag and sat on the cot as my head pounded and my stomach roiled. God, I was in bad shape, because I'm not much of a drinker. This was not good.

I found some clothes and decided what I needed most, other than six more hours of sleep, was food and coffee. I'd be a goner if I didn't eat. I had to get to the kitchen, and breakfast was likely long over. I'd have to throw myself on Val's mercy and plead with her to feed me. I laced up my boots, and bending over made my head spin more. After the room returned to its proper orientation, I called Marty. I hoped she and Miss Tits had enjoyed their last night in bed and managed to sleep a little. They'd have the afternoon for sleep. Then they were going to be up all night for the next four nights.

"Come get me at Bates," I said with much less than my usual good cheer.

"Roger," she replied.

I threw out the scotch in my water bottle, rinsed it, and filled it with water. Then I splashed some on my face for good measure. It was showtime, and I needed to get on with it.

"You drive," I said as I climbed into the passenger seat. I had my shades on and a baseball cap pulled down over my forehead. It was a very bright morning.

"Sure. Where to?" Marty asked. "You okay?"

"I'm fine. Go to the kitchen. I need to eat."

"Breakfast was over forty-five—"

"Never mind. Let's go." I was not in the mood for argument.

"Righto. Tina's out at the gate."

That news gave me another wave of nausea.

The bouncing of the golf cart made me feel even worse. There was a lot of activity on the road and elsewhere. My watch said it was ten till ten. Mother fucker, I *never* slept this late. I felt like I was about a mile behind the eight ball and losing ground fast. Coffee was essential, then food, preferably protein.

"Get out to the gate and make sure they're all copacetic, then come back and get me in a half hour," I told her when we arrived at the kitchen.

Marty heard my tone, and from my look she obviously concluded that I wasn't to be trifled with today, because she only nodded.

I went in the back door and saw about two dozen women immersed in food prep. I searched for Val amid all the hubbub and found her in the walk-in cooler with another worker, stowing gigantic amounts of foodstuffs. The smell of the cooler made me gag, and I nearly lost it right there.

"Val?" I choked out.

She spun around. The glint in her eye said she was in total kitchen mode and I was not a welcome distraction.

"Lane, baby, what's up? Talk fast."

"I need some food and coffee. I know I missed breakfast but—"

Val stood with her hands on her hips and glared. "You're damn right you missed breakfast. This isn't a restaurant."

I took off my sunglasses so Val could see my expression of abject pleading. "I'm hurting. I got a little too drunk last night and I need to get to work."

Val was silent for what seemed like forever.

"All right. Tell Sunny I said to make you some eggs, and you can make your own coffee. Go ahead and use my Melitta, and girl, I'm doing you a big favor 'cause I don't let *no* one touch my Melitta. What's wrong with you? I didn't know you were a drinker."

Val must have caught the scotch fumes emanating from me. She wrinkled her nose.

"Thanks. I really appreciate this. No, I'm not a drinker. That's the problem. I need to talk to you later, but I know you're busy. I'm about to get really busy myself."

"Busier than a one-armed paper hanger, but you know I'll make time for you, *chica*."

"You're the best, Val." I hugged her.

After some eggs, toast, and strong coffee, I was feeling physically better and told myself to get on with it. Marty showed up as agreed.

"Look," I said. "I drank too much last night, and I'm slow getting started. Sorry I was short with you earlier."

Marty looked at me liked she wanted to ask another question, but all she said was, "Okay. Thanks for apologizing. It's all right."

"What's happening out there?" I hoped Miss Tits was keeping it together.

"Oh, you know. A couple of gals are here early, and they're so excited, they just want to come in. Billie's there and they're okay."

Billie was the box-office coordinator.

"I left Tina to keep watch and for reinforcement."

"Let's go take a look. I don't want the box-office people to have another headache. We'll do 'security' on 'em." I hoped that leaving Miss Tits by herself was a good decision on Marty's part. It was done anyhow, and there wasn't anything to say. I just had to go check out the situation.

By the time we arrived the entrance, it was about ten forty-five, and a line of vehicles stretched out for what I estimated was a mile. Jesus Christ. *Don't people read the fine print? Noon means fucking noon. How hard is that to understand?* My head still hurt, though my stomach was no longer upset. But I had a bad attitude already, and the festival hadn't even officially started.

Marty and I hopped off the golf cart. My foot twinged a little, but I ignored it though I reminded myself to be careful.

When I'd told Marty we'd "security them," it didn't mean tie them up, but it meant being a psychological backup for the front-gate girls. Women aren't usually violent or dangerous, but they can get demanding and difficult, and some can be real pains in the ass.

Billie was there, with Miss Tits at her side, wearing Marty's radio and looking official. They were deep in conversation with a couple in a dingy blue Datsun hatchback with a peace sign and a Gaia sticker. The back was crammed to the roof with stuff, and the license plate proclaimed them residents of Tennessee. The driver, who wore a straw cowboy hat, was doing the talking. Billie showed the practiced patient smile of a woman used to dealing with the public. I heard she was a customer-service manager for Oregon's state power utility. Hoo boy. I could only imagine how many disgruntled citizens she dealt with on a daily basis. And she spent her precious vacation days dealing with customer-service hassles in a different context. But that's what festival volunteers are like.

"So y'all are saying we drove all way the heck from Tennessee last night, but we can't come in till noon?"

"That's right. We're not ready. We don't open until then."

'Well, yeah, but we drove all night, so how about y'all take pity on us? We won't be no trouble. We'll just go park and pitch our tent and all. No sweat."

There's always someone who's convinced the rules don't apply to her. Or him. Here was one who also came complete with Southern sweet talk. I had no patience for this nonsense.

"Hey. My name's Lane,' I said, stepping forward. Tennessee stuck her hand out the window and said, "Pleased to meet you. I'm Andy and this here's Belle." She waved an arm at her smaller, non-cowboy-hatted companion. Her introduction sounded like pleasedtomeetcha. I reminded myself to not be condescending because of their accents. Truly, it wasn't their accents but their apparent sense of entitlement that I objected to.

"Hi, Andy. Belle. Allow me to explain our situation. Number one, Billie here's in charge of the gate, and we have to respect her method and her process."

Andy looked concerned, but I read her expression as faux concern. "She already said all that."

She nodded at Billie. "But we got tickets. Ain't no problem with that."

"Well, that's not the only problem. We are not set up for security yet, and we can't guarantee your safety." This was a bit of stretch, but I'd used this type of argument successfully in other situations.

"Well, shit. That don't matter to us, does it, Belle?" Belle shook her head and looked at me. I realized that those of us between Belle and Andy and what they wanted were all non-Southerners and began to get a bit anxious.

"Nevertheless, we've got to ask you to stay with your car, relax for an hour, and then we'll begin to let everyone in."

"How's an hour gonna make any difference?" Andy's voice had acquired an edge. She left her Datsun and stood in front of me, her girlfriend or whoever she was behind her

I pitched my own voice as evenly as I could and repeated exactly what I had already said. Not only do people not read, they don't often listen. Sometimes repetition helped.

Not this time. Tennessee Andy spit on the ground between us. "Well, y'all got kind of a attitude, don't ya? You ain't from the South, are ya?"

"Nope. San Francisco," I replied.

"Well, that explains it. You kind a think 'cause you're from the gay capital a' the world, you're a little bit better than the rest of us here in the old backward Southland."

Belle put a hand on Andy's arm. "Andy, honey, let it go. It's okay."

"You know, a Southerner knows how to compromise. I hope the rest of y'all don't act like this." She glared around the half circle of me, Billie, Marty, and Miss Tits.

"Look. This isn't about me being from SF. It's just our policy."

"Well, back in Tennessee, we don't take well to people telling us what to do."

"Andy. *Come* on." Belle pulled her arm.

I should have let the lover or friend or whatever she was handle Andy, but my headache started to pound. Six women were staring at me, waiting for what I would say next.

"Well. Tennessee rules, or lack of them, don't apply here. Now I'm gonna ask you one more time. Please get back in your car and wait."

This came out sounding a lot harsher than it normally would, due to my throbbing temples and dry mouth and generally being over these two.

'What if we don't?"

Oh, swell.

Miss Tits spoke up suddenly. "You know, Andy? I'd like to talk to you alone for a sec. Let's take this conversation over here." She took Andy's arm and led her out of earshot. Marty glanced at me and I shook my head yes, and she followed.

The four of them talked for a few moments, and there was a lot of nodding on Andy's part.

When they returned, Andy said, "Come on, Belle. Let's go." She gave me one more dirty look, and they climbed back into their car and Andy folded her arms.

Billie visibly relaxed. "Thanks, women. I wasn't sure I could talk her into cooperating."

"You're welcome. Tina, please stick around for a while. We'll come back and pick you up for lunch."

Miss Tits started to pout a little, but Marty kissed her warmly and said, "We'll be back. Just hang for a little, okay?"

Back on the road, I asked Marty, "What the fuck did you say to Andy from Tennessee to get her to back down?" I was both pissed off and impressed that Miss Tits had jumped in at the crucial moment and helped make sure things didn't turn ugly.

Marty grinned. "Lane here has a hangover, and she's not in the mood for any crap. We'll get you a backstage pass to meet one of the singers. Just drop it, okay, and don't make Lane mad. You don't want to mess with her, today."

"I'm grateful, I guess. Bribes aren't my favorite way of doing things."

"I know, I know. I had to improvise. What *is* wrong with you anyhow? You look like shit, and I don't think it's just 'cause you drank a little too much last night."

"I don't want to talk about it. Take me to Medical so I can get some aspirin."

"Oh, right. You need a little TLC from Alison." Marty smirked.

"No. That's not it, and I said I didn't want to talk about it. Okay?"

Marty looked at me in silence. She wasn't used to me being cranky. Normally, I wasn't. But I sure as heck needed an attitude adjustment. Tennessee Andy was right about that much. I don't know if I exactly wanted to see Alison, but I wanted relief of some sort.

CHAPTER NINE

When I walked into Bates, the three musketeers were all there. They looked at me expectantly, but I could only see Alison. I wanted some sign from her. Sign of what, I didn't know. Did she care about me? Had she ever? I wanted her so much I was going nuts. It was way more than sex, though there was that. I wanted her to love me. That was the truth, and I wanted to know what I had to do to make her love me. Probably the list didn't include her running into my presumed sex partner at the bathroom. And I wanted to explain that, but now obviously was not the time.

"Hi. I came for some aspirin."

"Aspirin, ibuprofen, or Tylenol?" Leah asked in a Nurse Hard Ass tone before either Angie or Alison could say a word.

"Aspirin, please, three." This request earned me a frown from Nurse Hard Ass, but I didn't care what she thought.

I kept looking at Alison, who wouldn't make eye contact with me. Nurse Hard Ass handed me the aspirin, plus a cup of water.

"Are you okay?" she asked, very solicitous. I wanted her to leave me alone.

"Yes, thanks. Just a headache."

Alison raised her head and looked at me, finally. What was behind those sapphire-blue eyes? Pity, contempt, anger?

"Allie, can I talk to you for just a sec? Outside?" I glanced at the two other women, who looked at both of us with great interest, as though we were about to put on a show.

After a long time, she said, "Sure." Her tone was clipped.

I turned and walked out with Alison right behind me. I purposefully went a good distance away from Bates. The walls have ears, I thought idiotically. I needed to get out of the rising heat and go lie down in a dark room, but that wasn't going to happen any time soon.

"Hey. Look. About last night."

"You don't owe me any explanations, El—Lane." Good. She was getting used to my actual name. Bad. Her tone was dismissive and cool.

"Nonetheless, I would like to offer one, if you're willing to listen."

"Not right now. We think a lot of women will be coming by as they arrive."

I didn't think that dozens of festies were about to descend on Medical, but I didn't want to argue with Alison.

"I'm going to be pretty tied up myself, but after dinner, maybe we could meet by the lake just for a little bit."

"You're certainly fond of meetings, aren't you?"

"Don't know about that, but I need to talk to you." I tried to calibrate my tone to just enough pleading to not be abject but still reach her.

Something softened in her features that gave me hope.

"Okay. When we're done with supper, meet me at the lake." That had a nice sound and called up a lovely image, but I was too much of a wreck to truly enjoy it.

I waved good-bye and drove away on my golf cart. Next order of business was having a talk with Val and, oh yeah, actually doing my work as security coordinator.

❖

I stopped in at Nadia's domain and kibitzed with her and her people a little bit. Another aspect of being a festival volunteer is checking in with various people. I love to see people do their work. The volunteers, without exception, worked as a labor of love. We were essentially creating an entire city of women for several days, and we liked doing it. It was gratifying.

The aspirin kicked in, and I was starting to feel closer to normal, not super-high energy though. I prayed for no big incident for the rest of the day. That morning's encounter was enough. I took a tour of the land and stopped by the day stage and the craft area, and then I went out to the parking areas. Magda said she'd noticed nothing unusual, and neither had anyone else.

"Do you have a couple of women to sit out here tonight and how late?"

"Oh, for sure. The festies will be arriving past midnight, but we'll be around."

"Good. How about after midnight?"

"Maybe. We'll see who signs up."

She referred to the giant bulletin board set up near the kitchen and dining hall for the festies to sign up for their work shifts. I'd have to come up with a plan for my volunteers as well. Marty would have the night shift, but I wanted to make sure we got some folks who seemed reliable. That could be hard to determine at a first meeting.

"I'll try to get a couple of Security members to help."

"That would be dynamite."

I swung by and picked up Marty and Miss Tits and took them to lunch. No further problems with the gate had occurred, thank the Goddess.

As we waited to eat lunch, I gave Marty the keys and told her to go ahead and cruise around until mid-afternoon. Then she could go take a nap to get ready for her overnight. At the word "nap," Marty and Miss Tits glanced at each other.

"I mean that you should sleep, not screw." They giggled. Give me strength, I swore silently. But it was up to them how they wanted to spend their downtime.

Val was ready to take a break, and we went out on the back porch.

"How's it going?" I asked. It was really not all about my problems. I cared for Val and wanted her to have a good festival.

"Oh, you know. It's crazy, but it's good. We have to feed the multitudes, and we will. The health department stopped by this morning. We passed inspection."

"I had no worries about that," I said, and I meant it.

"Thanks. Now what's on your mind?"

I told her about the previous night, and she snickered.

"I know Tanya, and I think she's working her way through every woman on the crew."

"She wasn't happy when I put the brakes on."

"No doubt. Too bad, but she certainly has plenty of others to choose from. The question is why? What stopped you?"

"I stopped because I'm still in love with Alison."

"Oh, my Goddess."

Val unleashed a string of curses, then grabbed me by the shoulders, shook me, and fake-choked me. It was a good thing my hangover was almost gone.

"I know," I said morosely. "What the fuck am I going to do? She doesn't want to get into the past. She's been friendly with me, but now she thinks I'm a slut because of Tanya."

"I think you're crazy, but what the fuck? Love *is* crazy."

"What am I going to do, Val?"

"Do you know what the definition of insanity is?"

What was she talking about? Was I insane? I didn't think so, though I'll cop to having some insane *moments.*

"No, I don't, but I think you're going to tell me, and what does that have to do—"

"Hold on, girl. I'll explain."

I waited with a big frown that made Val laugh. I liked to make her laugh, but that wasn't my purpose at the moment. I needed answers, and I needed help.

"The definition of insanity is doing the same thing over and over and expecting different results."

"Huh." I suppose that made sense.

"We often say it about alcoholics in AA who are trying to get sober but refuse to change their ways. It's applicable to a lot of other types of behavior though," she said acerbically.

"So tell me. What does this have to do with Alison and me?"

"Hmm. I think I might have some insight into that for you."

"Please, Val. I'm desperate."

"You're in a sorry state, that's for sure. Okay. You've said that you've tried to talk to Allison about the past?"

"Yes. I apologized. I wanted her to apologize. She did, but it didn't make much difference in the way I felt."

"Right. You need to let go of what happened. You need to stay in the present. The way you describe how you've been talking to her, you sound like a real drag, if you ask me. She thinks you slept with Tanya. Well, you can clear that up, but then you need to court her. You need to show her who you are now, who you could be with her if she cares to find out."

"Yeah. I'm the girl who sleeps with the likes of Tanya."

"No, you're Lane, who loves Alison. Maybe there's still something there with her. You told me about your musical interludes and your little swim."

"Yes, but those were short moments. I don't know what she's thinking." I sounded so whiny I was disgusted with myself.

"Lane, baby, just be nice to her. Stop trying to have serious heart-to-heart talks. If she brings up Tanya, just explain that it didn't happen. Show her how much you care about her. You've got to get going, though, because the festival is going to be over as of Monday. That gives you four days, including today."

"Should I tell her I'm in love with her?"

"That's a big step, and it might be too much right now. I'll leave that up to you."

"Four days," I said, appalled at the enormity of the challenge.

"Four days," Val repeated. "Give it your best shot, slick. I've got faith in you." She clapped me on the back, then kissed my cheek. I wish I had as much faith in myself as she did.

I sat by myself on the back step for a while and smoked a cigarette, thinking about what I could and should do. For one thing, I was going to pray for a lot of medical emergencies that required security help. Other than that, I hadn't a clue. Then a sudden realization hit me. I'd never had much love for talking about relationship issues with my girlfriends. Probably one of the reasons why they always broke up with me. With Alison, talking was *all* I wanted to do. Well, not quite all, but way more than was normal for me. That meant that I was truly still in love with her.

This insight was devastating. I was in far worse trouble than I'd been when I was eighteen and trying to figure out how to seduce her and failing. The stakes seemed even higher than before. What a eureka moment. My approach to relationships had always been to let them happen with no thought. With Alison, I was acting with intention. If intention was all it took, I would succeed, but it was way more complicated and also included another person: Alison. Yet Val was right. I couldn't just drown her in requests for processing. It obviously wasn't working anyhow. I was going to have to show my intentions, but I didn't know exactly how this would work.

What I did have was a date with Alison that evening, and I surely needed to plan something good, according to Val. I went off on my golf cart, my mind humming along with its little rubber wheels rolling on the dirt road as I drove through the middle of the festival.

When I asked her to give me twenty minutes to discharge my coordinator duties before we could leave, Alison gave me a noncommittal shrug. She lingered off the side as I waited for the volunteers to find me. I held up a piece of paper that read SECURITY to help them. Marty and Miss Tits and I went over our plan for the first evening of festival, but it largely hinged on how many people volunteered to help us.

A small group of four showed up for work.

I said, "This isn't a difficult job. You'll mainly function as eyes and ears. Two of you will go the backstage area and help with crowd control. You'll check wristbands and ask the stage manager Nadia for help if you need it. Two of you will be out and about in the audience. Keep aisles cleared, and just watch for anything that looks like a problem. Call us if necessary. Marty or me. If we don't get any more volunteers, is it possible a couple of you would be willing to spend the night on the main stage?"

I saw a couple of nods. Marty would finish their marching orders and teach them how to use walkie-talkies.

Alison watched the whole thing dispassionately.

I gave the golf cart to Marty and Miss Tits, and we walked the ten-minute distance to the lake. That's one of the things about festival that you get used to. Unless you have a golf cart, you have to walk everywhere, and it takes time. In this case, I wanted to walk with Alison. Somehow it seemed less impersonal than using the golf cart, and my foot felt okay finally.

"What did you want to talk to me about?" Alison asked me. Her tone sounded neutral, but I heard a hint of weariness.

"Nothing. I just wanted to spend a little time with you." I gave her my winsome smile and got a small one in response. I wanted to hold her hand while we walked but was nervous. I told myself to take it easy and move one step at a time.

"Oh," she said, and I detected some surprise.

"Actually, I was hoping we could just hang out. Maybe go to the evening performances together." I grinned a bit wider. Gratifyingly, Alison looked a little off balance, skeptical maybe, but at least she hadn't shut down.

"What about Tanya?" she asked in a manner that suggested I had something to answer for. I suppose that was true, and I was willing to do that. I had plumbed my psyche enough to be able to answer non-defensively.

"I didn't sleep with Tanya," I said simply. "It wasn't right for me. I'm asking you because I want to spent time with *you*."

"Oh." This time that tiny word was charged with a whole lot more feeling. *No. Alison, my love. I'm not a slut, though I was momentarily impersonating one last night.*

"What do you say?"

"I'm on duty," she said, as though that was a reason to say no.

"As am I. We have radios, and we're reachable if necessary." I made sure to keep my tone neutral.

"I guess." She sounded as though I'd asked her to do something she truly didn't want to. I hoped that wasn't the case.

I picked up her hand. "I'd very much like it if you would."

She stared at her hand captured between my two hands. I waited.

"All right."

"Fabulous. Do you want to ride or walk?"

Alison looked thoughtful.

"Ride. If you don't mind. And you ought to still stay off your foot as much as possible."

"Very good." I grinned triumphantly and called Marty.

We had to wait for a bit, and I hadn't planned on more small talk. We were stuck in a somewhat strained silence. I fought my tendency to want to fill up empty air with useless babbling.

Finally, Marty and Miss Tits showed up, and Marty had some things to report regarding festies setting up camp outside the designated areas. Miss Tits chimed in with her admiration of Marty's ability to handle these situations. After Miss Tits's performance at the gate that morning, I was almost ready to concede she wasn't as useless as I feared she'd be. I adjusted my opinion of her and silently admonished myself to think of her as Tina. And as Marty and Tina were doing all the talking, neither Alison nor I had to say a word.

"Thanks a lot for taking care of that," I said. "You two ought to take it easy and watch the show. I'm here for the night where I think most of the action will be."

Marty nodded, though she gave Alison a sort of sidelong look.

At the stage, I marveled at the size of the audience. It looked as though most of the festies, all two thousand strong, were already here and psyched to get the party started.

I stood by the stage with Alison at my side but didn't touch her. Automatically, I scanned the crowd and noted a couple of young women on either side of the seating area looking serious and watchful. I was pleased to see one walk over and move someone who had plopped herself down right in the middle of the fire aisle. Good work. The new volunteers should do nicely.

Arden walked out on stage to a huge cheer. She took up the microphone and said, "Welcome to the first annual Southern Women's Music and Comedy Festival. We're glad you're here."

I glanced at Alison's profile, curious about what she was thinking, but I didn't ask. My goal was for us to just *be*, as in we were a couple enjoying the show. We might both be technically on duty, but barring anything amiss, we could pretend. Or at least *I* could pretend we were on a date. I longed to know what Alison was thinking but resolutely quashed the urge to ask. *Keep your friggin' mouth shut.*

The first performance was a local favorite, and Alison said, "I've seen her. I like her songs a lot."

I smiled benevolently. Secretly, I'm not that big a fan of women's music. It's fine, and I appreciate the cultural phenomenon, and I want my sisters to have a good time, but mostly it's just too insipid for me. I like hard rock and new wave.

I whispered in Alison's ear, "You want something to drink?"

She gave me a questioning look.

"Backstage. We have permission as workers to get soft drinks."

"Oh, sure. Yeah. Can I get a coke? Dr. Pepper, if they've got it."

"But you said Coke." I was thoroughly confused

She looked at me like I'd lost my mind. "Yeah. All that stuff is coke."

"Huh?"

She looked at me with benign contempt. "In the South, we call soft drinks coke. Then you name the brand or whatever. I meant coke as opposed to water."

"That doesn't make any sense."

She smirked. "It doesn't make any sense to you 'cause you're not a Southerner."

Instead of Southern charm, I was being treated to Southern superiority. Guess I'd just go with the flow instead of starting an argument. I was trying to seduce her, not annoy her.

"Righto. One Dr. Pepper coming up."

I ambled around the left side of the stage to a large tented area. At the entrance, I was again cheered when one of the security girls asked to see my wristband. Belatedly, she recognized who I was and looked embarrassed.

"You're doing fine. No need to be sorry," I told her. I showed her my wristband.

The backstage area was humming, but a cursory glance told me access was being controlled.

Some lesbian feminists object to us exerting that sort of "elitist" process. I have no patience with that kind of attitude. The women who perform for our pleasure need their space, and the stage managers try to keep things running professionally. There's simply no reason why everyone who wants to be backstage has a right to be. That was Arden's philosophy, and I concurred, being the control freak I am. It was one of the things that endeared Arden to women's music artists.

I found the drink coolers and located a can of Dr. Pepper and bottled sparkling water for myself. Sodas, as we call them in California, make my teeth hurt and coat my tongue. Give me water, bubbly or flat.

Back out by Alison's side, I handed her the soda with a flourish and a big grin. She took it from me and murmured thanks.

Actually, it was relaxing and sweet to just stand there near Alison and watch her enjoy herself. It was full dark, but her face was illuminated by the stage lights

In profile, her straight nose, smooth forehead, and pointed chin were shadowed but clearly visible. I was in the presence of the two Alisons again—my camp buddy Alison and the adult Alison. I loved and wanted them both.

"Do you want to sit down?" I asked. "Maybe disabled would let us join them for a moment or two." I pointed to the area up front where the wheelchair gals sat. There were some chairs for other folks as well.

She tilted her head. "Does everyone just automatically say yes when you ask them something?"

I wasn't sure how to interpret this question. It could be a real one or a little tease.

"You know, not everyone, but enough of the time, I suppose."

"Too bad it won't work on me." She was definitely teasing me, and I took the bait.

"Why not? I can't believe you're unpersuadable. I'm not working hard enough. I'll have to refine my skills."

Her response was a look made of skepticism and challenge.

This was becoming interesting. What was up with Alison? Could she harbor a tiny bit of a yen for me and I'd just been so mired in my angst-ridden curiosity about the past to notice? I remembered our dinner on Tuesday evening. It was looking as though Val's advice to shut up and be charming, attentive, and romantic was correct.

"I'm okay where we are, thanks." She took another sip and returned her gaze to the stage.

I pretended to listen to the concert, but instead, I was busily constructing scenarios where I could move this process along faster. There were, for example, four nights and five days, counting Monday. If I hadn't achieved my goal by Sunday night, it was over. And what was my goal? It wasn't merely to make love with Alison. No, I was way more ambitious. I wanted her to be in love with me and promise to spend the rest of her life with me. That was all. Very basic, clear-cut. *Right.*

I must have shaken my head, because Alison asked, "What's the matter?"

I was startled out of my fantasizing and could only mutter "Nothing" and show a noncommittal face.

Amazingly, she was watching me and noticed what I did, which also gave me hope.

The night was winding down. My program announced that the band onstage was the last of the night. It was eleven, which was good since the routine part of me wanted to head back to my little room in Bates Motel and crash. I didn't seriously think Alison and I would end up sleeping together tonight That would have to wait, but I fretted about kissing her.

First things first. It was time to leave and also keep the chivalry going.

"Let me give you a ride home. I hadn't noticed Angie or Leah around, which was good, since that meant Alison *needed* a ride to her cabin.

She yawned and stretched. "Okay. I'll take it."

Next dilemma: Marty and Tina had the golf cart, and I didn't want them along for the ride. Music festival was a constant stream of logistical challenges anyhow, and throw in attempted seduction, and you've got major complications.

"I'll be right back."

I walked away and spoke into my radio. "Marty, come in."

"Hey, Lane."

"Bring the golf cart back to the stage, please. I need it for a few minutes. Then you can take it for the night."

"We can give you a ride home, no—"

"In a little bit, but I need to do something else first."

"Oh. Okay." She sounded dubious. I would be too, if I was in her spot. I might need to clue Marty and Tina in on my plan, but that thought didn't thrill me.

I walked back to the front of the stage where Alison was standing exactly where I'd left her. That was nice.

I touched her arm. "We'll be going in a minute, as soon as Marty brings the cart."

She nodded vaguely. She appeared lost in thought. What about? I longed to ask.

I looked up at the gorgeous night sky. In my peripheral vision, I saw Alison do the same and silently cheered. Starry nights are made for romance.

"Lane?" All at once, one of our security volunteers appeared right in front of me, panting and a little wild-eyed.

"What's up?" Damn. I'd forgotten her name. Needed to work on that.

"Can you come quick? Some girls are fighting over here."

She pointed to the back corner of the audience area. Other than stray light from the stage lights, it was black. I couldn't see.

"Okay. Sure."

Alison was right there at my side, and before I could say anything, she said, "I'll come with you."

We followed my volunteer, and in a few moments, we were peering into the dark trying to see what was happening. I'd forgotten to bring a flashlight. Idiot. I needed to remember that and make sure to remind Marty, but those thoughts flew out of my head as we arrived at a typically chaotic scene.

The volunteer's partner was ineffectually trying to pull one woman off another one. They were yelling incoherently, and one was slapping randomly at the other one, who cowered.

Alison barreled right into the fray with me behind her, as though we'd practiced for days. Each of us grabbed a combatant by the arms and backed up.

"Okay. Women. Stop," I said as sternly as I could. Lucky my voice is sort of deep, unlike the ineffectual squeaks a lot of women produce when they try to yell.

I pinned the arms of the butchier half back, and Alison had her counterpart—girlfriend?—in hand.

"The party's over, everyone," I said to the onlookers. "Go on back to your campsites."

My volunteers stood by, looking shaken.

My prisoner struggled, and I whispered in her ear, "I'll let you go, but you have to settle down."

She stopped writhing.

I turned to my volunteers "Good job, you two. Head home, and thanks for your help." They started to talk, but seeing my face, they fell silent, and one said, 'Okay. Bye."

Alison was examining the other woman for wounds. "What's your name?" she asked.

The girl mumbled, "Bridget." She looked deeply embarrassed.

I dropped the arms of the other one. "You want to tell me what started this? Begin with your name," I asked the scowling woman, who was staring at her girlfriend looking half angry and half worried. I could smell alcohol.

"It's Ace," she said, as though she was making an admission of something. Whatever angry haze she was trapped in was fading away, and she was likely embarrassed.

Alison looked up from her examination of Bridget and back at us with a set expression. "I'm taking Bridget back to Bates," she said, and reached for her radio.

"You'll stay with me," I told Ace.

She started to look panicky and said, "No. I got to go with her and see—"

"Come on." I took her arm and marched her several feet away. I turned, and she wouldn't make eye contact.

"Okay. I'm not a shrink or a social worker. It looks like you two have a bit of a violence problem."

"No, we don't! It's just she's a big flirt."

"Yeah, you do," I said harshly. "Get some smarts. You might want to find someone to help you sort your problems out."

Ace looked sullen and stupid. Not a great look.

"I've got a bad temper, and well, Bridget, she don't deal with me very well."

"Huh. Looks to me like you're the one who doesn't deal with you very well."

"You a cop?"

"Nope. Not one of them either. I'm Festival Security. I'm just another lesbo like you, but I try to keep people from getting hurt."

"Well. No one's hurt." She didn't sound all that sure. "So can I go?"

"I'll take you to Medical since I'm going there as soon as my ride arrives, but you're going to behave yourself. No more bullshit. Sober up, and if you love that girl and want to keep her, I suggest you get your act together."

"Lane? Where the heck are you?" It was Marty on the radio.

"Coming back to stage left now. A couple moments."

"Let's go," I told Ace.

"Take us to Medical, please," I said to Marty. She looked quizzical but obeyed.

We proceeded in silence, and when we arrived, I told Ace, "You stay out here and I'll come get you."

Tina's eyebrows went up at my tone, but she was learning. She didn't ask any questions either.

I found Alison sitting next to Bridget, who reclined on one of their cots.

When I walked in, she looked up at me, her face troubled. "How's the patient?"

"How are you, Bridget?" Alison asked.

"I'm all right, I guess."

"She's just a little shook up. No physical injury, this time," Alison said sternly.

"Bridget? Ace is outside. Do you want her to come in?"

"Yes!" she said. I could see she'd been crying.

"Allie? What do you say?"

"I think Bridget ought to stay here for the night." She fixed the woman on the bed with a glare that silenced the protest she was about to mount.

I asked Alison, "May I bring Ace in for a moment?"

Alison nodded.

I stood on the top step and gave Ace a sign to come with me. Marty and Tina lounged on the golf cart.

All four of us squeezed into the tiny room.

'Hey, baby." Bridget held up her arms. Ace went into them, and they hugged. I wondered about the psychology of abusive relationships. It seemed something only heterosexuals ought to be bothered with, but that was ridiculous. Lesbians are every bit as capable of heinous behavior as straight people.

Alison and I stood back to let them have a moment.

"Alison wants me to stay here. Just tonight, baby."

Ace started to bristle.

Alison cleared her throat. "I think it would be a good idea if we found a counselor to talk to you two."

That surprised me.

Ace glared at the both of us. "We don't need any counselors. We're fine."

"It is clearly not true that you're 'fine.' Don't even try it," I said, my voice cold and harsh.

Ace started to speak but wisely changed her mind.

"I want to keep Bridget under observation for the night. Come back tomorrow morning, Ace." Alison was clearly concerned about

Bridget's health and wanted to separate the squabbling lovers. I agreed.

Ace kissed her tearful lover and marched out the door without another word. I followed her to make sure she actually left.

I told Marty and Tina, "Go ahead. I'm fine. I'll call if I need you. Have a quiet night." Marty grinned and saluted.

Back inside, Alison was sitting in a chair, and I fetched another chair and joined her.

"We only want you to get some help. We're not trying to break you up," she said.

I added, "We know Ace loves you, but she has a hard time showing it, right?"

Weepy, Bridget nodded, then asked suddenly, "Are you guys a couple?"

Startled, Alison and I looked at one another, and to my great dismay, my face got hot, as did Alison's. The sight of her blush nearly canceled out my embarrassment. *I'll be darned. She got unnerved at that question. Huh.*

"Nope," I said with as much cool as I could summon. "Just good friends."

"Oh. I thought…never mind."

Thought what?

Alison stood up. "Get some rest. I'll talk to you in the morning."

We walked outside without having to even say anything. It was like we could read each other's minds, like we used to way back when.

Alison clenched her fists, then rubbed her face distractedly. "Man," she said.

"You all right?" I patted her shoulder. I wanted to take her in my arms but didn't want to scare her.

"I guess. This is such a horrible situation. I never expected to run into anything like this at a women's music festival."

"That it is, but I'm more worried about you."

"I'll be fine. I'd like to actually go home now."

"Shit. I sent Marty off with the golf cart."

"It's fine. Angie must be around somewhere."

Come to think of it, I hadn't seen them for hours. Not that I wanted them around. *Hmm. What did that mean? Very intriguing.*

Alison used her walkie-talkie to find them. We had a few minutes before they would show up, and I pondered what I should do.

We sat on the steps of Bates, our knees touching lightly.

"I had a nice evening. Up to a certain point," she said, lightly teasing.

"Me too." I gave Alison my best wistful, tender grin.

She held steady eye contact with me. "Don't," she said.

My blood chilled. "Don't what?"

"Don't look at me like that."

"Like what?" I was terrible at feigning innocence.

"Don't look at me with all sad-eyed, oh-I-want-you-so much. I know you want me, but it's not going to happen."

'No-not?" I was astonished. And embarrassed.

"You're like a puppy dog," she said in a tone that implied puppy dog was a bad thing.

"No, I'm not." I was stung and irritated.

"Yes, you are."

Wow. This was a stupid argument.

"Stop it. I'm not." And I dove in and pressed my mouth against hers.

She flinched for a second, then relaxed into the kiss, and I moved my mouth around. I didn't use any tongue, but I kept us in a tight lip-lock. She kissed me back for just a few seconds, and then she wrenched herself away.

I turned her head to make eye contact with me. "I think you're mistaken about me. Further, I think you liked that kiss."

I know I did. My labia started to swell the second our lips met.

"You're the one who's mistaken." Alison spoke with such bitterness, I mentally flinched. "You don't know what you're doing."

"Yes. I know exactly what I'm doing. I'm in love with you. I was in love you all the way back when we were kids. It never went away. It went into hibernation, but when I saw you, it came back to life."

"You're out of your mind," Alison said.

"No. I think I'm very much in my right mind. Tell me you don't feel it."

"Whether or not I feel something for you is not important. I'm not the one for you. I can't ever be."

"Never? How come you're so sure about that?"

We glared at each other.

And at that precise moment, Angie and Leah showed up. Their timing was impeccably bad, and I hated them.

We must have looked like we were either about to tear each other's clothes off or start throwing punches. Leah and Angie stared at us with identical expressions of avid curiosity.

With surprising calm, Alison said, "Hey. 'Bout time y'all got here. I want to get to sleep." There was possibly the slightest tremor in her voice, but I could have been imagining it.

She got up from the step and walked to the golf cart, saying over her shoulder, "Make sure Ace doesn't come in here and try to kidnap Bridget tonight."

Alison's Southern accent was so pronounced, I wondered if my kiss had rattled her. If that was true, it was a sign of progress, and I suppose it was gratifying. I was thrilled to receive some sort of response, though that was all the gratification I was going to get at the moment.

"Right," I said, not knowing what the hell else to say. We never got to finish. It was maddening how often our conversations were interrupted.

They drove off, leaving me brimming with sexual and emotional frustration.

CHAPTER TEN

After the kind of day I'd had, I should have fallen asleep right away, but no such luck. I lay in the dark thinking about Alison's lips and the way her hair smelled. Also, the ambiguity of her behavior. *Still stuck on that.* I reprimanded myself. Val had said to just be nice. I *was* being as nice as I could possibly be, aside from the kiss, but I wasn't getting anywhere. Day one down and three to go.

So I'd managed to kiss her. Honestly, this wasn't our first kiss. The first kiss had happened as a sort of surprise, just like the latest one.

July 1972

It was the weekend in between session one and session two, so no kids and we had a night off. The rest of us went out without Alison again. She said she just wasn't up for drinking and wanted to stay in camp and read.

I was irritated mainly because I just wanted us to be together whenever possible. But I also wanted to have a good time.

I stood on the steps of the unit house. The others were waiting down the hill.

"Allie. Come on. It'll do you good. We need to split for a while, get away from camp and into the real world."

She came out of the door onto the porch with a book in her hand. "El. I'm not into it. Not right now. Go ahead. Have fun. I'd just bring everyone down."

My shoulders sagged. I knew once she made up her mind, she wouldn't change it. Normally I liked that about her. But not tonight.

West Virginia drinking age was handily only eighteen. We went to some dive country-western bar in Wheeling, where we drank a lot of beer and fended off the local boys who thought a couple of dances meant we were easy picking.

We were pretty wasted when we returned. Tigger told me I ought to sleep down the hill in one of the extra cots in her unit, but I refused and hoofed it the three-quarters of a mile up to the Alpine unit, where Allie was. I guess all the beer I drank gave me the energy.

She woke up when I flopped onto the mattress next to her.

It was almost completely dark in the unit house, but I could see her face a little in the moonlight.

"You okay?" she asked, half asleep.

"I missed you," I said, suddenly very maudlin in that way that drinking too much beer makes you.

"I missed you too," she said, sounding even more morose than me.

"You could have come."

She rolled back over on her back, and I propped myself up on one elbow and looked down at her, trying to figure out what she was thinking. This was almost a full-time occupation for me. Since the beginning of the summer, she'd been mostly silent and unreachable when we were alone. She could be cheerful and energetic around the kids, but that was it.

I couldn't state my feelings either because I was afraid of saying out loud, "I love you." I knew what it meant, but I didn't know what she felt. In the moonlight though, and sufficiently drunk, I spontaneously acted on what was in my head and kissed her.

She kissed me back, but only to a point, and then turned away, saying, "El, go to sleep."

How I wanted to ask Alison about that kiss. But Val said to just forget about the past and concentrate on the present.

I flip-flopped on my creaky, uncomfortable army cot.

Tomorrow was another day. I'd have to keep up with my romance offensive and look for openings, for chinks in her armor. I was convinced I'd seen some that evening in her flirty teasing and her reaction to my kissing her. Somehow I had to inch us forward without acting like a stalker. I had to find a way to talk her out of this "I'm not the one for you" BS.

I must have dozed off because loud knocking on my door jerked me out of a sound sleep.

"Yeah, yeah. I'm coming." I turned on the table lamp and put on some shorts.

Then I threw the door open and said, "What's up?" It was Tina.

"Hey, Lane. Sorry to wake you up again." She actually looked pretty excited to wake me up.

I waved it off.

"Marty sent me down to get you. Hope it's okay if I drove the cart."

"Fine." I kept rubbing my face, trying to wake up. I looked at my watch. One fifteen a.m. Christ.

"Marty says to tell you we caught some snipes, and she wants you to come meet them."

I perked up. "What sort of snipes? The human kind?"

Tina giggled, and I considered reinstating the Miss Tits nickname.

"She just said for you to come with me."

Well. If Tina was giggling, it couldn't be that dire.

Fifteen minutes later we arrived at the far end of Artemis parking lot, where we'd conducted our snipe hunt a few days before.

In the dark in the woods with only a flashlight to illuminate your surroundings, things can take on a surreal quality. Add some night fog, and you got a spooky scene.

As we got off the cart, I recognized Marty by the light of her super-strong flashlight. She was standing near two other figures. I could tell they were human and female, but that was it.

'Hi, Lane. Sorry we had to wake you, but I figured you'd understand when you found out why."

"Snipes," I said. "The real kind?"

"Close to it," Marty said. She waved her flashlight. "Meet Robbie and Millie." She spotlighted each girl as she said her name.

"Hi," I said.

Each of the girls replied, "Hey," with identical sullen tones. It was hard to tell, but they looked like they could be around fifteen or sixteen.

Marty answered my unspoken question. "Robbie and Millie were trying to sneak into the festival." She took hold of Millie's wrist. Millie tried to resist, but Marty was bigger and stronger than she was. Marty showed me the lack of plastic wristband.

"Well," I said. "You two live around here?"

"Yeah. We do. About four miles that-away. In town."

"So what are you doing here?"

They glanced at each other, then back at me. I began to understand what was afoot.

"You thought you might sneak in here and blend in and maybe get some nice woman to take pity on you and take you away?"

Their faces fell.

"It seemed like we could, you know. We gotta get out of this town before we get killed." The word sounded like "kilt."

"You're girlfriends?" I asked, already knowing the answer.

"Yes. Won't you help us? We didn't mean no harm by sneakin' in."

"You've been hanging out for a while and checking out the scene. We found your little pile of cigarette butts. You ought not to be smoking." I felt absurdly like their mother or a kindly aunt.

They just looked away, obviously embarrassed.

"Look. I understand your predicament, but we could get into real trouble if we let you stay. You can hang out 'til morning, and then we're taking you back to town, and you can't come back here unless you bring a parent or guardian with you. I know that's probably not gonna happen. I'm sorry, but that's the way it is. "

They were clearly despondent and I was sympathetic, but I couldn't help them for the reasons I told them. If their folks got involved, Arden could get sued or arrested.

"We really ought to take you back to town right now, but I think it can wait until daylight. You can come with me and get some sleep. I'll even let you sleep together."

They grinned happily.

"Or you can hang with Tina and Marty, but you'll have to be up all night."

"Um, can we sleep somewhere?" Millie asked.

"Yep. Marty, can you take us all back to Bates?"

"Righto."

After I got them settled in one of the treatment rooms, I fell back on my cot, too keyed up to go back to sleep, which left me nothing to do but fret about Alison. I tossed and turned for a bit, then gave up and washed my face and put my jeans back on. I thought I might just call Marty and drive around with her awhile. Then my radio spoke up.

"Lane. Sorry. Can you come out to the front gate? We've got a problem." Marty's usual cool had deserted her.

Uh-oh. What now? "Can you come pick me up?"

"Negative. Please walk down, and hurry."

I hoofed it out to the front gate. Thank goodness it wasn't that far away.

As I approached, again I was left with trying to discern who was there and what was going on. My mouth went dry as I realized that one of the dimly lit figures was taller than anyone else, and I could see the outline of a trooper hat. *Shit.* It was the sheriff, and it wasn't hard to figure out why he was here.

As I approached, I could hear a lot of strained small talk.

The trooper shined his flashlight into my eyes, temporarily blinding me.

Marty said, "Sheriff, this is Lane Hudson, head of Security."

I stuck my hand out. 'Hello. Nice to meet you."

"We've met."

Then I recognized him. It was Deputy Trent, the one with the toothy, humorless grin. Okay. This was just great.

"Yes. I recall. What can I do for you, Deputy?" I asked with as much amiability as I could muster.

I was shining my flashlight on him to return the favor and could see he wasn't smiling this time.

"I'm lookin' for a couple a potential runaways. Maybe you seen them?" He described our two young guests.

I knew what would happen if I lied and Trent found out. We'd have a huge problem. But I didn't want to have to send Millie and Robbie away with him. I needed to stall him a bit.

"There are over two thousand women here. If your two runaways are here, we'd probably not know about it. I haven't heard a thing, but I'd be glad to take a good look around in the daylight and let you know. Not now though. That would just upset everyone, since it's the middle of the night. If they're here, they're safe. And if they're here, we'll find them. In the morning."

He looked very skeptical. "Their parents might take exception to that. All right. I'll be back tomorrow."

"Sure. At that point we might be able to help you. Feel free to come back first thing."

Without another word, he turned and stalked back to his cruiser.

After he left, I congratulated the gate security girl on calling in Marty right away and Marty for keeping her head, not letting him in and calling me.

Marty asked, "What do we do?"

"We need to talk to Arden and Becky first thing. Don't wake them up now. I hope our two runaways have some sense and stay put in their cots until tomorrow."

"Yeah. Me too," Marty said grimly.

When I got back to Bates I checked, and they were asleep curled up together on one of the cots like a couple of sleepy kittens.

It made me think of Alison and me when we were that age. Seemed like eons ago, yet not. I was sorry I had to boot them out but happy they had one night to be together and safe.

❖

Predictably, Arden was annoyed and apprehensive. It didn't help that it was six a.m. I'd had only about another three hours of sleep and wasn't feeling that great myself. I was nervous about having to turn the girls over to the law, though. I wanted to do something different.

"You get those kids out of here ASAP," Arden said.

"Roger. Can I borrow one of the vans to drive them?'

"Sure. Sure. Just go." She waved her hand.

Then she said to Becky, "Isn't Catherine, Willa's lover, a lawyer?"

"Yes. Should I go find her?"

"Yep. Bring her up here. I want to be ready. In case."

I heard this remark as I slipped out the door. Marty drove me back to Bates, to find our two runaways, whom I had looked in on not twenty minutes before, but they were gone.

"Marty, you can go to sleep. I'll handle this."

"No way, man. I'll help you look for them. Where do we start?"

"Well, first thing, let's get another golf cart. I'll see if we can borrow Medical's."

That meant I had to first go to Angie and Leah's room and wake them up and then beg them to use their golf cart.

As it would happen, they wanted to know why.

"What if we need it? What's going on?" Leah looked especially irritable, either because she wasn't good in the morning or it was me asking.

"We've got two fifteen-year-olds hiding out somewhere, and we have to find them before the law comes back looking for them."

"Oh, my Lord. All right, but we'll help look. Angie, call Alison and tell her."

Marty and I went off together with Tina, who also refused to go to sleep. We decided to split up the camping areas and go on foot and check back at the crossroads in an hour.

I went around asking random people if they'd seen any teenage girls by themselves and giving their descriptions. "Nope," they all said.

Becky's voice came over the radio, "Lane?"

I had a feeling I knew why she was calling. "Yeah, Becky. What's up?"

Becky dropped her voice to a whisper. "Sheriff's here."

"Right. I'll be there as quick as I can."

"One of their fathers is here too," she whispered.

Oh crap.

"Righto. Tell them we're still looking. Is Catherine there?"

"Yes." Becky obviously didn't want to say much on the radio, and I understood.

I was about to call Marty when I heard Alison's voice.

"Lane? This is Alison."

As if I didn't know. "Hey. I'm kind of busy."

"Yes, but I think you might want to come over to my cabin."

The light went off in my head. She had the kids.

"Right. Marty, you hear that?"

"On my way."

When we arrived at the workers' cabins, I spotted Alison sitting outside on the steps with Millie and Robbie. Relief flowed through me, and the next thing I wanted to do was kiss Alison.

"So? You couldn't stay put like I said to," I said by way of greeting.

They moved closer together and just stared at me sheepishly. Again, I felt just like one of their parents, and I didn't like it.

"Look, the police are here with your dad."

"Whose dad?" Millie asked nervously.

"Don't know, but seriously, you've got to come with me and deal with this."

Alison put her arm around Robbie. "Come on, honey. You're gonna get us all in trouble. Let's go with Marty and Lane. Delaying isn't gonna help anything."

They looked at me like *I* was the one responsible for their dilemma, but I quashed my annoyance.

They unwound themselves and slowly stood up.

"Hi, Allie," I said. "How's your day so far? Mine sucks."

She grinned sadly at me.

"Alison, can you come with us?" Millie asked.

Alison raised her eyebrows and made eye contact with me. I asked Marty to wait back at Bates for me.

I thought for a second and said, "Sure." If that was what it took to get them to cooperate, fine. I was unaccountably annoyed, though, that the two runaways seemingly trusted Alison more than me.

The two teenagers had to share a seat in the golf cart as we drove back to Arden's house. The sheriff cruiser parked outside looked ominous.

"All right," I said to Alison. "I'll take it from here."

Millie piped up. "Oh, please. Can Alison please come with us?"

"Uh." I was nonplussed. Also I was feeling a bit like my territory was being encroached upon.

I looked at the three of them, who stared back at me. Alison wore a neutral expression, but the two kids were pleading.

"Sure," I said. "Fine." I didn't sound too gracious.

Once again, the two law-enforcement guys were seated in the living room. This time, a beefy, distraught-looking man sat between them. When he saw us, he leapt from his seat.

"Millie Jean Winters, I'm gonna beat your butt. Your mom 'bout had a heart attack—"

Sheriff Tanner put hand on the man's shoulder. "Steady, Rick. We'll get this figured out, but no one's butt's getting beat just yet." Rick's face was nearly purple, but he stayed put, instead turning to Arden and saying, "This is all your fault."

"Rick," Sheriff Tanner said. "Can you just cool it for a New York minute till we sort this out?"

Rick opened his mouth to say something else but apparently thought better of it.

Sheriff Tanner said, "Let's start again with introductions." He was good at defusing a tense situation, that's for sure.

"Good to see you, Millie, Robbie. Y'all okay?" The sheriff sounded surprisingly gentle.

The girls nodded, seeming unable to speak. Becky brought in some more folding chairs, and we all sat down.

I glanced at the deputy sheriff, who glowered at me. I was very relieved that his boss, Sheriff Tanner, was present.

All of us had a seat, and the sheriff took his time gazing at everyone in the room one at a time. He was one of those guys whose look said he could tell what you were thinking.

"Let's start at the beginning. You two kids want to tell us what the heck you thought you were doing running away like that?"

The two miscreants looked at each other, obviously gauging just how much to reveal.

"We heard about the festival, and we just wanted to, you know, check it out."

"Y'all got no business bein' anywhere near all this craziness." It was Rick again.

"Rick, I ain't gonna tell you again. Just hush, and let's hear what the kids got to say before we jump to any conclusions." Sheriff fixed him with a hard stare.

That reminded me that Alison and I and the two girls had had no chance to concoct a consistent story. We were going to be on very shaky ground if it came out that we knew the girls were here and I had lied to the deputy sheriff last night.

My mouth was dry and my temples hurt. I looked at Willa's lover and hoped she was a very good lawyer. She'd been listening intently to the back-and-forth but hadn't said a word.

Millie and Robbie began to speak in turn, in small, shaky voices. They admitted they'd snuck in to the festival but only revealed that they wanted to participate, not that they were trying to run away.

"So," Robbie said. "They caught us and said we could stay till morning, but then we had to leave. They gave us a place to sleep. We didn't want to leave in the morning, so we snuck out of the motel and went to look for somewheres else, and then she found us."

Robbie pointed at Alison, who blushed. Very prettily, I thought, even through my anxiety.

Sheriff Tanner looked at the kids for a few moments, obviously wondering if they were telling the truth.

Deputy Trent spoke up. "I was told by this individual"—he pointed to me—"that she'd not seen the two minors." He put some emphasis on the word minors.

"When we spoke last night, I had not." I prayed that Mollie and Robbie wouldn't attempt to correct me, and I was rewarded. They knew enough to keep quiet unless asked a direct question.

"You refused to let me search for them." He sounded like he was pissed.

"Deputy? Excuse me." Willa's lover spoke up. "I'm Catherine Williams, attorney. I believe you're familiar with search-and-seizure laws? The festival was under no obligation to allow you to enter a private event such as this in order to follow a suspicion. You offered no evidence nor produced a warrant."

Wow. Catherine was as clued in as I hoped.

"Ahem. Yes, but I had hoped they would be cooperative since it was a couple of minors involved."

"Nonetheless, they were within their rights to refuse to let you in."

"You can try that argument out on a judge, Counselor, if you want. You had a couple of minors on site, and you're not legal guardians. You're—"

"Hold on a second," Sheriff Tanner said. "Dwayne. Let it go."

Daddy Rick had been following this back-and-forth with ill-disguised impatience.

"There's been a kidnapping here, and I want to know what you're going to do about it?" I thought he was going to bust a blood vessel.

"Whoa. There's no evidence of kidnapping," Catherine said.

"I don't see any reason to think that, Rick," the sheriff said calmly.

"Mr. Winters?" Alison spoke up a little hesitantly. "I want y'all to know I had the girls with me last night after we found them, and we took real good care of them. They're fine. And I bet they're sorry they got everyone so upset."

She was pouring on the Dixie, and when she stopped talking, she looked right at the kids.

After a moment, they both nodded. At the sound of Alison's voice, Daddy Rick began to visibly calm down. Deputy Trent still glowered, but Sheriff Tanner looked thoughtful.

"We're sorry y'all got scared. We didn't mean to do that," Millie said. "Daddy. Please don't be mad."

His face had finally faded from red to pink, and he puffed out his cheeks, but he was clearly mollified.

"I think you ought to just go on and take the girls home," Sheriff Tanner said.

"Let's go, you two," he said to the girls. And they all left.

Sheriff Tanner said to Arden, "I guess y'all know y'all dodged a bullet on this one. Next time, you'll call us right away."

Arden said, "Absolutely. You have my word."

Alison and I made our way back to Bates on the golf cart.

"Why didn't you call me?"

"They asked me not to. They thought you were going to turn them in to the cops. They were afraid of you."

"Afraid of me? Jesus Christ." I was almost yelling.

"Cool down, Lane. You're not a Southerner, and you don't get it."

"No, I'm not, but I'm supposed to provide security for the festival." I was feeling peevish and tired. "We coulda got in a lot of trouble. We almost did."

"But we didn't. You're not the only one with all the answers."

"Yeah." I knew she was right. "I'm sorry I got upset. Hey, you were great with the father. You jumped in at the right time and probably saved our asses. He looked at you and heard you talk, and it settled him right down." I didn't say that it helped she probably looked like some local beauty queen as well as talked like one.

"Yeah. Why don't you get some sleep? You look all done in."

She was taking care of me again, and part of me liked it, but it was just way too confusing, and I had to not become too carried away with hope.

Alison patted my shoulder, and that felt good. She even followed me into my room at Bates.

'Would you stay for a few minutes?"

"Yes. Just a few."

I lay down on my cot, and Alison sat next to me and put her hand on my head. She just rested it there. It felt good, not arousing but just good, and it calmed me down.

I actually didn't have time to sleep. When I woke up an hour or so later with a start, Alison was gone. I called Marty and told her to come get me.

"You ought to go take a nap."

"Nah. I'm good for now. I sent Tina to grab one, and I'll get her up and sleep some later. Don't worry about it." It was useless to argue. Just as Alison said, I didn't have to try to control everything and everybody.

Friday, we ran around putting out little fires. Lost children and more keys locked in cars. I had a Slim Jim to help with that. My old mentor Sid had shown me how to do it. Retrieving car keys from locked cars made me feel like a Girl Scout all over again.

One fire was an actual fire, just as I had predicted. I got the call around noontime.

Somebody in the camping area nearest the day stage found a worker with a walkie-talkie. This was one of those rare times where I wasn't close by an incident. I floored the golf-cart accelerator, but the excitement was over by the time I got there.

When I found the location, I could see a couple of dykes stomping their feet on the smoky ground, to the amusement of several onlookers.

"What happened and to whom?" I asked in my "security" voice of everyone in general.

The two foot-stompers looked at each other, and I knew they were the perpetrators. I'll say one thing about lesbians. If they start something, they finish it.

"We was heatin' up the coals for lunch," dyke number one said. "And Lindy here wasn't lookin' where she was going. The next thing I know, they're all over the ground."

Dyke number two shot dyke number one a dirty look. "You make it sound like it was all my fault."

I cut in. "No one's in trouble. How about you tell me the rest of what happened. Let's start with your names."

They calmed down, and we made sure the fire was out. I left them to contemplate raw hot dogs for lunch. Or they could have gone for sauteed tofu and bean-sprouts salad at the kitchen. I'm not sure which would be worse.

I checked our sign-in sheet at the kitchen and met with a few volunteers, then assigned a couple to help Magda's parking detail later. One of the volunteers was Sarajane, the local from a few days before.

She told me she hadn't heard about anything around town, but that didn't mean anything to me. Sarajane didn't go to any of the bars in town where guys might get a little too chatty and boastful while they drank. I liked her attitude though. She had a subtle don't-mess-with-me air I appreciated.

I kept finding reasons to go back to Bates so I could check on Alison and kept thinking about her hand stroking my hair as I fell asleep. She was busy with patients. With the festival opening, they had a lot of visits for small problems: forgotten Tampax, bee stings, and minor cuts and bruises. Of course, Angie and Leah were there as well, which put a crimp on what I could say or do.

I did my best though. I watched her in action, and when I got a chance, I whispered, "Do you have a date for the concert tonight?"

She didn't answer right away. She looked pleased though, for a second, before her expression reverted to neutral.

"I told Angie and Leah I'd stay here tonight, and they could go."

"Well. Can I point out that ninety-nine percent of the women will be at the main stage? We can rig up a sign or something to tell people where you are."

"Oh, Lane. I need to stay here." Alison definitely had a huge good-girl streak.

"Okay. I'll keep you company." She gave me a funny look but shrugged and said, "Suit yourself." Not exactly the response I was looking for, but I'd take it. Something about her manner suggested she was only pretending to be indifferent.

"Great. After dinner?"

"You mean supper, right? Dinner was at noon."

I sighed. "Yes. That's what I mean. I'll just have to talk to the volunteers after...supper." I called Marty and then went to the crafts area to make an appearance.

I had a chance to lie down again for a while. Honestly, the sleep deprivation would have knocked me out, except the prospect of seeing Alison alone later gave me energy.

CHAPTER ELEVEN

I took my guitar out to the infirmary waiting room, and Alison seemed happy to do some singing. We ran through some old camp songs like "Michael Rowed the Boat" and "If I Had a Hammer." They made both of us giggle, and Alison's laughter enthralled me. It had such an open, unforced quality. Some girls bray and wheeze, and it sounds awful. Alison's laugh was light and almost musical. It struck me that since we met on Saturday night, Alison had barely cracked a smile, and here she was now in a light mood. It intrigued me, but I kept my questions to myself. I hoped that if I was patient, I'd find out more.

I took some minutes to retune my guitar for a special song, and Alison watched me. When I played the introductory chords, she stopped smiling and looked at me gravely.

I started to sing Joni Mitchell's "Case of You." She joined me, and I faded out and let her take over, since her voice was much better than mine. That song made me deeply happy but morose and wistful at the same time.

When we finished the song, Alison sat with her head down. She looked unhappy.

"Alison?" I whispered.

She looked up and directly at me, her lips drawn down and her eyes cloudy.

I put my hand on her cheek, and she covered it with her own hand. Emboldened, I leaned in for a kiss. I kept my mouth still. I only wanted to see what she would do, but the touch of our lips was amazing, and I never wanted to break contact.

She did after a few moments.

"Lane. I—"

"What? What is it? Do you not want me to kiss you?"

"It's not that. I do want you to kiss me. I like you kissing me."

I decided not to bring up what she'd said the night before about me wasting my time. I concentrated on courtship and not sliding into overtalking or asking dumb questions.

I kissed her some more, and she put her hand in my hair and massaged my scalp. I was becoming so aroused I couldn't breathe. But then she broke off contact and put her face in her hands and wept.

I was startled and anxious by this turn of events. "What's wrong?"

She spoke brokenly between sobs. "I just can't. I know what you want. I know how you feel. I do. But it's not right for us. I'm not the person you think I am. I know you said you love me and that you forgive me for that night, but you don't know the whole story."

"Alison. Look at me."

She slowly turned her head toward me, sniffling.

"I love you so much," I said. "I loved you when we were kids, and I love you now. It was rough after we parted. I felt a lot of anger and pain. I mostly was able to forget you, but it took a long time. But now that we're together, it's come back. Every single feeling I ever had for you is right up in my face, and every single one of them is stronger than ever. Please. I never really got over you. We're adults, not confused teenagers anymore. Tell me what's wrong. Talk to me. If you love me, and I believe you do, you can tell me anything."

I hoped my words and my desperate and sincere tone would convince her.

She shook her head. "Oh, Ellie. My friend, my rock. You have no idea. "

"Then tell me. Tell me you love me."

"I do love you," she said, but her voice sounded resigned, not tender and loving, and that chilled me.

"Then what is it? We have a chance to start over, a chance to really have something together."

"I know you want to think that, but it isn't true. I'm not worthy of you."

"What? Why would you say that? That's ridiculous."

"I'm a damaged person. I'm not someone who can truly give herself to love."

"I don't believe that."

"If you found out what I'm really like, you wouldn't want me."

I took her by the shoulders gently and made her look at me. "You're not making any sense, Allie."

"I can try to explain, but it's not that easy for me to understand either."

"I don't care. Just tell me. Let me be the one to decide how I feel about what you say."

Val had said something like this to me once, and after I thought about it, it made sense. She'd said something else too: *Don't try to make a woman tell you something she's not ready to say. We all have to decide what to reveal and to whom on our own time.*

"Alison. I want you to tell me things when you want to. But I'm confused. One minute you're friendly, even a little flirty. You're like you were before and even better. I love who you are now like I loved you then. I love both Alisons. But then you close down and get quiet and kind of reject me. It's really hard to deal with."

"My poor Ellie. I'm sorry. I think about us a lot. The shock of seeing you, well, it was a just a lot for me to take in. I knew when I saw the name Hudson on the staff list that it was you. I knew it in my bones, and it terrified me, but it was also like a miracle. I wanted to believe I could set things right with you, but I also keep chickening out. These past few days I've thought about us."

"You knew it was me? I kept telling myself it couldn't possibly be you," I whispered. "Yet deep in my heart, I knew it was you, too. I was a wreck for a month just thinking about it."

"Me too." Alison paused and sighed. "I know I haven't been acting normal. I'm kind of all over the place.

That was an understatement. It was also not that different from how she'd behaved during our last summer together. Nevertheless, I waited for her to continue.

"I wasn't all that sure I wanted to come to the festival, but Angie and Leah wore me down. I guess you kind of get the idea I'm trying to come out?"

"I do. I hope you'll tell me more about that. Hey, how much of our story did you tell Leah and Angie anyhow?"

"I, uh, just said you and I were really close, and you had a crush on me. When we got the list, I wondered if it was you, and we kind of talked about what if it was you. That's all."

"What is with Leah, and why does she always act snippy around me?"

"Oh, she's okay, but she sort of has a crush on me." Alison looked resigned. "Angie knows about it, but she doesn't take it real seriously. She knows nothing's going to happen. Leah likes to tease me all the time."

Alison's tone said nothing would ever happen with Leah, and that reassured me if for no other reason than I couldn't picture Alison having any interest in such a shallow woman. It now made sense that Leah was so hostile to me.

"Anyway, they wanted me to be around a lot of women at the festival and see if I could start to feel safe and come out of my shell a little bit."

To me, there was no safer place on earth than a women's music festival, unless the outside world intruded, which it rarely did. Otherwise, it was like a living dream of being part of a matriarchy, a society built by women, run by women for women, and based on the values of love and feminism. Was it perfect? No, far from it, but at least we had ways of working on our conflicts that made sense. How could Alison not feel secure at a festival?

"Do you feel safe?" I asked.

"On the one hand, yeah, but I'm afraid of women," she said simply. "They make me nervous and unsure of myself. I've tried to date. I've gone to bars, and it was terrible. They were awful, superficial, everyone drinks too much, and the worst women would hit on me."

"I'm sorry, Al. That's awful." I could imagine the amount of attention she'd get on a crowded Saturday night at a dyke bar.

"The only couple I know is Leah and Ange. I know you don't like them—"

"It's not that. It's that I think they don't like *me*."

I knew that Leah, at least, didn't like me, though Angie's attitude was ambiguous. I didn't want to argue about them.

"That's just silly. Of course, they like you, but they're just like mother hens with me."

"The chick's gotta leave the nest and fly sometime," I said, trying to be not too sarcastic.

That drew a little grin from Alison. "That's something a Southerner would say."

"Well. Maybe that means I'm learning. Tell me. Now that you've been at the festival for a while, how do you feel?"

"I'm getting to that. Lord, you can be awful pushy."

She favored me with such a vexed look, I grew embarrassed. Val had warned me, and here I was still being obnoxious.

"Sorry. Let me let you do it your way. I'll shut up."

"Goodness, yes. I'm trying to talk to you."

I clamped my jaws shut and waited.

Alison had recovered from her earlier dismay and looked almost cheerful. I think she was just enjoying ordering me around and me obeying.

"I have to say I wasn't real sure about the music festival, but I thought what the heck have I got to lose? And aside from you being here, it's been real nice. Like Leah and Angie said it would be."

I decided to let that part about "nice except for you being here" go right by me. I believed I understood what she meant, and she wasn't trying to be mean.

"It took me a couple days, but I got into the spirit, and yes, just being around women, talking to women who aren't drunk and trying to pick me up, feels great."

That made me recall my behavior Wednesday night, and I felt ashamed again. She had to think not only was I a slut, but a drunken one at that. And that thought, in turn, kicked me right back to the last time I saw her on that horrible night in August of 1972. And on top of all this, her ex-husband was a drunk and an abuser. Sheesh. It was a miracle she even liked me a little bit.

I wanted to start explaining myself all over again, but mindful of Val's warnings and hopeful that Alison seemed to be opening up to me, I stayed silent.

She sighed, a deep sigh of what seemed like bewilderment. "Here it's like I'm wrapped up in a nice cotton-wool blanket. Safe and surrounded by women. It's way different from regular life. I see why women love women and love the music festival. Y'all are nice to each other even if you're fighting."

She laughed, as did I.

"But it isn't real," she said. "We have to go back to our lives, which don't look a thing like they are here."

"I know what you mean. It's true that this isn't the real world, but in a way, the festival charges my emotional batteries, and then I can deal with my life. But I have it a little easier since I live in San Francisco."

"Yeah. I bet you do. Not me. I've got to go back and live in Atlanta."

I didn't want to trouble her or scare her, but I still wanted to know more about how the festival affected her, particularly regarding sex. My curiosity was self-interested, sure, but I wanted her to talk to me. She'd gone quiet again, and I took a few moments to form my question.

"Allie—?"

"You want to know if I'll sleep with you? That if all this sex stuff going on and all the naked women are going to get me in the mood?"

This was a bit more direct than I expected. Was she psychic? I suppose not. I'd just kissed her, so I guess my intentions were clear enough.

"I uh—maybe, but there's a lot more to it than that." I was rendered incoherent by her question and by the wave of arousal that washed over me at the phrase "if I'll sleep with you."

"You're damn right there's a lot more to it than that. I've thought about it, for sure. Yeah, I liked you kissing me. I liked our swimming adventure. I was real pissed off when I thought you and Tanya...But I told you I'm not the right woman for you. It's not you, El-Lane. It's me. I don't want to start something I'm not ready to finish."

She'd gone full-bore Southern on me.

She continued. "I told you before, we've got too much history. Some of it's sweet, I'll admit, but I'm not who you think I am. You have this image of me in your head of that nice little teenage girl you hung out at camp with. A lot of stuff has happened since then, and, well, it's taken its toll."

I was speechless and didn't know what to think. When it came down to it, I didn't want to believe there was anything about Allie that I couldn't handle, that I couldn't love, but without knowing more detail, how could I be sure?

"Alison. We have a history together. Also I've got one that doesn't have anything to do with you, and you've got one that has nothing to do with me. So what? Why don't you just tell me and let me decide if whatever terrible things you've done or whatever horrible things that have happened to you make any difference to me?

"I sincerely doubt they will, but without knowing, you're right. I can't be sure. Isn't it kind of unfair to beat around the proverbial bush about it and hint about things without actually being willing to tell me? Once upon a time you trusted me, and you still can. You can't just reject me without me knowing why. If I can't handle what you tell me, I'll say so and we can say, 'Good-bye, nice to see you again.' Maybe we can keep in touch, but please, Alison, please, just tell me about you. Give me a chance to respond, and then we'll see. As your friend, I think I deserve that." She looked at me for a long time. We sat on the cot in my room, my guitar silent, leaning against the bed frame. A little bed-table lamp cast a dim light, and her face was in shadow and hard to read.

"Look at me, Allie," I said and pulled the lamp over to shine it in my face. "Tell me."

She stared back at me, her expression a mixture of fear and hope. Which emotion would win? She had her hands clasped around her drawn-up legs as she sat on the cot resting her back against the wall. It was an oddly graceful position but so clearly self-protective, I was afraid her fear would win out. I knew for certain that back in her past were things having nothing to do with me but that still had traumatized her and made it almost impossible for her to let down her guard and say out loud what she'd experienced. It saddened me immensely to think of how much she'd suffered. I was sure I was the one person she should feel safe to talk to.

"Give me a cigarette," she said suddenly. "Those things must be good for something if you're smoking 'em."

I handed her a cigarette and put one in my mouth, then lit them for us. Whatever would help her get started, I was all for it. I'd deal with the consequences of smoking in a nonsmoking room later if I had to.

"I'll even give you some scotch if that'll help."

"Lord, no, thanks. I can't abide the stuff. Anyway, we're supposed to be working."

"True." After my recent experience, I surely didn't need any alcohol.

She took a deep drag on her smoke and let it out, then coughed.

"Gah. This is nasty." She took another drag and closed her eyes. Then she took a deep breath and opened them and looked right at me. "Okay. Do you remember when we started the summer we were counselors?"

"Oh, yeah. I've never forgotten it, any of it."

"Me neither." She spoke so harshly I got alarmed. But I told myself to just keep my editorial opinions to myself and let her talk.

"Did you think maybe something was a little off about me then?"

"Oh, boy, did I ever. But then you'd act normal, and I'd think, 'Oh, nothing's wrong.' What did I know anyhow? I was just a naive kid."

"But then there was the night at the end of the season and—"

"I apologized and you apologized, and I'm okay. We were both just totally confused and said and did things that weren't cool. I'm—"

"Yes, but there's stuff I couldn't tell you at the time, and even thinking about it now makes me feel sick to my stomach. It was bad, Lane."

She got my name right. I was pleased, but the way she said it seemed like it meant something other than she was just finally getting used to it.

"Don't you remember how much persuasion it took for you to get me to agree to stay with you at the motel until the next day when your parents were going to pick you up?"

"Yes."

August 1972

I wasn't entirely telling the truth when I asked Allie if she could drive me to the Motel Six where I'd stay until my dad picked me up the next day. I told her some story about my mom and dad just not being able to come that day. The truth was I wanted us to be alone, entirely alone, because I wanted to sleep with her. I wanted her so much it was like a physical pain. I had told my folks I had to stay an extra day and where I'd be.

She hemmed and hawed around it a lot but finally said yes.

We got a quick bite to eat, and I suggested we get something to drink—a little wine. I knew I was going to need some help to get the courage up to do what I wanted to do, and I hoped it would help her relax as well.

She'd been quiet through dinner. I thought she was sad because camp was over and we had to part. I was sad as well, but I wasn't going to miss out on my last chance with her. Who knew if I'd ever have one again.

We sat on the double bed sipping wine from plastic cups and talking about the summer and about going to college in a month. I sneaked an arm around her shoulders and squeezed slightly. I was very nervous and hoped I could manage this with some sort of smoothness.

She didn't look at me. I put a finger on her cheek and turned her head to kiss her. Our wine-scented lips molded and explored. She was somewhat limp, but I took that for agreement and went on. We both got warm and sweaty since the room was August-hot and there was no air-conditioning. We slid down together on the bed. I was mesmerized by how her body felt, how our bodies felt together. They seemed made to be close, as close as two humans could get. I felt like all the years of our friendship, the many hours we'd spent talking, singing, just being together had led us to this moment. I'd reached the point where I had no more words, no more songs, no more thoughts. I had only one way to show her how I felt about her. If we could make love in whatever fashion that ended up being in my slightly hazy conception, then I could bind her to me forever.

I had no idea except my own limited experience. I was flying blind, but I was convinced we could figure it out. We kissed for a very long time, and I dared to push the shirt she wore away from her shoulder so I could kiss her neck. My lips on her collarbone felt as good as our lips pressed together. I took the natural and logical step, to me anyhow, of tentatively touching her breasts, still covered by her shirt and bra.

"Allie?" I whispered in her ear. "Would you take off your shirt? I'll take off mine and we could—"

"No, I can't, I—" She spun out of my arms and turned over on her side, her back to me.

"Allie?" I touched her hip.

"Leave me alone, please, El."

"But why? You like this, don't you? You love me. You said you loved me!" It was amazing how fast my sexual arousal morphed into unreasonable anger.

"I don't love you, not that way. Not the way you want."

"But what about all the stuff you said? You said—"

"I was only trying to make you happy. I didn't mean it."

"What? How can that be? How can you say that?"

"I don't know. I'm sorry. But could we just go to sleep and not talk about it anymore?"

I jumped off the bed and stood over her, almost speechless with frustration and shock.

She was crying, and that should have caused me to settle down and just offer her comfort, but it enraged me. I couldn't absorb that she didn't love me the way I thought she did. Some other person had taken over Alison's body. It wasn't her.

"Well, this is just great." I marched into the bathroom and slammed the door. I swept every bathroom item on the sink onto the floor. I pounded my fists on the door, and I'm fairly sure I yelled. Then I sat on the toilet and sobbed.

I heard a light knock on the door and then Alison's voice. "Ellie? I think I ought to go."

I flung the door open and said far too loudly, "All right. Just go, if that's what you want. For the record, I never loved you either. Don't ever try to talk to me again. Don't write. Don't call."

She said with surprising calm, "All right. I suppose that's the best thing. I should go now." She turned away.

I put my hand on her shoulder, and she froze.

"No, Allie, I didn't mean it. Don't go. I'm sorry I yelled and all that stuff. We can talk."

She looked at me sadly. "I'm going to leave. It's best for both of us."

She picked up her purse from the dresser and walked out the door of that crummy motel room, and I never saw her or heard from her again.

The memory of that horrible night swirled in my brain. It was fragmentary, but I remembered all the emotions attached to it, all the lust, the anger, the frustration, and finally, when she left me standing there in that crummy motel room, the deep sense of grief and defeat.

I said, "Yeah. I recall that night, but like I said, I was young, you were young, and we had no idea what we were doing. God. Everything went wrong that night."

She smiled sadly. "It's good of you to take such a forgiving view of it. But I want to tell you what happened to me that summer. I didn't leave you at the motel because I was mad at you. I left because I was afraid. Actually, I was terrified."

"Allie, there's no shame in that. I don't hold it against you. Quite the opposite."

"It wasn't you I was afraid of. I loved you as much as you loved me. I lied then when I said I didn't."

I was becoming very impatient with Alison's evasions and partial information, but I wanted her to tell me, and it had to be on her own terms.

"But now?" I dared to touch her hair gently in what I hoped was a comforting gesture.

"I'm going to tell you everything. I've been keeping it to myself. I've never told a soul. Not Angie, not Leah. Nobody until last year. It was bad, I had nightmares, I was on anti-depressants for a while. I finally went to a counselor and…" I nodded for her to go on.

My radio squawked, and since we were on the same channel, hers did too.

I heard Marty say, "Hey Lane, we need you. And—" I heard some background noise, faintly, and the name Alison.

Adrenaline replaced the expectation of hearing something profound from Alison. It was time to leap into action.

"Marty? What's up?" I asked, catching Alison's eye. She was looking at me in a watchful, concerned manner.

"Hold on." More muffled indecipherable sounds.

"Lane, we need you and Alison to come out to the Artemis parking lot ASAP. We've got a situation."

That was part of our discipline: we didn't get into specifics on the radio because we didn't want the whole festival crew and Goddess knows whoever else to hear what the problem might be until we could stabilize matters. I could tell from Marty's tone that it was something fairly dire. And she'd asked for Alison as well. But her voice also had a funny undercurrent, almost as if she was trying not to laugh.

I asked Alison, "Do you need backup from Leah or Angie?"

"I'll see. I don't want to call for them unless it's absolutely necessary. They wanted to enjoy themselves for just a few hours." She leapt off the cot and disappeared down the hall.

I put my shoes on and grabbed my radio and my flashlight and followed her, and in less than a minute we were on Medical's golf cart and speeding—or at least trying to speed since the blasted thing went only thirty-five miles an hour—up the road toward the Artemis parking area.

It was odd to have a "situation" out in the boondocks of the festival since we could hear the night's performance still going on, and theoretically, everyone ought to be there. But never underestimate the power of festies to be somewhere you don't expect them to be and doing something they're not supposed to be doing and that you would never expect them to.

Alison drove, and she looked like I felt. She was leaning over the steering wheel and pressing the gas pedal to the floor, trying to get the cart to somehow move faster. She'd thrown a bag of medical supplies onto the seat behind us.

"We just can't seem to ever not have an interruption when we're in the middle of some deep conversation," I said.

"I know. We've got the worst timing." She turned to me and grinned briefly.

"I want you to finish telling me whatever you were going to, tonight, I hope."

"I really have to before I lose my nerve. But first things first."

"Righto." I clicked on the mike and said, "Marty? Our ETA is about ten minutes."

"I hear that. See you soon." I knew Marty could keep it together. I wouldn't have picked her for the night shift if she wasn't competent.

After much radio talk and waving flashlights around, we finally found Marty and Tina. Tina was standing next to two women, who were sitting on the ground looking abashed. Marty pressed a bandage to the leg of one of them. A mangled lawn chair sprawled nearby, and both festies were shirtless, which was somewhat odd for nighttime. I couldn't help smiling at the incongruous scene.

"Hi, women. Is everyone okay?"

The two festies looked up at me with the strangest expressions, but they didn't say a word.

"Okay," I said, drawing out the two syllables. "Let's let Alison here have a look at your wounds. T, Marty? Over here."

I motioned with my head for them to follow me. We walked far enough to be out of earshot, and I turned and looked at my two volunteers.

Marty laughed and shook her head. Tina did exactly the same thing, as though they'd practiced it as an act.

"What?" I was somewhat amused but also irritated because they'd dragged Alison and me away from what promised to be a vital conversation.

Marty said, "We were just making a circuit of the festival and went by the camping area there. As we drove by, we heard this scream and like a thumping and cracking sound."

Tina picked up the story. "So we stopped and walked toward where we heard the sound and yelled, 'Is everything okay? Anyone hurt?' We heard them say, 'Over here,' and we finally found them. You know how frigging dark it is."

I just nodded for her to continue. "When we found them, they were laying on the ground next to that lawn chair. The one girl was holding her leg and moaning. The other was rubbing her head, so we did first aid. The one with the hurt leg was bleeding a bit, but no too bad. I don't think the other girl has a concussion, but that's Alison's call. We asked them what happened."

Marty looked at Tina, and they both really started to laugh.

I laughed with them. I couldn't help it, but I managed to get myself under control. "Come on, girls. Tell me."

Marty said, "They were trying, they wanted to—oh, my God." She burst out laughing all over again.

Tina wiped her eyes and said, "They said they wanted to 'see if we could do it in a lawn chair.'"

And she dissolved in laughter but finally choked out, "The lawn chair broke."

I laughed again.

They needed Alison's medical skills, but mostly they'd brought us out here to give us a laugh. Marty and Tina didn't need backup for this situation. They were trying to cheer me up. It was sweet, but they had no idea what they'd interrupted, and I couldn't be mad at them.

Sex in a lawn chair? What would these festies think of next?

"So the chair broke under them and they got hurt. Somewhat."

"I think mostly they just feel stupid," Marty said.

"You think? All right. Let's go back and see what Allie has to say."

Alison was bandaging the one woman's cut leg. The other one was watching.

She told her companion, "Honey. I think we're gonna need to buy a new chair."

And she laughed too. It seemed all was well.

"I hope you two have learned your lesson," I said as sternly as I could, but it was hard because I wanted to break into loud guffaws as I pictured the two festies trying to have sex in their flimsy chair. And the inevitable result.

The girl with the cut leg said, "It was goin' okay until I tried to put my finger up you. I think I sprained it when we fell. I told you to take off your pants, but you were 'no, no, you can do it.'"

With some heat, her girlfriend said, "I said I didn't wanna put my bare butt on that nasty plastic chair 'cause my ass would end up havin' a waffle pattern on it."

"Oh, Holly, you're such a girly girl. That wouldn't last more 'n a minute. Geez Louise."

All of this was said in buttery Southern accents, which made it even funnier to listen to, but I'd had enough and didn't want them to start arguing.

"Okay, okay, Spare us the play-by-play. We're glad you're all right. Alison? They all good?"

Alison had been giggling quietly the whole time, and she nodded.

CHAPTER TWELVE

We rode back to Bates in silence, and of course, Angie and Leah were there. We went inside and had to tell them what had happened, and everyone had a good laugh. But I wanted Alison and me to pick up where we left off. I tapped Alison's shoulder and motioned with my head for her to come outside with me. I felt Leah and Angie stare at us as we walked out.

I could tell Alison was tired. We'd gotten the call at such a crucial moment, I was afraid she wouldn't want to go on. I was really tired as well, but I wanted us to finish our conversation.

I didn't say anything. I just looked at her and waited.

"This is so hard, Lane. But I want to tell you. Where can we go to talk?"

"How about my room?"

She raised her eyebrows. "And we can keep three feet on the floor?"

I laughed. "Sure."

Alison curled up at the end of the cot and rested her back against the wall, using my pillow. She looped her arms around her knees, just as she'd done when we were kids. I put the flashlight between us, and the moon shone through the window. Her face was in shadow, but I could make out her features and read her emotions well enough.

"I knew you were in love with me, because of how you acted around me. You were watchful. All the time. You always made sure wherever we were, whatever we were doing that we were close."

"What did you think when I got in bed with you in the middle of the night?"

"Nothing. I mean, it didn't seem weird to me. I felt safe with you." She giggled.

"You *were* safe with me. Then."

That prompted a smile.

"I loved you too. Please don't ever doubt that. You were the one thing in my life I never had to worry about."

I wondered about the meaning of that last sentence but didn't ask. She loved me. That was important for me to hear. It relieved me to hear it. I didn't have to feel like I was crazy or living in a fantasy land. I wanted much, much more from Alison than that simple declaration, but it was a start.

I stayed quiet to give her the space to go on with her story. At last she was willing to talk, and I didn't need to mess it up with my endless questions. I heard Val's voice in my head telling me to shut up and be patient.

"My mom...was difficult." Alison almost choked trying to say those words. "It wasn't until a year or so ago, after talking to Angie about my mother a lot, that I went to see a counselor. It helped finally to tell someone what it was like. I always tried to hide it because, well, you're not supposed to hate your mother. I didn't exactly hate her. I loved her, but it was, you know, complicated."

I had just one question I had to ask. "Did the counselor know you're a lesbian?"

"Nope. We didn't get into that," Alison said, rather dismissively, I thought.

"Okay. Sorry. Go on." That wasn't the right answer, in my opinion and could portend trouble, but I let it go. It wasn't up to me.

"Anyway, from the time I was little, my mom made sure I was the most perfect little girl in the world. If I failed to meet her standard of perfection, she let me know. Madeline had rules for everything: how I dressed, who my friends were, what hobbies I could have. Thank the Lord she approved of music. I don't know how I would have survived otherwise."

She laughed the kind of laugh that really ought to be a sob.

"When I was in high school, she was real picky about who I dated. It turned out almost no boy would meet her requirements, which in a way helped me because I wasn't much interested in boys."

I laughed.

"She was also fine with the Girl Scouts, since that was all about honor and honesty and being clean in thought, word, and deed. All that stuff."

Still laughing, I said, "Sure. What parent wouldn't love that?"

"But something happened. I think it was April or May in '72. Right before we were going to start camp." Alison's voice changed. It took on a sort of monotone quality.

I waited, keeping my eyes fixed on her face. She paused, looking into the middle distance. We had the lights off, and in the glow of the flashlight, she looked sad. She paused for a long time.

"She found the letters you wrote me. I had saved all of them from the first year we met."

I was dismayed, horrified, really. I remembered those letters. I didn't hold back any of my feelings. Everything I thought and felt about Alison was in those letters. They were love letters.

"Oh, no."

Alison took a big breath, and I could tell she was reliving the emotions she'd had at the time. "Oh, yes, and Madeline was *not* pleased. In fact, she was so distraught when she confronted me while waving the letters in my face, she threw up. Right there at my feet. Then she screamed about how disgusting I was, how disgusting you were, that it made her sick."

"Oh, God. Alison." This was beyond horrible, and I felt like it was all my fault.

"She screamed at me some more and demanded that I not go to Triple Creek. I managed to talk her out of it by saying I'd signed an employment contract and had promised to work and couldn't renege on that. She caved, finally, but she told me I wasn't to have any contact with you. I promised her I wouldn't, which was impossible, but I managed to convince her I realized the error of my ways and I'd behave properly, etc."

The light bulb switched on in my head. "*That's* why you were so flaky that summer."

"Yup."

"Gosh, Allie. I don't know how you managed to function at all."

"It's a weird kind of place to be. On the one hand, I was the Alison who loved you, but I was also Madeline's daughter. I had to find a way to be both. And I thought I did. Until the point you wanted us to have sex. Then it all sort of broke down. The problem was, of course, I loved you and I wanted to be with you."

"Why didn't you tell me? I would have understood. Maybe I could have helped you."

Alison shook her head, regretfully. "I don't think so. No. Telling you would have made it worse. I went through the whole summer thinking somehow, my mom could see what I was doing and know what I was thinking. Crazy, huh? But that's how I felt. The counselor told me that was normal, that I wasn't crazy. We internalize our mothers so thoroughly, we think they're always with us. That's great if you have a loving and supportive mother, but not if your mother is like Madeline—an evil, demanding, controlling bitch."

Wow. Alison was bitter, but I didn't blame her. I felt so awful, though, because of my part in being too honest in my letters so that Alison's mom found out about us. And even if I didn't know what exactly was going on with Alison, I didn't have to get so mad at her when I didn't get what I wanted. I kept quiet though and let Allie continue her story.

"When I left you in that motel room, I wasn't so much leaving you as trying to run away from myself. I was caught between two impossible alternatives. I was either going to surrender to you and my mother would somehow find out and she'd kill me, or I was going to hurt you terribly. Guess which one I chose?"

"Now I understand. I was devastated at the time and figured you didn't love me."

"I did love you, though my mother made me hate myself for loving you. If that makes sense."

"It all makes sense, Allie. A horrible kind of sense but still..."

"You know my terrible secret. Do you still want to be friends?"

I took her hand. "More than ever." More than friends too, but I left that part out. "What happened after that?"

Alison withdrew her hand and returned to her original position. "Oh, you know, not much. I went to college, then nursing school. My mom found Tom and decided he was the one I was going to marry. She knew his folks, so she thought he was the perfect match."

"Where was your dad in all this?"

"Oh, he was around, but you bet he never tried to tell Mom what to do. She'd make him miserable if he tried anything like suggest she not tell *me* what to do every second. She'd say, 'Oh, Robert. Don't be ridiculous. You don't know what you're talking about.' I guess she's a real Southern belle, because she could put so much contempt into that sentence."

"You were absolutely stuck with no way to make a choice between me and please your mom. I am sorrier than ever about how I treated you."

"I sure as heck was, and when she ordered me to marry Tom, I did. But you don't need to be sorry, El. You getting mad at me was a normal reaction after that whole summer of me acting so crazy."

"Okay, but why did you marry Tom, really?"

"Ah, you know, thanks to Madeline, my self-esteem was nonexistent, and I hoped getting married would cure me of loving you. But he had a personality very much like Madeline's. No wonder she liked him. He was super charming, at first."

I was so sad for Alison I wanted to cry. She'd truly had a screwed-up life. Who was I to try to fix that? I was just arrogant enough to think I could, but I knew I couldn't.

If Alison was going to be able to love me, she would have to be released from her past. Her very next words confirmed that realization.

"You see? Now do you understand why I can't be what you want me to be?" In the semi-darkness, I could still see the tears on her cheeks and hear them in her voice.

"Yes. I think so."

"Do you really? What I did to you is unforgivable. Worse was what I allowed my mother to do to me. First, she got me away from you by guilt-tripping me. Then she got me into that hideous marriage. I allowed all of it to happen and didn't make a peep. I didn't do one thing, one single tiny thing to prevent any of it. I could have rebelled against my mother, but I didn't. I chose to go along. I'm a spineless person."

Then she started crying in earnest. I moved to sit next to her and put my arm around her. I felt guilty for only thinking of myself, only thinking about how much I wanted to sleep with her. I was kind of a heel.

"Alison, baby. Shh. I still forgive you. Unconditionally. You know I do."

"You do?" She actually sounded genuinely surprised.

"Of course I do. None of it's your fault." I kissed her forehead.

"All of it's my fault." She cried harder.

I hugged her until she calmed a bit. Then I went and found some Kleenex and gave it to her. "You're even beautiful when you're blowing your nose."

I could see her roll her eyes even in the dark. "You'd think I was beautiful no matter what state I was in."

"You're right," I said cheerfully. "I'm glad you told me the story. It makes things much clearer. I thought you didn't like me."

"You idiot. Of course I like you. It's because I like you that I didn't want you involved in all this mess."

"That's where you're wrong. I can't change any of it. I can't even talk you out of feeling bad about yourself. But I can say from the bottom of my heart that none of it matters to me. I still love you. I've always loved you. I will continue to love you even if you can't love me back. But I want you to love me back, Alison. There's just one problem."

She was wide-eyed and stopped crying. "What's the one problem?"

"You have to forgive yourself."

She was momentarily speechless. "The counselor said the same thing. How did you know what she said?"

I was pretty proud of myself, I must say, for figuring that out.

"I didn't, but it just makes sense to me. Look. I'm not trying to tell you what to feel and what not to feel, but you're as stuck in your misery and self-recrimination as you ever were under the thumb of your mom. Right?"

"I suppose so. The counselor said stuff like that, but I didn't really believe her."

"You just needed a second opinion," I said rather grandly. I was thrilled that she'd stopped crying and just seemed confused but curious. "And now that you've told me the truth, I totally understand why what happened, happened. I'm serious. I forgave you before I knew the whole story because I didn't want that between us.

"I never thought you would forgive me, even when you said you did, because you said it without knowing the whole story. I told you everything, and now all you've got to say is I need to forgive myself?"

I just grinned at her. I seemed to have broken through the wall.

"Huh. I need to think about this, and I better go to sleep. I'm beat."

To say I was disappointed would be putting it mildly, but I kept my feelings to myself. We weren't going all the way tonight. Well, we still had two more days.

"Okay. I hope you can sleep after all this."

"Me too. I feel better though. I've been carrying this around for almost a week, ever since I got here and saw you. Honestly, when I saw your name on the list and knew it was you, in my bones I wondered what I would say or do when I saw you. I went back and forth so many times the last few months about whether I wanted to see you or what you would think of me I almost lost my mind. I was really screwed up. I was sure when we met, you wouldn't want to talk to me. I was afraid to talk to you."

"So was I," I whispered. "I didn't know it was you, but I really hoped it was but also terrified if it would turn out to be you.

And then it was you, but you didn't exactly act happy to see me, but that I kinda understood. Now that you've told me everything, I'm good."

She looked at me for a moment. "We both were feeling the same way."

"Allie, I think you've been carrying this story around for a lot longer than a week."

She stared at me for a second. "Yes. You're probably right."

"I wish I could give you a ride to your cabin."

No, I didn't. I wanted her to stay right where she was except to take her clothes off and lie down on my cot. But wisely, I didn't say so.

"I'll be fine. It's the safest place in the world to walk around by yourself at night."

"Nowhere safer."

"Good night, Alison," I whispered and kissed her lightly on the lips, steeling myself to not go further. Her lips were soft and pliant. I held her gently. Where I got all this restraint was a mystery.

I pulled away before things could get too heated, and she opened her eyes. In the dark, I could swear I saw a little spark of arousal. I was sure I felt her hesitate as I released her from my friendly hug.

"Good night. Thanks," she said, very softly, and then she was gone.

❖

It was a tribute to just how tired I was that I fell asleep almost immediately and didn't lie awake pondering Alison's latest revelations and what to do next. But that ended as soon as I woke up with a snap early Saturday morning.

I had a million questions for Alison. Some of her story didn't entirely make sense. For instance, why did she go to the Motel Six with me, surely sensing what I had in mind? Was she almost ready to go through with it?

Maybe I was closer to achieving what I wanted than I realized. It was a breakthrough for her to tell me all that she revealed.

The poor girl was sure traumatized, and how she would hate me referring to her as "poor girl."

I didn't want to push her into doing something she didn't want to do, i.e. make love with me, but on the other hand, I was fairly sure she wanted to. She just needed a tiny bit more incentive. Also, a girl like Alison would most certainly think if we did it, we ought to stay together forever.

I was almost ready for that, but I didn't know how to accomplish it in a practical matter. There was also the little problem of me and my history of relationships. I have no self-confidence issues when it comes to most things. I feel like I can do anything, and mostly that's true.

When it came to being a real honest-to-goodness full-time lover, though…evidence of my inability to be good at that was the trail of disappointed women I had left behind me. I considered myself quite virtuous because I didn't cheat on them. Well, that was something, but it wasn't everything, or they would have stuck around longer.

How could I drag Alison into something that wouldn't last for more than a year or so? That would be majorly painful for both of us. After all this time, all this drama and pain, we get together only to split up? Ouch. That would hurt worse than anything else we'd endured up to this point.

I was cruising on adrenaline so I decided to get up and take the shower I'd missed on Thursday morning. What was I going to say when I saw Alison? Nothing. She could tell me where we were going next. In the meantime, I needed to follow a routine of some sort so I could stay sane.

I went to take a shower and found the place overrun with festies, even though a sign on the door said, WORKERS ONLY 8-8:30. It was 8:05. This royally ticked me off. The festies were supposed to hold off taking showers for just a little while to give us a chance to get on with our workday. It had been announced from the stage the night before as well. And I didn't have a bullhorn with me, so I improvised.

I pounded on the doorframe really loudly three times and got most everyone to look at me.

"Listen up. I want all of you who are not actually in a shower and don't have one of these wristbands on"—I pointed to my blue wristband—"to leave right now. Those of you in the showers, finish up quick." I got results. Grumbling a little, the interlopers got themselves together and left. A couple of workers grinned and said "thanks," clearly happy to have the showers depopulated. They could have done what I did themselves, but no one likes to be the bad guy. I don't either, but I'm willing to be one, if necessary.

I looked around the nearly empty shower room. Lesbians have a reputation for not being too particular about body hair. Possibly true, but not universally so. I found plenty of evidence of leg-shaving littering the shower stalls, along with other detritus such as soap fragments, scrunchies, and toothbrushes. And a whole other jumble of clothes and miscellaneous items lay on the benches that faced the showers. The floor was wet and cold, and the whole place smelled like a damp armpit.

The showers at music festivals are disgusting.

I finished as quickly as possible, then put on my favorite purple-and-green gym shorts and a purple SF gay-parade T-shirt, and I added a SF Giants baseball cap. No mirrors were available, but I knew I looked good. I was hoping the shower, clean clothes, and a decent night's sleep would energize me. I was planning to take up my campaign to win Alison's heart, mind, and body.

I had my lingering misgivings, however.

I purposefully didn't seek her out, though it was hard to keep away from the Bates infirmary. Instead, I jumped in the golf cart and started driving around, hoping for distraction. It was the middle of the festival, so tonight would bring the best performers onstage, and apparently, we were going to end the evening's festivities with a full-moon ritual. I assumed that would involve some drumming, a lot of chanting, and likely the blossoming of lots of sexual energy. I should have been psyched because that would aid my seduction of Alison. But I wasn't that jazzed, because I feared the consequences should I be successful.

This was new for me too. I wasn't one to give much thought ahead of time to the aftermath of sex. I guess that's how I ended up in all those relationships. We'd get in bed, and the next morning, I was somehow in a couple. I let myself get drawn into something intimate without conscious thought. Maybe that was part of my problem. I couldn't tell the difference between raw sexual chemistry and the kind of emotional and intellectual connection that keeps people together.

This wasn't unusual among the women I knew. We were all looking for love, and either we didn't find it, or we did and it wasn't what we thought it would be. I heard a lesbian say once that we were all deprived of adolescent dating and the room to make mistakes and try out romantic relationships with different people. Therefore, we had to go through our adolescence in our twenties or thirties or whenever we come out. It made sense because I didn't know very many people who were any good at staying together. I think maybe the only long-term couple I knew of was Phyllis Lyon and Del Martin. But I didn't *know* them. They were gay-rights icons, and I saw them a few times in San Francisco, where they happened to live.

It felt different with Alison, though. I felt like another person with her, a better person, a woman more capable of commitment. I was being more positive and making a choice rather than just allowing things to happen willy-nilly. Maybe that was the key.

As I drove along the road, I looked at all the festies. Many of them were in couples, walking about holding hands. Not only that, they were couples who looked alike and dressed alike, down to their identical fanny packs and hats. Lesbo Tweedledums and Tweedledees. I was certainly not surprised. I'd been to enough festivals and understood where all this came from. Given the opportunity, lesbians loved to be *seen* as couples.

Most of us can't be out this much in their regular lives. We have to be in the closet to a greater or lesser extent. I sympathized with their need to be recognized as couples. Among our kin at the festivals it was perfectly safe to be seen for who we are. I was glad I lived in San Francisco, though, where it wasn't such a big deal, but even there we have to live in the straight world, and it's still alienating. We may have less of chance of getting beat up, fired, or simply grossly insulted, but we're all still strangers in the strange land of straight society.

Not all couples at festival behaved like twins, of course, but that's what my mind chose to see and got me to thinking about myself and Alison. What would it be like to stay with one woman for the rest of my life? Was I nuts thinking Alison was that woman? I guess I thought all the other girls were "that" woman too. But with Alison I felt qualitatively different. It was like she was in my DNA. When I thought of Alison, I thought about eternity. Before I mostly just didn't think about anything at all, except what we might be having for dinner on a given day. That may sound cavalier, but that's the way my mind worked. I didn't think of the future. I must have just been surprised too often when my girl of the moment left.

Maybe I could achieve forever with Alison.

Or maybe she'd leave me like all the rest of them did, scratching my head about where I went wrong.

But there was still the question of what she wanted. I thought I'd witnessed Alison having some sort of emotional breakthrough last night, but I wasn't sure.

A radio call from Becky interrupted my woolgathering.

"Lane. You need to go out to the S/M camp. Come by the house and pick up Judy. She's made a complaint, and I said you'd look into it."

"Righto." I was actually glad for something concrete to do, even though it was more like mediation than any real security issue. I would have to soothe whatever feathers were ruffled and try to get a consensus among the disagreeing parties. Leather women were used to having objections to their "lifestyle," a fact I found ironic since a great number of people took issue with the lesbian lifestyle. But leather and S/M pushed a lot of buttons with some women. They seemed to equate it with violence against women, though that isn't what it's about.

One of the leather dykes I knew in SF told me that sex was the one area of her life where she could exercise full control and freedom of choice. She also liked the fantasy and role-playing. I admired the fact that S/M practitioners took elaborate care in structuring their "scenes" so that no one got hurt in the literal or emotional sense or treated by their partners in a way other than what they agreed on. There was something to be said for that, since women so often committed emotional violence against one another. I was still not interested in sex that involved actual pain; therefore, I never responded to the invitations I sometimes got. I'm strictly vanilla, though I saw the appeal.

I retrieved a decidedly agitated woman from Becky and Arden's house. Becky, ever diplomatic yet efficient, said, "Lane will take care of this for you." She gave me a look that said both "tread lightly" and "I'm tired of listening to this chick ramble on. It's your turn."

I fixed Judy with a big, empathetic grin.

"Hi. Why don't you tell me all about it while we drive back to your campsite?"

Judy was tense-eyed and clasped her hands together as she talked.

"Yeah. Last night I got up to go to the PortaJane, and I didn't walk three feet before right in front of me was a woman tied to a tree and another one whaling on her with a whip."

"Did you say anything?" I asked.

"Nah. What the heck am I gonna say? 'Hey, stop that!'?"

Well, you could have apologized for the interruption and gone on your way. But...no.

Judy had a whole lot more to say about how terrible it was that women did those things to one another and why do you allow it at festival, and so forth. I was secretly impressed that there were leather dykes in the South, though I shouldn't have been. San Francisco might be the cutting edge for gay culture, but the rest of the country joined in, if only in a small way. Atlanta evidently had a huge gay and lesbian community, and a few of them would inevitably be into S/M.

"Show me where this happened," I said to Judy.

She found the exact tree. I examined my map and saw we were right on the boundary between the S/M area and general camping. Likely the S/M dykes didn't know that.

"I'm going to go have a talk with the women over there, and we'll try to make sure something like this doesn't happen again."

"I'm coming with you," Judy said with finality.

Oh, brother, that's all I needed: an argument.

"Sure, but let me do the talking, okay? Please let me try to smooth things over?"

That's another thing about lesbians. They're opinionated and don't feel the least shy about telling you what's wrong with the way you live, think, eat, love, or dress. You'd think that our outsider status would make us sensitive about making those sorts of judgments about each other, but not always.

Judy tightened her lips and narrowed her eyes, but she nodded.

A few leather women were hanging around their campsite. The four leather dykes regarded our approach with interest. They, of course, were taking advantage of festival to sport their leather and metal and show off their piercings and scars and tattoos. They certainly had the right to do that.

"Good morning, women. I'm Lane. This is Judy."

I could see that Judy was staring at them like they were space aliens.

I received a chorus of "his" and "hellos" back.

"I'm from Festival Security, and Judy here lodged a complaint about some S/M activity.

Their faces, which had been neutral to friendly, immediately clouded. The tallest woman spoke up. "This is our designated area."

"I know. I think maybe the boundaries aren't terribly clear. I'm certainly not here to boot you out or tell you to stop doing what you want."

I had tensed up, but as they absorbed what I said, their body language and facial expressions changed. Oh, good. They understood I wasn't the enemy. And, thank the Goddess, my complainant was keeping silent.

"And what do you want?" This came from someone else.

Fair question.

"I want to look at the boundaries and make sure everyone agrees. I came to ask if you would please, if you're going to hold scenes outside, make sure you're on the other side of your camping area. Over there." I gestured to the back of their little circle of tents.

They looked where I pointed.

"Just so one of your neighbors doesn't interrupt you by mistake." I added a winning grin and heard a few snickers at that comment.

The tallest leather dyke smiled broadly and said, "Anyone's welcome to join in, if it's agreeable to all concerned."

Leather people, I noticed, were kind of like evangelists. They liked to recruit.

"Come show me where this all occurred."

We all took a short walk in the woods.

"Here," Judy said, and the tall leather dyke nodded. We checked on the map and then found a sign that had fallen off its tree. I reposted it

"We can agree that you'll keep behind this sign?"

The leader said, "Sure, okay. We can do that. No sweat. Thanks for stop—"

"Y'all are sick. That's all I gotta say," Judy said.

Shit. She just couldn't keep it together and keep quiet.

"What y'all are up to is violence against women."

Tall leather dyke had likely heard this before and didn't appear angry.

"I'm sorry you think that, but it's not what's going on."

"Judy," I said. "Are you okay with what we've decided? They'll keep their activities as far away from traffic areas as possible."

"Yes, but—"

"I think we better go." I took her arm.

"Thanks very much," I told the leather dykes and hustled Judy away.

I walked her back to her tent. "You're cool now?"

"Yeah, I guess so," she said, not very graciously. "Thanks for talking to them."

"You're welcome."

"But I might call you again."

"Sure. By all means." I really hoped not.

CHAPTER THIRTEEN

I circled back to Bates and the infirmary, hoping Alison would be there. She was, and Angie and Leah were there as well, along with a slew of festies either getting their owies bandaged or waiting for their friends or lovers to get *their* problems tended to, and it was a zoo.

I stuck my head in the door and caught Alison's eye. She looked up from taking someone's temperature and actually beamed at me. What do you know?

As usual, she looked smashing. She had on another sleeveless shirt, blue this time, flip-flops, and white Bermuda shorts. Her tanned arms and legs practically glowed with health. I knew intellectually that tans weren't proof of health, but wow, did Alison ever look good.

She finished with her patient and came over to me. Was her walk more sexy today? Was I hallucinating from heat or lust or lack of sleep? No. I'd actually slept the night before. That wasn't it. It was Alison, or more accurately, it was how I felt about Alison.

She kissed my cheek and took my hand, swinging it gently. I ignored the stew of emotions in my brain and just looked at her.

"Hello, Lane." Those two words had never sounded sexier than when they came out of Alison's mouth. I thought about our swim of a few days before and suddenly wanted to repeat it as much I had ever wanted anything. With my sexual fantasy added, naturally.

"Hi," I said, rendered nearly speechless by her presence, her voice, and the way she looked at me. "You look, um, busy," I said, my words coming out of me with difficulty.

"Last night," she said with a shy smile.

"Yes. Last night." I echoed her idiotically.

"I slept well. I wouldn't have predicted that."

"Good. Me too."

She hadn't let go of my hand. My palm was heating up, as was the rest of me. I was ready to toss my nervous speculation aside for a chance to enjoy her body, to make love to her until she swooned, to have what I had wanted many years before. Then I chided myself for being so shallow, but it wasn't really just all about sex.

"You have to work now?"

Her question startled me. "Um, yeah. Until sometime this evening after the concert, when things settle down."

"Can we be together tonight?"

"Together? What do you mean 'together'?" My mouth dried up and my stomach tensed.

Alison looked at me as though I'd said something pornographic. "Together as in the same space at the same time. What did you think I meant?" she asked sharply, but her eyes were twinkling.

"Nothing. Never mind. We can just hang out at the concert and then, well, whatever." I attempted to sound nonchalant, but inside I was anything but. She'd asked *me* to spend time with *her.* This a first and it was astonishing.

Alison lowered her eyelids, squeezed my hand, and then let it drop. "I've got to go," she said.

"Okay, see you later." I tried to sound casual, but I felt a stomach-flipping surge of anticipation.

❖

The rest of the day was pretty calm as festival days go. When I bumped into Marty at dinner, she asked me if I'd be available in the evening, and I wanted to say no, but it would be unusual for me to say that. Whatever was going to happen with Alison would happen. We'd be in the same place at the same time, as she said. I was in a fever of speculation but had to be realistic. I had no idea what she really wanted. It looked like we might have to talk more, and though I understood the need for talking, it wasn't all I wanted to do, but I'd have to see how things were going to play out. This was such an unusual place for me to be. I rarely gave any thought ahead of time to sex. It happened or it didn't. I dealt with the consequences when I had to, the consequences often ending up with me being tied to someone I shouldn't be.

This was a whole different mindset for me, and the stakes were much higher because I stood to win the love of my life or lose her forever. I had turned this possibility over in my mind all day long, and the more I thought, the more scared I became. I suppose I was experiencing a flash of insight or an epiphany or whatever you want to call it. All I knew was I was different and Alison was different as well. The wariness in her manner was gone. She hadn't touched me in an especially seductive way, but my nerve endings and my psyche interpreted her touch as sexual. Meanwhile, I cautioned myself to be careful.

By dinnertime, I was a huge bundle of nerves. Alison actually sought me out and, in her shy but sweet manner, asked me to sit with her. It was like we were already lovers and meeting for a meal and a little time together in the midst of our festival duties. She seemed to be promising something momentous would happen later. Or at least my overactive imagination presumed so. I thought she was smiling at me more than usual.

I conferred with Marty and we made a plan. We had a few more volunteers to help ease the problem of having to be too many places at once.

Alison had gone back to the infirmary, we were to meet in an hour, and I needed another pep talk from Val. Again it was a matter of sprinting around the kitchen with her and talking at the same time.

I told her what had occurred between Alison and me.

"What do I do?" I asked. I was indecisive and flummoxed, another odd set of emotions for me.

"What do you mean what do you do? How should I know?" I could tell Val was tired. No wonder. I estimated she worked a minimum of sixteen hours a day. She was a monster of energy, but even she had her limits.

"Don't you have anything to suggest? I'm a wreck here, Val."

"You can't control everything, you know. You can't plan *everything, chica.*"

"I know, I know, but I could lose her. It could be the end."

"It doesn't sound like the 'end' to me. It sounds like the beginning. It sounds like you've chased her, and now she's caught you."

Val chortled at her own wit, but it didn't amuse me.

"What the heck does that mean?"

"I don't think you've ever had all your emotions engaged, your mind and your heart both longing for one woman, along with your body, of course." She grinned lasciviously at me, and for once, her expression didn't make me think about fooling around with her.

"Yeah."

That was it. I was in such a frantic state about Alison because, not only did I want her, but I loved her, and I felt like I was going to lose everything if we didn't get together. The rest of my life *sans* Alison looked very bleak. But Val was right. I had no idea how to handle this situation. This wasn't a security issue where I could use my authority and no-nonsense persona to achieve an end. I had to let go of all my preconceptions and all ideas of trying to induce Alison to do what I wanted her to do and be who I wanted her to be. Worse, I had to be me and hope that was good enough. I had to trust myself.

"You're going to have to take a leap of faith," Val said. "You don't know what's going to happen. You don't need to repeat your past with women over and over. You're scared that a future with Alison actually might happen and you'll screw it up. This fantasy you told me about is going to become reality, maybe, and you don't know how to handle that possibility. I don't know what I would do in your shoes, if that makes you feel any better."

"I don't. You're right," I said, anxious and hopeful in equal measure.

"For starters, try to be a little lighthearted and a little happier. She's not going to want you if you're a sourpuss. That's not attractive. Just like you stopped all your processing bullshit. That worked, didn't it? I told you to just be nice, and when you were nice, she came around."

"I think it's a bit more complicated than that, but yes. She did."

I didn't feel the need to violate Alison's confidential revelations about her mother by telling Val.

"So it's a big night, right? We've got Cris Williamson and Teresa Trull performing together, and we've got a full moon, and there's going to be a major ritual around that. You know what the full moon does to women, don't you?" Again, Val grinned widely.

"Makes them nuts and makes them do stupid stuff," I said irritably, thinking of more unsafe hijinks amongst the festies. Or more arguments like the one I had moderated in the morning with the S/M girls.

"No, silly. Wondrous things can come to pass during the full moon."

I wasn't sure I believed all that stuff about the full moon, but I surely knew that when you got a bunch of horny and high-on-life lesbians together out in the woods, anything could happen. Throw in music and mind-altering substances, and you had the recipe for chaos, my least favorite state. But Val was trying to tell me it was all going to be fine. Even more than that, it might mean my dreams could come true.

I was there first, and I looked for Alison. When she came into view at the far end of the seating area, I watched her the entire time it took for her to walk toward me. She was smiling at me. That in itself was enough to send me over the edge. I couldn't actually tell if it was a generic friendly smile or something else, but I chose to believe it was more than friendly. Every nerve in my body was on full red alert. I was never this keyed up when I responded to some sort of safety situation at an event. Nor was it like a little sexy dancing with a cute girl that presaged sex. The way I felt about Alison and *with* Alison was at a whole other level. Seriousness, intention, emotional awareness. These were new feelings for me to experience in connection with a possible sexual interlude. That was it. It wasn't going to be in interlude. I wasn't going to slide into bed with a new acquaintance. I wanted and hoped and seemed to be on track to winning the one woman I never even thought I would see again, let alone sleep with, never mind spend the rest of my life with.

We met once more at stage left near the performer's tent. Alison hugged me, rather somberly, I thought. I managed to return the hug without losing my mind. Val's term "leap of faith" kept popping up in my consciousness. Alison had changed to jeans, as had I. No more hat or sunglasses for me either.

"Well, are you looking forward to this evening?" I asked her, sounding very silly to myself, but that was all I could I come up with.

Alison looked at me thoughtfully. "Very much. I can't quite describe it, but I have a sense that this is going to be a special occasion for us."

"For us?"

"All of us." She gestured to encompass the entire crowd of women who were filtering into the seating area with their friends and lovers and chairs and coolers and blankets and all their other gear. I automatically noted that security volunteers stood at each corner. Marty had managed to recruit a few extras as well, after she conferred with the priestesses about their needs for the ritual. I had minimal participation in the evening's plans. That's why I had Marty and her trusty squeeze Tina.

I was willing to admit I was wrong about Tina being a lightweight. She'd turned out to be pretty solid. I'd made a lot of unfair assumptions about her and given her a demeaning nickname. This fact gave me an entirely irrelevant spark of hope about myself and Alison. If I was wrong about Tina, then I could be wrong about myself.

"What are you thinking about," Alison asked, startling me out of my ruminations.

"Nothing," I lied. "Just looking at the security setup."

"Stop worrying. Marty's got it under control. You need to relax, honey."

"You called me honey," I said in wonderment.

"Don't get excited. Southerners call *everyone* honey."

But Alison's eyelids dropped as her voice grew throaty. The combination gave me a small sexual frisson, not much more than the motion of grass in a spring breeze. Miniscule but unmistakable.

"How are you feeling after last night?" I asked carefully, aiming my gaze on her face so she'd know I was fully present and not thinking of anyone or anything else.

"Lighter, I guess. Relieved. After carrying all that stuff around for my whole life, finally saying it, especially to you, made it *seem* like some old tempest-in-a-teapot thing." Her "thing" sounded like "thang." "But I'd had this whole scene in my mind of how you might react, and you were nothing like I thought you'd be. I guess I'm just a Southern belle at heart since I thought it would be all dramatic and you'd push me away and say you never wanted to see me again. I think I've just always grown up expecting the worst-case scenario 'cause that's what usually happened. Old Madeline and her histrionics, then Tom's yelling and worse. But you just looked at me with those puppy-dog eyes and said I needed to forgive myself. That was such a simple and clear solution, but I never believed in it even when the woman I paid to fix me said it. I needed to hear it from you."

"I'm glad you told me because it makes a lot of stuff clear to me that was a fucking mystery at the time." I said this as neutrally as I could since my heart was about to explode. Even the "puppy-dog eyes" dig didn't faze me. It seemed Alison had truly broken through the fog of her self-hatred.

"Don't use bad language."

Alison's reproof was mild and delivered with a certain amount of tenderness. I didn't mind, but I did need to watch out for the swearing. It was one of my many nervous habits.

"Okay," I said.

"Like I said, you pretend to be tough, and I don't think you are."

This was almost a non sequitur, but I sort of understood. Use of bad words was equal to ersatz toughness in Alison's mind.

I swallowed. "Maybe not. I think there's a way I have to be in the world to get by. I don't want to be that way with you. You're the same, aren't you? One way to the rest of the world but another with someone you…trust?"

Alison looked sad and thoughtful. "Yes, I am, now that you mention it. I've been self-protective my whole life. With my mother, my teachers, my husband, pretty much everyone. Not you, though. It practically killed me to have to hide things from you."

That made me sad for her all over again, and I put my arm around her shoulder. "You don't have to do that anymore."

She looked at me for a few moments. I couldn't read her emotion, but she hadn't moved away from my embrace. We stood there just looking at one another. I was deeply conscious of the way her body felt under my arm. I could smell her light, soapy scent, and I shivered.

"Good evening, women." Arden's voice boomed out suddenly. I'd been so absorbed in Alison, I hadn't noticed her walk onto the stage, nor had I felt the attention of the audience shift from their private conversations. I was that fixated on Alison and me. We could have been by ourselves on an island in the middle of the Pacific Ocean rather than in a crowd of lesbians in the Georgia woods.

I dropped my arm and joined the applause. Our moment had passed, and who knew what the evening would bring. I knew what I wanted, but I schooled myself to be patient and wait and see. Val's jolly predictions about the full moon came back to me. I glanced at Alison, who was listening intently to Arden. She must have sensed I was looking at her because she half turned to me with a knowing expression before turning back to the stage.

❖

I watched Alison enjoy the music. I liked the two headliners better than I liked most other women's music acts. Cris and Teresa were good separately, but together they had a certain chemistry that was hard to beat.

"Is this your first time seeing women's music performers?"

"Nah," she said. "I told you, silly."

"Oh, right. You did."

I forgot *that*? What a dimwit I am.

"What about now? These two?" I gestured at the stage. Around us the crowd of women was clapping and shouting.

"They're great. It's something, isn't it? To have singers that are actually talking about loving women. You don't have to substitute pronouns."

"Yep. Mainstream culture can be such a drag because it has little to do with us and what we feel and how we live, how we love. We exist on a kind of plane apart. When we come together at a music festival, it's like reuniting with our tribe, and *we* get to be mainstream for a few days. And dream of the day when this might be 'real life,' instead of that other life we have to inhabit all the time."

"I think that's what I've been trying to put into words. At first I was just nervous and felt out of place. That's also why I kind of acted weird with you. That and our history, of course."

I thought it might have had more to do with internalized homophobia, but I kept that theory to myself.

"Ah, yes. Our history."

"I never gave 'lesbian culture' much thought. I kind of understood it at Diane Davis's show, but that was just a couple of hours long. This is four days straight, or rather not straight."

She giggled at her own pun, which was endearing. Alison was just Alison to me, a being in herself apart from anything or anyone else who'd always amused me and cheered me, and she still did. But remarks like that reminded me she was also a newly out lesbian. In our little music festival cocoon of dykedom, the outside

KATHLEEN KNOWLES

world seemed far away and just not worth thinking about. I knew very little of Alison's life since we'd parted, and I had acquired only a little more information since our reunion. If I was going to go for a lifetime with her, what did that mean? It was too much to contemplate. I sternly told myself to stay in the moment. That was all I had and all I needed.

The show was over and it was completely dark. My watch said it was eleven p.m. The full moon was high up over the circle of trees around the main stage area, and I gazed up at it. No clouds obstructed it, and the silvery glow was reflected everywhere: on the stage canopy, women in the audience, on the leaves of the trees. The stage lights were switched off, and other than a few flashlights here and there and the light coming from the performers' tent, it was dark. I gazed at Alison's face, grayish in the moonlight. She looked ghostly and had grown very quiet. I didn't see a need for any more small talk between Alison and me.

The audience was a bit restless. You couldn't have that many women in one place and have them be completely silent, but still, they were much quieter than I'd ever seen a group of two thousand or so women be. We all grew silent and less fidgety as we waited for what would happen next.

We watched stagehands bring out a table draped in some sort of colorful cloth. Then they carried out a large ornate candle, a mirror, a huge quartz crystal, and a bowl of water and placed all of it on the table. I could feel the energy change. The moonlight was reflected in the mirror and refracted by the crystal. The night magic oozed into me, mixing with my heightened perception of Alison, who was close enough to touch but not touching me.

Nadia walked to the microphone and said, "Our priestess has asked that we remain silent out of respect for the Goddess and only speak when she prompts us to speak. The ceremony will begin in just a few moments. Thank you."

The light in the performers' tent was turned off, and Marty's security team stood guard around the crowd. I counted eight in total. That was a good number of women willing to give up being participants to become observers.

We heard them before we saw them. Four women, all in blue robes, marched up the middle aisle chanting in some ancient language and waving small, burning torches. I smelled sage. One of my exes was a sort of Wiccan and had performed a purification ceremony on a flat before we moved in. To get rid of the leftover negativity of the previous tenants, she said. That may have helped, but *we* still generated enough negativity of our own and broke up the next year.

Alison had moved closer, and we were almost touching. I could sense her body heat. Was she frightened? I doubted that. But she was, if not tense, then intent and alert.

"What are they doing?" she whispered.

"Purifying the area with sage for the ceremony, I guess."

The four junior priestesses, or whoever they were, crossed paths at the front by the stage and walked down the outer perimeter of the viewing area, waving their sage torches. They switched to English.

We prepare the earth for she who brings the Goddess to life. The sky waits for her. The wind and the fire celebrate her. She is the Goddess on earth. She comes to us.

I swear that every woman in that audience went dead silent. All the festies were waiting quietly. I never would have dreamed that could be possible.

Then we heard drums. The crowd was on its feet and turned around. From our vantage point near the front, Alison and I could see them approach from the rear.

Two women wore purple robes, and the one in the middle had on a robe fittingly the colors of the moon: gray and silver. The two in purple looked like priestesses as they clasped their hands and bowed their heads. The high priestess, however, looked straight ahead. It was the same one who'd consecrated the festival on Wednesday evening, but tonight she truly looked like a goddess.

They marched up the center aisle to the beat of the drums from the periphery. The solemn and stately cadence was almost funereal but not quite. They walked right past Alison and me to climb the stairs on stage left. As they passed, I inhaled, and I'm certain Alison did as well. I could just hear the intake of breath through her nose. We each felt the power in ourselves and flowing between us: the power those three women brought as they swept by us.

The moon-robed priestess stood behind the table with its ritual objects, her attendants flanking her. I didn't recognize any of them. They must have arrived at festival within the last couple of days.

My mind tends to run to trivia when I don't want to engage emotionally or when I'm frightened. I wasn't precisely scared at that moment, but I was thinking something profound was going to happen, and normally I would want to back away. But this time I refused to be the detached, remote security person. I decided to participate. This was about Alison. And me. Wherever she was going, I wanted to go too.

The high priestess spoke.

Welcome, women to the Esbat ceremony for the Full Moon. I am Ishtar. I take my name from the Mesopotamian goddess. In Wicca, we worship the Goddess in all her forms from all cultural traditions. Blessed be.

The priestesses and most of the crowd echoed her.

She spread her arms wide and turned her face upward and toward the moon.

Goddess of the moon, queen of the night,
keeper of women's mysteries, mistress of the tides,
you who are ever changing and yet always constant,
I ask that you guide us with your wisdom,
Help us grow with your knowledge,
And hold us in your arms.

She lit the candle, and the glow of its flame blended with the moonlight in the mirror and the crystal. I'm not a spiritual person, but at that moment I became one. If there was such a thing as the Goddess of the Moon, I was sensing her.

The priestess lifted the candle, then the crystal and the mirror.

Take time to reflect upon yourselves and the gifts you have in your lives, whatever they may be.

Alison and I turned and looked at each other at the exact same instant and for just a moment. But the intensity was too much, and we glanced away.

The high priestess returned the objects to the table and lifted the bowl of water. She turned once again to the moon and lifted the water toward it.

The moon is the symbol of the mother and she watches over us day and night.
She brings the changing tide and the shifting of light to night.
She brings the flow that changes women's bodies.
She brings the passion for their beloved to lovers.
Her wisdom is great and all-knowing, and we honor her tonight.
Keep your watchful eye upon us, Great Mother, until the cycle returns once more.
Bring us to the next full moon in your love and light.

She took a sip of the water and then gave it to each of the other priestesses, who each drank and then returned the water bowl to her.

She raised the water to the moon once more and then poured it out on the ground. I understood the symbolic offering of the water blessed by the Moon Goddess to all of us.

The festies were still silent, which was some sort of miracle. I wondered how the down-to-earth, practical Southern lesbians took all this New Age-y rigmarole? Maybe, like me, this night they were believers.

I stole another look at Alison, and her face seemed other-worldly in the moonlight, as though she was fully immersed in the rite. I saw no doubt or resistance. I turned back to the stage and the priestesses.

Ishtar said, "I now invite you all to join with me. Stand with your arms crossed over your chest and your feet together, and be ready to receive the Goddess."

Alison and I did as we were told

Ishtar turned back once more to the moon, and we all followed her. She spoke each sentence, then gave us time to repeat it.

Goddess of the moon, you have been known by many names in many lands in many times. You are universal and constant. In the dark of night, you shine down upon me, bathing me in your light and love. I ask you, oh Divine One, to honor me by joining with me and allowing me to feel your presence in my heart.

Ishtar opened her arms and spread her feet apart, prompting us all to do the same.

I am the Mother of all life, the One who watches over all. I am the wind in the sky, the spark in the fire, the seedling in the earth, the water in the river.

I am the vessel from which All Things spring forth. Honor Me from within your heart! Remember that acts of love and pleasure are My rituals, and that there is beauty in all things. Honor Me on this night of the full moon. I have been with you since the moment you were created and shall remain with you always. Let there be beauty and strength, wisdom and honor, humility and courage within you. If you need Me, call upon Me, and I shall come to you, for I am everywhere, always. Honor Me as you seek knowledge! I am the Maiden, the Mother, and the Crone, and I live within you.

*I look down upon the sands of the desert, I crash the tides
upon the shore, I shine on the mighty trees of the forests
and watch with joy as Life continues every cycle. Be true
to Me, honoring that which I have created, and I shall be
true to you in return. With harm to none, so it shall be.*

A wave passed through me, and the hair on my arms prickled.
I closed my eyes, startled. I might have walked through some
sort of veil. I opened my eyes to see I was where I thought I
was, Alison at my side. The audience was still quiet, staring at
Ishtar.

"We have concluded the rite. You may sit and meditate or
speak amongst yourselves. We will have some music to dance to if
that is your pleasure. The night is yours to do with as you desire."

She folded her hands again, and as she and her helpers walked
off the stage, we heard the drums begin again, and this time some
pipes or some other wind instruments joined them.

I finally turned toward Alison, and we reached out at the same
time and began to dance in a slow circle. I had seen videos of
Deadheads dancing at concerts, and around us some other women
danced liked that. We imitated them, weaving in and out and around,
sometimes together and sometimes apart. I'd danced in plenty
of clubs and bars, but this was something different. Meditative,
mesmerizing, hypnotic, and well, yes, very sexy. Sexier than any
of that other sort of dancing I'd ever experienced. I thought of
the line from the priestess saying the moon goddess brings lovers
together and looked at Alison.

Somewhere along the way, she'd taken her hair out of its
barrette, and it waved freely as she moved. I shouldn't have been
surprised she was a very good dancer, very graceful. I had forgotten
about the moon goddess, and only Alison held my attention.

I took her hand and wound her into my arms, and she didn't
resist. I wanted to kiss her, but I stayed with the spirit of dancing
and only brought our heads together so that her hair was in my
face and I was surrounded by her. Our cheeks touched and she
whispered in my ear, "Yes. Now."

I drew my head back in astonishment. "Now? You mean…? You and me?" I thought it would take some more seduction on my part and more time.

She smiled at my confusion. "You're too funny. And so slow sometimes."

"What are you talking about?" I asked, tilting my head. I thought I grasped what she meant, but I wanted to be certain. My heart was about to jump into my throat, and my knees were weak.

"Lane, honey, get with it. Don't you want to honor the moon goddess with me?" She draped her arms around my neck and brought our faces close.

"Honor the moon goddess?" I repeated stupidly. "Didn't we just—"

"Yes," she said. "Let's keep honoring her." Then she kissed me slowly, took my hand, and led me to the Medical golf cart, and we left the crowd of women, who would no doubt be dancing into the night.

CHAPTER FOURTEEN

D idn't someone once say, "Be careful what you ask for. You may get it."

We hadn't said a word since we left the stage. I was so overwhelmed by the rush of feelings, I truly didn't know what to say and decided it was better to quell my tendency to babble and just do what ought to be easy: follow my instincts. It's not like I hadn't had sex before with many other women.

But this time it was Alison.

I was about to get what I'd wanted for such a long time. My desire for her had never truly gone away. It was dormant but had awakened with a snap just a week ago. My anxiety receded to a dull background buzz and then finally disappeared. I couldn't wait until we returned to Bates. In the passenger seat of the golf cart, I gripped the metal bar of the seat and mentally urged the golf cart to go faster.

We crashed through the back door of Bates and into my room. She whirled around and threw herself into my arms, and we kissed, hungry and frantic for contact. I guess Alison was as crazy with lust as I was. I wouldn't have predicted that, but I wasn't complaining. She pushed me onto the army cot, which gave a rusty-nails-on-blackboard squeal. I didn't struggle for dominance as I usually did but instead let Alison top me, which she did with gusto, pinning my arms and keeping me still with full body contact. I was unable to think coherently and didn't care. The phrase "let the Goddess direct us both" floated dimly through my mind. I only knew that at last Alison was in my arms, our naked bodies were glued together, and I was ready.

Alison was kissing and nipping the skin of my neck just under my jaw, when from somewhere on the floor, a radio piped up. "Lane, do you copy?"

It was Marty. Why had I not turned the fucking thing off?

Alison collapsed on me with an exhalation of pure frustration. "Oh, my Lord. Whatever could she want?"

From underneath the delicious weight of Alison's hundred and thirty so pounds, I groaned. "Don't know but I better find out."

She clumsily rolled off me and sat at the end of the army cot, while I pawed through the pile of clothes on the floor until I found my jeans with radio attached to my belt.

"Hey. I'm here. What's up?" I was pleased to note my voice was steady.

"Sorry, but I need your help. Medical too. I can't seem to raise Angie or Leah. Do you know where Alison is?"

I looked at Alison in the moonlight, who was grimacing and rolling her eyes.

"Yep. Where are you? We'll be there ASAP." Marty gave me directions, and I turned off the mike.

Glumly, Alison said, "I gave Leah and Angie the night off. They're probably still dancing. Or they came back to do what we were about to."

I started putting my clothes back on, and after a moment, Alison did as well.

"We've waited for fifteen years, so I guess another few hours won't make a difference," I said, mostly just to keep myself positive.

I felt like a balloon that had been pricked with a pin. Deflated. I was afraid Alison would be the same. Worse, she could change her mind altogether. Her next sentence confirmed that fear.

"Huh. That's nice, but I was ready, and I don't want to lose my nerve."

I put my arms around her and kissed her cheek and forehead. "You won't. Half of the thrill of sex is the anticipation of it."

"I wouldn't know. With my ex-husband, all I ever felt was dread."

Whoa, her mood had radically changed, and I became a little uneasy, but we needed to reorient ourselves. We had a situation, and I didn't think it was attempted sex in a lawn chair because Marty's tone was dead serious.

There had to be something about the damn Artemis parking lot, because that's where we headed. When we pulled up, a small crowd had gathered, but I was glad to see that Marty had snagged a couple of onlookers to form a barrier between the crowd and the situation. Tina was off to the side leaning against a car with none other than our friend Bridget, who was weeping, as usual. Where was Marty? What now?

Alison strode into the middle of the crowd and knelt by the figure on the ground, and I followed her. It was a woman I didn't know, but she wore black leather chaps, a wife beater and a bandana, and nearby was a motorcycle. She could have been one of the leather dykes from that afternoon, but I wasn't sure.

To the woman nearest me, who, like all present, stared at the injured person on the ground, I said, "Can you tell me what happened here?"

She didn't move her gaze, but she said, "I think it was a lovers' quarrel or something. She—" and she pointed at Bridget "—might know more."

Oh, boy, more Ace and Bridget drama. Wonderful. Alison was examining the fallen woman and asking her how she felt. One of the rapt onlookers said, "Should we pick her up for you and get her in the golf cart?"

Alison turned and said, crisply, "No one's doing anything exciting until *I* say so."

That was my girl. Or who I hoped would be my girl.

I sauntered over to Tina and Bridget and addressed Tina. "Hi, T. Where's Marty?"

She pointed to a truck a few feet away, where Marty was leaning into the cab. I decided to address the Bridget half of the couple first.

"Hello, Bridget."

Bridget raised her red eyes to my face.

"What happened this time?" I didn't want to be mean, but really? Twice in two days was starting to be a pattern.

Tina patted her arm gently, but she didn't answer.

"Where's Ace?" I asked the two of them, but mostly Bridget.

Tina spoke up. "Over there in her truck, and Marty told her she better not move or she'd be in big trouble. Marty gave her such a look, she almost lost her shit. She actually listened to Marty and sat there, but Marty decided she ought to stay with her so she wouldn't do anything *else* stupid."

Tina amused and pleased me with her hard-core safety attitude. With Marty in charge of Ace, I could wait to deal with her.

"Was she drunk?"

"Think so," Tina said.

I drilled a stare at Bridget. "Tell me what happened."

"I wa-was just talking to Stoney about her bike and stuff, and next thing I knew, there was Ace in her truck, and I jumped out of the way, but she hit Stoney and the bike and knocked 'em both down. Some women came over and pulled the bike up, but Tina told 'em don't move her, and Marty took Ace off, and they said for Tina to call you. Again. I'm sorry." She looked so ashamed, I felt sorry for her. As sorry as I could feel for a woman who would willingly stay with someone so screwed up that she tried to run her down with a truck.

"Well done," I said to Tina, who grinned very gratefully. I might have given her the impression I thought she was a total lightweight, and that wasn't fair.

"Well. I don't exactly know what to say to you, but you realize that you and your lover's behavior are causing a lot of trouble."

"I know. I feel awful. Ace just gets so mad at the least little thing I do if it's not her idea. I wasn't doing anything except talkin' to Stoney." She sounded a mite defensive.

"Ace won't listen to reason. She just goes off."

Tina and I looked at each other but didn't say a word. We didn't have to. There was nothing we could do, really.

"Stay with her," I told Tina. I walked back to the little knot of women surrounding the injured Stoney, sidled in, and knelt next to Alison. "What's the verdict?" I asked her.

"I don't think she's badly hurt. Just a few bumps."

From the ground, Stoney said, "Lemme get up. I'm fine."

"Not so fast. Just let Alison here tell you when it's okay."

She lay back down with an irritated air. "Is my bike okay?"

Typical. The motorcycle was more important to her than her own well-being.

I went over to look at it, and it didn't appear to be damaged except for some scratches. Oops, the footrest was bent. That had likely absorbed the brunt of Ace's truck bumper.

I reported this to Stoney. Alison had allowed her to sit up but not stand.

"Fuck. I'm going to get that bitch—"

She started to stand up, but I put a hand on her shoulder. "Whoa there, my friend. Cool your jets. You're not going to get anyone. Let me handle it." I gave Alison a look that meant "keep her in place." Alison nodded that she understood exactly what I meant.

This time I walked over to Marty. "Hey," I said to her back. She was still leaning into the cab of the truck

She turned around and moved to the side. "Hey, Lane." She shot me a rueful smile. I moved in close and looked through the open window of the driver's side of the truck.

Ace was slumped over, head down and, as usual, exuding the odor of stale beer.

"Hi there," I said in a neutral tone. "We meet again. This is getting to be a regular thing."

She didn't look at me. She stared at her steering wheel. "Yeah, well. Shit happens." Her mouth twisted in what looked like regret and defiance mixed together.

"That it does, but you seem to be a shit attractor."

She tossed her head and snorted.

"Wanna tell me what happened?"

"Me and Bridg left the concert. It was boring anyhow. I don't need that New Age crap. We came up here to party, and there were a few other women around as well. So we were just hangin'. Next thing I see is what's-her-ass in the leathers over there flirting with my girl."

"And your first thought was to run them down with your truck?"

Funny how ridiculous a sentence like that can sound to even the most stubbornly clueless. Ace actually looked embarrassed.

"Well…no. I just wanted to scare her and teach Bridg a lesson. I kind of miscalculated and couldn't stop in time.

"Again, you need help, my friend. I'm almost ready to boot your ass off the land, but I can't do that unless I clear it with Arden first."

"Please, don't. I'm sorry. I won't do anything else. If I have to go, what will happen to Bridget?"

She was actually contrite? I doubted if what she said was anything but self-serving. I wasn't exactly as jaded as a cop would be, but I'd heard enough nonsense in my time.

"The good news is, when you're surrounded by this many women, there's usually someone who can help with whatever your problem is. We can take care of getting Bridget back home. Where do you live?"

"Texas, near Houston. But—"

I turned the screw a little. "Ought to be simple to find Bridget a ride home. There must be a ton of Texas lesbians here." I smiled sweetly at Ace, who grimaced. At least she was acting chastened. I was bluffing somewhat. I didn't truly want to separate them, but I wanted to put some fear into Ace.

"Okay. Come with me, and we'll go have a talk with Arden Weinberg."

I radioed Becky and got Marty to drive us to meet them at their headquarters.

I made Ace shut up while I described the situation. When she got a chance to give her side, you wouldn't believe how sweetly sorry she sounded.

Arden looked at us for a long time without saying anything. "Well, I won't kick you off the land, but if there's any more problems, I will. I don't give a crap what happens in your life, but while you're on our land, you're not going to make any more trouble. Clear?"

"Yes."

"We're going to have Security keep an eye on you. Stay out of trouble."

"I will."

Ace seemed to be relieved and grateful, but I was suspicious. Now I had to find a way to keep track of her, but I had an idea.

As we drove her back up to their campsite, I said, "Whatever work crew you signed up for, forget it. You're on the Security night shift. You'll need to stay sober. And awake."

Marty snickered. "Oh, thanks, Lane. Well. Let's get you some coffee, and I'll tell you where you'll be and what you'll be doing."

Ace asked, "What about Bridget?" It was very touching how worried she was. I wanted to grab her by neck and give her a good shake and tell her to get a grip or she was going to lose Bridget. But like I said, I'm not a social worker. Also, I was done with this situation, and I wanted to find Alison and continue what we'd begun.

"Don't worry. We'll drive her back to your tent and tell her what's up with you. You can hang out with her during the day. 'Course you'll need to sleep sometime." I grinned at her.

"Yeah. Okay."

"You'll be fine. Seriously, though, you ought to get some help with that anger you got going on."

"Yeah, yeah. I know."

I had my doubts, but this was done, and it was time to get back to Alison. But before I did that, I wanted to make a stop. As much as I enjoyed the idea of the consummation of our love occurring on an army cot, it wasn't very practical. That was made clear when we started. I could foresee we'd fall off unless we paid attention to our positions, and that wasn't how I wanted it to go. We weren't the size of fourteen-year-olds any longer, and we required some more space. I needed Marty and Tina to help me, though.

Marty was in the driver's seat of the cart and asked, "Back to Bates for you?"

"Yeah, but I need to make a stop first." I climbed into the backseat and directed Marty to drive over to the workers' cabins.

"What?" Tina asked.

This was a major problem with festival. Yes, you could have sex almost any time with almost anyone, but it was not going to be a secret. In fact, eventually almost everyone would know who you were screwing.

I put my head between the two of them and looked from one to the other. "Okay. When you called, Alison and I were just about to…you know."

"No way." Tina squealed with delight. "See, honey. I told you."

Marty just gave me a knowing smirk.

"So, I'd like to get her mattress and her sleeping bag and take it down to Bates. Please."

For some reason, they decided not to give me any grief. I guess the story about being interrupted hit a nerve.

Naturally, when we arrived at the infirmary, Angie and Leah were there. Swell.

"Take me around the back," I said. "And please try to be quiet."

With their help, I managed to quietly drag Alison's stuff into my room.

Back outside, I thanked Marty and Tina. "Better go check on Ace," I said.

"Roger." Marty winked. "Have a nice honeymoon."

I rolled my eyes. Marty and Tina were okay. They only wished me well. The next phase of the gauntlet was getting Alison away from Leah and Angie, and I had no idea how to do that. I went to the front door of Bates.

They were all in the infirmary. Alison had likely filled them in on the evening's events. Bridget sat next to Stoney, who reclined on one of the cots, looking just fine. Maybe there was something there. With a girlfriend like Ace, who could blame her?

Their issues, however, weren't my problem. I had a much bigger dilemma.

"Hi, everyone," I said, but I looked right at Alison. She met my gaze, but her face was blank. It's likely she didn't want Leah and Angie to know what was going on with us. I didn't either, but I had no idea how to work around them. There was longish pause.

Alison said, easily, "You know? I think all's well here. Y'all don't have to stay up. We'll take Bridget and Stoney back to their tents." She looked right at me.

Oh. The "we" was Alison and me. Drat. More delays. But I suppose it was a good plan.

"What about Ace?" Bridget asked, and she looked genuinely fearful.

"She's going to be on Security tonight with Marty. Arden told her to behave, or she would be kicked off the land."

Bridget's eyebrows went up, and she said, "You okay with going back?" She addressed this question to Stoney, who had brightened up even more.

"Oh, yeah. I'm fine."

"Well. That's it. Then let's hit the road," I said. *Please let nothing else happen tonight.* My watch said it was half past midnight.

"Good night," Alison said cheerfully to Leah and Angie. "See you in the morning. You'll drop me off at my cabin. Right, Lane?" Damn, she was a cool one, more so than I would have expected. Alison had been in control during the situation, and she was still in control.

"Oh, absolutely," I said, trying to keep my voice neutral and not bust out laughing.

It seemed like a long ride back out to the general camping area. We said good night to our two passengers and turned the golf cart around.

"How are you doing?" I asked Alison, a bit anxiously. I could only afford quick, sidelong glances because I was driving with nothing but the dim little headlights on the golf cart.

"Good grief. I feel like all the wind has been taken out of my sails. I don't know if I can just pick up where I left off."

"I went and got your mattress and sleeping bag. I thought it might be more comfortable and safer if we were, um, on the floor."

"Yes. I was giggling to myself, thinking about us doing it on an old army cot, but a mattress on the floor is just as fitting."

"Yeah. I think so too."

I touched her shoulder, squeezing it just a bit. "Are you okay?"

Alison didn't look right at me, but she put her hand on my waist. "I don't know. We'll see. What about you-know-who? Will they know if we're in your room at Bates?"

I did know who she meant: Leah and Angie. "Not sure. I think we can sneak in the back without them hearing us. Their room is nearer to the infirmary end. Marty and Tina already know, though."

"Oh, pissant. Really?"

"I had to get their help to fetch your stuff. Sorry." I hoped she'd understand and not be discouraged. We didn't need anything else to slow us down.

"Is the whole damn festival going to know about us?"

"Yeah. Probably."

She huffed and crossed her arms.

We arrived at Bates, and thankfully, the infirmary was dark. It looked like Leah and Angie had gone to bed, and I breathed a little easier.

We crept in the back door and into my room. I had hastily arranged the mattresses and the sleeping bags on the floor, and I must say, they looked inviting. Alison stopped in the doorway to stare. I reached over and pulled her into the room and shut the door as quietly as I could and leaned against it and took a big breath.

Alison stood by the bed with the full moon glowing in the window behind her, which made her blond hair look silvery. She spread her arms and I went to her.

What a difference a couple of hours made. Our headlong drive toward sex had been brought to an abrupt halt, and we had to start over again.

All that magical, full-moon goddess energy was gone and with it our forward momentum. Poof.

We simply hugged for a few moments, and that was fine. Our bodies melded together, conforming like two pieces of a jigsaw puzzle. I inhaled again to relax myself, and Alison did as well. Both of us taking that action at the same time aroused me, but it was comforting too. I was no longer feeling frantic or worried. As far as I could see, neither was Allie. I stroked her hair and gently kissed her a couple times.

I took a step back, and she put her arms around my neck, and I put my hands on her waist.

I said very quietly, "I never thought I'd see you again, yet here you are. I never thought we could get over what we did and said to each other, but it looks like we managed. I *don't* want to screw us up anymore. Not ever again. I want you more than I ever wanted anything in my life. I'm not eighteen anymore, though, and I know our actions have consequences. I want us to be okay."

I put my hands on either side of her face. I could see well enough in the moonlight, and I searched her face for clues.

"Lane. I…" She sighed. "We're okay. I know I love you and I want to make love with you. Can we just do that and leave all the rest until later? Tomorrow?"

I nodded, and we took our clothes off for the second time that night and lay down on the bottom sleeping bag, then pulled the other one over us. We embraced, touching head to foot. I didn't need to worship the goddess of the moon or goddess of anything else; I had a goddess in my arms. I rolled us over and pulled Alison on top of me. We promptly slid into the gap between the two mattresses, but I didn't care. Alison's hair wafted over my face and neck, just as it always had in my fantasies. I put both hands on her butt and squeezed. She made a quiet little sound and pressed into me. The phrase "coming home" leapt into my mind. After a long time away, I was returning home to Alison, where I'd begun when I was only twelve.

I didn't need to make any show-offy moves as I had sometimes employed with other women. In any case, I'd left all my toys back in San Francisco. I rolled us over again but, instead of pinning her, lay beside her and touched her all over, memorizing her body. I rubbed my palm over those remarkable breasts, and her nipples hardened and darkened to a rosy color I could just make out in the silver-blue moonlight.

Alison thrashed her legs and moved restlessly. "This is nice, but you better do something more 'cause you're driving me nuts."

"Right," I whispered against her neck and stuck my hand between her legs. I kept it slow and easy at first, stroking her labia and clitoris until she was nice and slippery. Alison put her arms around me and held on like she was drifting in an ocean and I was saving her life. When I finally entered her, she gasped and groaned. With the help of my thumb on her clit, she came quickly in a flurry of deep, guttural moans. That's my favorite moment, hitting the sweet spot and hearing and feeling a woman come around my fingers. My mind whispered in wonderment, *It's Alison.*

I stopped moving my fingers but stayed where I was for a few moments and then started over until she came again, harder than the first time. I removed my hand but kept us wrapped up in a tight embrace and kissed her face and neck as she calmed down.

"That's never happened to me before," she said finally in a tone of awe.

Yikes, thirty-two-years old and she'd never had an orgasm? It made me want to give her several more right then to make up for lost time.

"I'm happy I was able to do that for you." I didn't brag about being the first, though that crossed my mind, but this moment wasn't about me. It was all about Alison.

She kissed me hard, and her tears wet our cheeks.

"You okay?" I asked.

"I sure am. Never better." I touched her hair and moved it away from her face.

"Al—"

She rolled over on top of me. I was conscious of the hard floor under me. Only a thin layer of flannel and canvas was between it and my ass. But it didn't matter.

"Did anyone ever tell you you talk too much?"

"Well—" She shut me up with a deep kiss and then moved her lips from my mouth down to my breasts.

I didn't need any prompting to stop talking. If making love to Alison was a miracle, her making love to me was cataclysmic. I had the longest, strongest orgasm I'd ever had, and I immediately wanted another one, which she provided. Either she was the quickest learner in the world, or somehow she already knew exactly what to do. But this wasn't the time to wonder about that.

CHAPTER FIFTEEN

Sunlight in my face woke me up, and the first thing I saw was Alison's back. Alison and I were in bed together. Wow. I wanted immediately to touch her, but I also wanted to let her sleep. I had no idea how long we'd spent making love or when we fell asleep. Time had become irrelevant. I had achieved what I wanted and it was miraculous, everything I hoped it would be.

We had been very easy together. I don't know what I had expected, but after all the buildup in my head, we'd made love like we'd been doing it for years. I couldn't really enjoy the moment though. I was too caught up in my fears about the future. Did she mean for us to go on, try to find some way for us to be together? I was so busy asking myself all these questions I couldn't truly enjoy how wonderful it was to be with Alison, how good she felt and tasted and smelled and sounded.

I must have made some movement or noise because Alison turned over and said, sleepily, "Hi."

I touched her cheek and smiled back at her. "Hi."

"Oh, Lord. What time is it?" Her sleepy eyes grew wide and alarmed.

"I don't know. Let me find my watch." I groped around and found it. "Eight thirty."

"Oh, gosh. I gotta get up." Alison threw off the sleeping bag and stood up, giving me a full, sunlit view of her body. I didn't have much time to enjoy it, however, as she began to dress.

"I could maybe get Val to give us some late breakfast, if you want to hang out for a bit," I said hopefully.

That she wanted to leave me that quickly disappointed and worried me. It was like she was regressing to the Alison who had first arrived on the land, apparently in so much shock to see me that she could barely be civil.

"Oh, that's okay. I'm not hungry. I better get up front and make sure no one's waiting for medical attention." She was fully dressed and combing her hair with her fingers.

I stayed under the sleeping bag and just watched and waited.

She knelt on the floor and kissed me—a nice kiss but way too short. "Thanks for a great night and all. You're wonderful, really."

And she flew out the door, closing it behind her.

I lay still for a moment, stunned. I couldn't comprehend the contrast between what my body felt like—satiated, loved, floating in a warm bath of sex hormones and sex scent—and my mind, which should have been in the same state but was instead in a stew of dismay and bewilderment.

I went to take a shower, and because it was long past workers' time, I had to fight my way through a swarm of festies and all the accumulated debris of three days of thousands of women showering in the tiny shower room.

I'd have to throw myself on Val's mercy again and ask her to give me a bit of food and also maybe pick her brain yet again on the subject of Alison.

"Hi, Val," I said when I located her. She turned from her chopping task with a grin that faded as soon as she saw me.

"*Chica.* What's the matter with you? You look like death *and* shit warmed over."

"I was with Alison last night," I said before I could even think about the way I wanted to frame what I wanted to say so it would be coherent and put me in a good light.

"Oh, wow!"

"Yes," I said dejectedly.

"But something's wrong. You should be floating on a pink cloud. You should be happy, but you're not." She touched my arm, instantly concerned.

"I know, but it's not quite what I thought it would be."

"You didn't try to have some kind of involved discussion with her, did you?" she asked, suspiciously.

"No! I swear it was all spontaneous, beautiful, sexy sex. Until this morning." And I described what had happened.

"Okay. That's a little off-putting, but hey. Maybe she's just embarrassed? Doesn't want to be all gooey? Really needed to get to work?"

"I really doubt that her work was the reason."

Val looked thoughtful. "Nope. Probably not. Just give her some more space and then go visit with her later, and again, don't be overbearing. Be gentle. Goddess, you're really a mess."

That was an understatement. I still wanted to orchestrate every moment and every one of her reactions.

"Right. No processing. Yet," I said.

"Yeah. You got it. But what about you?"

"What do you mean, what about me?" Although I knew what she meant, I didn't know how to answer because I didn't know how I felt. I was profoundly mixed up.

"Don't be stupid. You know what I mean."

"I'm in love with her, and I can't believe we just spent the night in bed together and I have no idea what's going to happen next."

Val didn't say anymore. She just looked at me sympathetically and patted my shoulder.

After I left Val, who gave me something to eat, Marty came on the radio and told me the rest of the night was peaceful. Then she asked me, "And how was *your* night?"

"Fine." And mercifully Marty didn't say anything more. I told her to just go to sleep for a while and we'd meet later.

At loose ends, I slowly drove through the festival, trying not to think, and most of all trying to ignore the magnetic force trying to drag me to the infirmary and Alison. I went to lunch and didn't see her, which was both disappointing yet sort of a relief. I was determined to follow Val's advice and leave her alone. She could easily find me if she wanted to talk.

Why in the hell hadn't she radioed me?

The afternoon warmed up, and my lack of sleep combined with emotional turmoil made me headachy and sleepy. It was a perfect excuse to go the infirmary and beg some aspirin, but all I did was go to my room through the back entrance.

There on the floor lay the two mattresses and two sleeping bags. *Super.*

I dragged my bag and one of the mattresses up onto the cot and lay down with my arm over my eyes to shut out the sun. My pillow smelled like Alison's hair, which made my headache pound harder.

My mind was buzzing too much to let me take a nap. All I could think of was the night before, plus wondering where she was and what she was thinking and what we were going to do.

There was a knock on the door. "It's Allie."

"Come in." My heart was in my throat and my stomach flipped over. *Hold it together. Be cool.*

"Is it okay if I sit down?" Allie asked, sweet and tentative.

"Sure." I struggled into a sitting position. She sat next to me, looking cool and beautiful and wide awake. She wore the same sleeveless pink blouse and tan Bermudas of a few days before, and they appeared to have just come out of the wash. She was amazing.

I felt like and probably looked like a used cleaning rag. I felt worse than I had the morning after the night of my ill-advised scotch consumption.

"Sorry I had to leave so fast this morning."

I shrugged, indicating the exact opposite of what I truly felt. My insides were screaming *Why? What's the matter?* But I kept quiet and waited for Alison to explain herself.

She picked up my hand and turned it over, then looked at it, stroking my fingers, smiling a little as though she remembered where they'd been just a few hours before. I certainly remembered. And it occurred to me that she was stalling and trying to gather her thoughts

"Last night was wonderful," she said. "I left so fast this morning because I was so overwhelmed I thought I might start bawling." She put my hand down.

Her withdrawal of her touch left me bereft.

"Love and I aren't on what you'd exactly call speaking terms," Alison said, her tone bitter. "So I still need to learn how to act when someone loves me. *Really* loves me, not fake-loves me."

She continued. "I believe you love me. What I'm not certain of is myself. Having never been loved, I don't know how to take it. I've got no idea how to act."

I cleared my throat. "Generally speaking, you don't split like you did this morning unless something went horribly wrong." I stroked her arm.

Her forehead wrinkled. "I know. That was rude and unkind. That's why I'm trying to explain it to you."

She clasped her knee and rocked her leg. "This morning when I woke up and figured out where I was, I was really overcome by what I was feeling. I'm in love with you, and that terrifies me. I'm afraid I still think I'm not good enough for you. I know I told you about what happened and all, and that made me feel better, but I wish that were enough. Also, this is embarrassing, but I guess I still can't wrap my mind around being a lesbian and all that means." She looked at me, and I could tell she was thinking about sex.

"You're saying it was *too* good?" I asked.

She batted my arm. "You're awful, but yes, it's kind of like that. You might need to get over me because I'm still not at all sure I can be what you want me to be. I'm sorry I'm acting like such a birdbrain."

"Is that all?" I asked. "You don't know if *I* can be what *you* want me to be? I've never been with a woman longer than two years. They all leave me eventually. I may not be a very good bet myself."

"How many are we talking about here?" Alison asked, her tone a bit suspicious.

I counted to myself for a minute. "Five."

"*Five?*"

She clearly didn't know that wasn't a huge number of girlfriends for a normal, red-blooded lesbian living in a big city. I think my number was lower because I didn't do that overlap thing. I didn't even count the also-ran dates, one-night stands, etc. It was just better to leave those out for the moment.

"They mostly said some version of 'you're just not there.' So I have no idea if it was me or if it was them. Since I'm the common denominator, I'd say it's me."

This was a glum epiphany. It was the ultimate version of it's not you, it's me. How was I ever going to be any good for Alison? That was the question I'd brought up to myself and then tossed aside in favor of finally, at last, being able to make love with her.

Alison wasn't the birdbrain. I was.

"In other words," I said, "you think *you're* not good enough for *me?* You have no idea."

I ran my finger down her other arm, noting it raised goose bumps. "I've got a question for you, Alison. You said last night was your first time?"

She chuckled and said "Yep," clearly pleased.

"Well, it didn't seem like it was. You were, um, really amazing."

"Leah and Angie gave me *The Joy of Lesbian Sex* for Christmas, and boy, I read that sucker over and over until I memorized it. I *can't* stand not being good at something."

I was momentarily speechless, and then I started laughing. "There's a little more to it than reading a how-to manual."

She frowned. "And just what are you getting at, honey?"

"Well. The book may have helped, but every woman is different, and it seemed like you knew exactly what to do with *me.*"

She just stared at me for a really long time without a word.

I said, "Can I ask you a couple of questions?"

She fetched the other pillow from the floor and put it behind her so she could lean against the wall. She put her legs over mine. "Sure."

I'd started to feel better since she'd come to talk to me. My headache had eased back and I wasn't as sleepy. "Why did you agree to go with me to the motel? Did you know what I wanted?"

She looked away and her forehead wrinkled. "I was afraid you were going to ask me that." She looked at me again. "But you deserve an explanation, and since I've finally started talking about myself, no reason not to keep going."

I reached over and squeezed her hand. "I'm so happy."

"I wanted to ignore my mom's voice in my head. I went back and forth so many times that summer between being terrified at what my mom would say if she knew how I was behaving and what I wanted, which was to be with you. So I agreed to go with you because I wanted to. I loved you."

This saddened me so much I wanted to cry.

She continued. "Summer was over and we were going to leave and maybe not see each other for a long time, so…It started okay, I liked it when you kissed me, really kissed me and we were getting as close as possible, and then my mother's face popped into my mind and I lost my nerve, and well, you know what happened."

"I do," I whispered, remembering how angry and frustrated I was instead of thinking about Alison's terror and shame, which I had no idea of but somehow thought I should have.

"I'm sorry, Allie."

"No. *I'm* sorry. I can't help but think if I were a stronger, braver person, I would have acted differently."

"Alison, no, it's not your fault. It's over, and please don't feel bad about it anymore."

"Right. I know that in my mind, but I still haven't gotten that self-forgiveness you talked about." She sighed and closed her eyes.

"Yet. You and I. Last night?" I asked.

"Yep. That was really something."

It took all my resolve to stay quiet, but truly there wasn't much more I could say. Alison had to go through what she had to go through. I couldn't help.

To my surprise and joy, she slid down next to me on the cot, shoving me over, but I didn't mind.

"Let's not talk anymore. Just hold me."

I was more than happy to do that.

❖

We must have fallen asleep. I woke up in a fog as Alison stirred and turned over.

"What time is it?"

"I don't know." I just wanted to stay exactly as we were, never mind the tiny cot and how sticky and hot we'd become.

"I better get up. She clambered over me, kissed me on the cheek, and left, saying, "I'll see you later."

I lay still for a moment, then put my shoes on and dragged myself out to the golf cart.

It was the last day of music festival. Normally, I'm a bit sad to see it all end but also relieved to return to my routine life. Not this time. I was afraid Alison and I were going to part and that would be the end of it. That wasn't what I wanted, but I didn't know what to do except wait and see. It would be awful if we had to part without at least settling something.

Magda called on the radio and said, "Lane, can you come up to Hera? Someone's locked their keys in their car."

"Yep. Give me a few." I looked in the storage boxes on the golf cart. No Slim Jim. I was going to have to wake up Marty. I called her, and she sounded scratchy.

It was not only me who was a bit weary.

I strode into their cabin and greeted Marty with, "Do you have the Slim Jim? The Lesbian Nation is leaving today, and I just got my first call about keys."

"And a gracious good morning to you too, Lane. I'm all right. Yeah. How about you?" She pulled herself up on one elbow.

"Want me to go with you?" she said and yawned. In the cot next to her, Tina stirred, barely awake.

"Yeah, come to think of it." I went outside to wait for them.

"Hi, T," I said over my shoulder when they climbed into the golf cart.

"Hello," Tina said. She wasn't her usual upbeat, talkative self, and I sympathized. Then she asked in an arch voice, "How about you?"

"I'm all right."

"Good, but what about Alison?" Marty asked, her eyes searching my face, questioning.

"Honestly. I don't know," I said. "Last night was good. We're up in the air, nowhere, and tomorrow morning, as you know, we're off to the airport."

"So what are you going to do?"

"Fuck if I know."

From the backseat, Tina piped up. "You know you have to convince her you love her."

"She knows I love her. That's not the problem."

"Well, you'll figure it out. I know you'll end up together, happily ever after," Tina said with deep conviction. I wished I had her certainty.

"I hope so. But in the meantime, we need to work on getting all these women out of here and on their way home."

"Right," Marty said. We went out to Hera for our first key rescue, and then we drove around some more. The last day of festival is always bittersweet and chaotic, and as Marty had correctly predicted, we had lots of car issues, lost keys, lost children, lost lovers, and even one lost vibrator. That item wasn't going to make it into lost-and-found.

I took a break to go back to Bates and see Alison for just a minute or two. Around Angie and Leah, both of us were inhibited. Without knowing for sure, I believed Alison must have told them about us. I got inklings of even more disapproval from them, especially from Leah, but maybe it was my imagination. Also, she always acted as though she disapproved of me, and her little nose was up in the air whenever she saw me.

They were busy packing all the medical gear, and I was basically just making eyes at Alison, when I heard a soft knock on the door. The four of us turned as one, and there stood Ace and Bridget. I groaned silently because I didn't want to deal with their BS anymore. I was done with them.

They walked into the room, and when I took a closer look, I realized no one was hurt or crying, and they seemed to be in a good mood and were holding hands.

"We just wanted to stop by and say so long and thank y'all." Ace was doing the talking for both of them, which was unsurprising. She must still think she had to act like an old-fashioned butch from the fifties and Bridget was the little woman. Yuck.

Alison had stopped her packing and given them her full attention. Neither of us said anything. We waited to hear what these two had to say. Leah and Angie just watched the whole scene with interest while they pretended to pack.

"I know I was a real pain in the butt," Ace said. "After that last thing with the truck, me and Bridg talked and—"

"I told her I'd had it up to here," Bridget sliced a finger across her throat, "and I was leavin' her behind if she didn't clean up her act, and she said, 'Okay, you win.' We talked to someone today at breakfast, some kind of therapist or somethin', and she told us we had to go find someone like her back home and keep talkin'."

I'll be darned. The femme had found her voice. Good for her.

Ace was grinning at Bridget, and she actually had a nice smile when she wasn't drunk and pissed off.

"Yeah. After being up all night and then sleeping for a couple hours, I kind of woke up after hittin' that chick's bike and said I don't wanna be this way, and Bridg here said, 'No, honey, you don't. Not if you expect me to stick around.'"

Alison and I exchanged triumphant grins, and I said, "Well, congrats on wanting to change. I hope you can make it. I wish you both the best." I shook hands with Ace, but she hugged me anyhow. So did Bridget, and then they hugged Alison and off they went, still hand in hand.

Angie and Leah stared at us.

Leah said, "Well, aren't y'all just the cat's pajamas. You're all 'can this marriage be saved'? For lesbians." She could have been admiring, or she could have been sarcastic. Both maybe.

"Huh?" I didn't understand her reference.

Alison said, "Never mind, Lane. Don't pay any attention to these two. They think therapy is for the birds and for Yankees. Southerners just think when you're upset, all you have to do is get drunk and have a good cry or break some dishes or shoot something, and you'll be fine."

I understood, but it also seemed like they just wanted to tease me and Alison. I wasn't in the mood to take that in stride.

"Allie, can we talk?" I asked.

We walked outside with Angie and Leah's eyes on our backs. Then, at exactly the same time, we spoke.

"Allie…"

"Lane…"

Then we laughed

Alison asked, "When are you leaving?"

"Tomorrow morning sometime. We have to drive to the airport early to make all our flight times."

"Do you *have* to leave then?"

I was so startled, I stuttered, "We…well. I don't know. I'm supposed to be back at work on Tuesday." I know my face registered mystification.

"The reason I asked is—is because I, um, wondered if you wanted to–or you could come back to Atlanta with me for a few days?" Alison's hope and hesitancy were adorable, and well, essentially she'd just told me there might be a chance for us.

Oh my God. Or Goddess. I would do whatever I could, whatever I had to be able to spend some time with Alison. My mind raced.

"I can reschedule my flight, maybe pay a fee, but the problem is work. I can't talk to them until Monday, obviously, to see if it's okay to take a few more days off."

"If you could, do you want to come stay with me for a little while?"

I gripped her shoulders. "I sure do. I just have to think about how to organize it."

She grinned, seeming relieved, and kissed me.

My mood lifted, soared, actually. The change in airplane flight was minor, but I didn't want to make trouble for myself at work. On the other hand, this could be a decision that would affect the rest of my life. I'm a rule follower, and I'm not a flake, but this was an unusual circumstance. Since I didn't want to lie, I started formulating what I would say to my manager. And I needed to call her right away on Monday. How the heck would I do that on Arden's phone, which wasn't her phone anyhow? And with the time difference, I would have to wait for a couple of hours before my boss would be at work. I needed a pay phone and a lot of change. I thought about it for a while and constructed a plan.

I radioed Marty to pick me up, and we went over to Arden's house, and I told Becky I wouldn't be joining them for the trip back to the Atlanta airport. Then I called the airline and rescheduled my San Francisco flight to Wednesday evening. That would give Alison and me a couple of days to try to figure ourselves out. I hoped it would be enough.

That night at dinner, Alison had me sit with Angie and Leah, who stared at me like I was some sort of creature from outer space. I supposed Alison had informed them I was going to drive back to Atlanta with them. They behaved like they were in the middle of one long eye roll and were just waiting to say "I told you so" when Alison and I busted up. I didn't want to give them the satisfaction. I would have groused about their behavior to Alison, but I decided it was better to keep my mouth shut. I'm not usually that discreet, but I didn't want anything I said or did to screw us up. The "us" of Alison and me was entirely too tenuous.

"We can squeeze your duffel bag into the trunk, but you're going to have to keep your guitar on your lap," Leah said with a certain satisfaction that made me want to slap her. What the heck was their problem anyhow? If they'd given Alison a sex book, why wouldn't they be happy she put it to good use?

However, I just smiled benignly and said, "It won't be the first time." Alison was holding my hand under the table, and I had a serious case of butterflies. Tonight was going to be a hell of a night, if I had anything to say about it. Alison appeared to be poised to make it memorable as well, if her little sidelong glances at me meant what I thought they did.

"Be ready at seven a.m.," Leah said severely as we said our good-byes after dinner. They weren't going to the farewell party.

"Oh, we sure will be," Alison said airily.

Angie wore a noncommittal expression, but Leah glowered. Leah's attitude broadcast her distaste for the whole scenario, but Angie seemed neutral, if not totally approving. She was clearly the more romantic half of their couple. I'd noticed there's often a dichotomy such as that in lesbian relationships. Lesbos are a practical species generally—sometimes too much so. I was almost always the practical one with my girls, but in this case, I was anything but. Instead, I was a throw-yourself-in-headfirst romantic when it came to Alison, except for the part where I wasn't good enough for her and was terrified of screwing it all up, as I usually did.

The party for the workers was a lot like the one the day before the festival—maybe even more uninhibited. Only this time, I barely drank at all, and I had no need to look for a sex partner. I already had one. I had found my new/old love, and all I had to do was figure out how to keep her.

Alison stayed fastened to my side and whispered in my ear frequently. Her breath tickled me. I was so keyed up I could hardly speak, and it didn't seem important to say much. I was planning to communicate a lot more nonverbally.

We danced a few times, and it was fun, but nothing reproduced the magic of the full-moon dance, not that it was necessary. We were hardly dancing anyhow. We were mostly just glued together and swaying to the music.

I said, "Let's go out for some air."

Alison said, "Let's go back to Bates. I'm done with this."

"Sure thing."

On the way to Bates, I decided to risk damaging our mood to ask Alison what was up with Angie and Leah. "What have Angie and Leah got against me?"

"Oh." She sighed. "I told you Leah's had a big old crush on me for the last few months. Well, she managed to kiss me one time. I told her off and threatened to tell Angie myself if she didn't stop doing that and tell Angie the truth. She did. She's still screwed up, but Angie's okay because I'm not about to do anything stupid like mess with a 'married woman.' I'm not interested in Leah that way anyhow. Angie handles it way better than I would."

"Oh, wow. Now I get why Leah has such a fucked-up attitude about me."

"Yeah. I thought she was going to have a fit when I told her about us. Angie isn't too happy either, but I said, 'Y'all get over it 'cause it's happening, and I'm a grownup who can take care of herself.'"

More dyke drama, only this time it involved me and not random festies. Oh, well. If it was going to be a tense ride back to Atlanta tomorrow, so be it. It wasn't my problem. Alison seemed fine, and that's all I cared about. Meantime, we had other things on our minds.

I'd found some duct tape earlier in the day and taped the mattresses together as much as I could. There was, I was pleased to note, still an almost-full moon, and its light poured into the little bedroom. Alison in moonlight was something I'd never tire of.

I said, "We can go slower this time. I *want* to go slowly, and I want to enjoy every second. And I have a few things to show you that I think you'll like."

"Hmm," Alison murmured dreamily, nuzzling my neck and running her hands down my back. "I'll tell you if I want you to go faster, but sure, knock yourself out, honey.

This gave me a nice little shiver of anticipation.

She patted my collarbones and sort of just looked me over like she was standing in front of a buffet and trying to decide what she wanted to eat first. "You know, I was kinda nervous about doing it, but once we got going, I was good."

"You were way better than good."

She patted my cheek and ran her hand down my neck and over my shoulder.

I kissed her cheek and whispered in her ear, "You were incredible."

She put her arms around me and whispered back, "Lord. You just turned my knees to jelly."

She sagged in my arms, but I didn't mind. I kissed her neck and said, "Let's go to bed." We locked our gazes as we removed our shorts and shirts and underwear.

The duct-taped mattresses almost held together, but we were so absorbed we hardly noticed. I let Alison take over right off. She touched me slowly, lightly, as though I was a fine crystal vase. I finally had to say, "Harder, darling. I'm not going to break." She probed me with her fingers until she found my clit, and I said, "There."

As I was recovering, she hugged me and asked, "Was that good?"

I kissed her. "The best ever." And I meant it. I've never had trouble with sex. I almost always could come easily and produce easy orgasms in my girlfriends, but something had always been missing. Some dimension I didn't know about and couldn't describe. When Alison made love to me, I finally realized what it was, what I'd been missing. I needed her. I needed my soul mate.

I rolled over on my side and pushed her gently back onto the mattress. "I want you to relax for a few minutes."

She must have seen the look in my eyes in the moonlight, and she asked, abruptly, 'What're you about to do to me? Should I be nervous?"

I laughed. "No. You'll be fine, but I like to take my time with this."

She looked at me, skeptically, but obeyed.

I started with her perfect breasts, using my lips and hands alternately until her breathing became ragged. I rubbed slow circles on her stomach, edging close to my goal. She was very slick and squishy, and some concentrated attention on her clitoris would have made her come quickly. I kept my touch light and slow because I didn't want her to orgasm just yet. She thrashed impatiently.

"You're driving me crazy," she complained.

"That's the idea."

She slapped the side of my head but not too hard.

I gauged she was ready and slid down her body. I pushed her legs open and knelt between them. Her open eyes scrutinized me. I ran my index finger lightly over the flesh of her inner thigh where it's the softest.

"Well?" she asked. "What's going on? Are you gonna do something or what?"

"Yeah. I'm going to do…something."

"Jesus Christ, just do it already."

I scooted down and settled her thighs on my shoulders. I opened her and blew a light breath on her clitoris, and she moaned and tensed her legs sharply.

I licked the inside of her thigh where my finger had just touched, and she made a sound in her throat. I took a deep breath and gently licked her labia and around her clit, avoiding the head. *Not just yet.*

She was sweet, but I detected a faint undertaste of garlic. That was to be expected, I suppose, and I didn't mind. It was Alison. The essence of Alison was in my mouth and my nostrils. I wrapped my arms around her hips to keep her in place and went for it. It didn't take much time. I stuck my finger inside her and curled it slightly to stimulate her from inside. She arched her back and slapped a pillow over her face as she screamed. Her orgasm went on for many seconds, each contraction coordinated with the beat of my heart.

I released her and rolled on my back gasping.

"Lane?" she said faintly.

I roused myself and crawled up next to her, watching her chest rise and fall as she caught her breath. She sprawled in the moonlight, her legs spread and her skin glistening. She was so beautiful, I had to catch my breath all over again. I snuggled in next to her. She flung herself on me, kissing me almost frantically.

"Whoa. You okay?"

"Are you nuts? I'm blown away. That was…something."

"I guess you liked it."

"You're…something."

"I am, aren't I?" I put my hands behind my head and smirked at her.

"Don't think much of yourself, do you?"

"Nope." I grinned even more.

She looked at me for a few moments, then said, "I'm going to wipe that shit-eating grin right off your face."

"By all means, please try."

And with that she threw herself between my legs and imitated my movements, the exact same things and in the same order. I'm a very effective giver of head, and she was an excellent student of the art. I came in a cloud of exaltation. I don't remember if my fantasies of Alison had included her going down on me, but they would from that point forward and forever.

CHAPTER SIXTEEN

Naturally Leah and Angie woke us up at dawn. "Y'all get a move on. We got to hit the road."

At least this time, Alison didn't bolt the second she opened her eyes. I was able to put my arms around her and bask in our sexual glow for a couple of minutes. And the shower room wasn't overrun by festies, so we could take a shower together. We didn't have time to fool around, but it was still pleasurable.

Thanks to Val and her people, we were able to eat a nice breakfast. And even if Leah and Angie were in a fever to leave, the many good-byes that all of us had to make slowed them down, and we didn't actually leave until around nine thirty.

To Val, I said, "I don't know what's going to happen, but I have you to thank for where I am, where we are."

Val shook her head dismissively. "Nah. I just let you figure it out for yourself. See you in September." She referred to the West Coast festival, for which we both were scheduled to work.

We hugged tightly, and Val kissed my cheek soundly, then pinched my ass. I'd tolerate that move only from her.

When I said good-bye to Marty and Tina, I hugged them both hard and said, "Well. See you in September." They laughed

In the car, the four of us were nearly silent. Leah only spoke when she and Angie had to exchange information about directions or things they planned to do later. I wondered if Angie had made Leah promise to not run her mouth on the way home.

I was really nervous about the phone call I was about to make because I'd never done anything like that before. I was glad we were all quiet, even if it felt like an uncomfortable silence. I used the time to formulate my reason for what was going to be an unusual request. I didn't want to be dishonest with my manager, but it was clear I had to be somewhat cagey about my reasons for not returning the day I said I would. My employer was understanding, up to a point, about employees' various personal issues. I was about to find out how far this flexibility would extend.

I knew my manager was an early arriver, so around an hour into our trip I figured would be late enough out West. I asked Angie, who was driving, to stop at a gas station. We all left the car to stretch our legs, and I went into the little convenience store and induced them to make some change for me. I took a deep breath, plugged the coins into the pay phone, and dialed my manager, Grace.

Much to my relief, she answered the call and I didn't have to leave a message.

"Hey, it's Lane."

"Hello! This is a surprise. Aren't you still on vacation? You're not due back until tomorrow, yes?"

"Yeah. That's what I'm calling about. I wanted to ask to extend my vacation to Wednesday. I'll come back Thursday."

Long silence.

"This is really awkward, Lane."

"I know," I said, brimming with guilt. "I hate asking, but I feel like I have to. Something's come up."

"I see. I'm not going to ask you what that something is, because it's not my business."

I never shared anything personal with Grace. She knew I was a lesbian, but we never discussed anything related to it. It was just a fact about me, and we didn't have any trouble about it. In the Bay Area, most people were out at their jobs without repercussion. I just wasn't a person who shared personal things at work.

I made a really quick decision without thinking about it. "I'm staying in Georgia for a couple of days because I think I've met the love of my life, and we have to, you know, talk."

I endured what seemed like a long stretch of silence while Grace hopefully absorbed what I said.

Finally, she said, "Wow. That's great. I'm happy for you. What's her name?"

"It's Alison and she lives in Atlanta. We, er, met years ago, and we met up again at the music festival, and well, it sort of clicked." The way I described it sounded lame, but it was accurate enough.

"Well, I'll be darned. I wish you the best. Please take some time. I do need you back Thursday, though. The trial at the University of Washington starts next week." She sounded like she meant what she said.

"I promise. I'll make it up to you somehow."

We spent a few minutes discussing my priorities for when I returned to work, but I didn't mind. I owed her for her graciousness about my abrupt change of plan. I plugged more coins into the phone as she went on for a few minutes about the next clinical trial I would be organizing.

I walked back to the car, excited and relieved. I couldn't wait to tell Alison the good news, but as I approached the three musketeers, I began to hear their raised voices and pick up on their tense body language.

"It's only because we care about you that we're pitching such a fit. This is about as crazy as it gets, Alison, if you're thinking that this thing with Lane is going to go anywhere." Angie was speaking, and her back was to me, but I got a good view of Alison's face, and it was clear she was furious

"You don't know that. You have no business trying to warn me off. Who do you think you are!" she said heatedly to both of them.

I stopped abruptly and waited.

Leah turned and spotted me.

"This isn't personal," she said. "We're just looking out for Alison."

Alison said, "The hell it isn't personal. You two have been about as negative as can be about Lane ever since we first got to the festival, and I'm tired of it. Y'all need to quit right now. All I'm doing is spending a couple of days with Lane. We need to talk, and you two need to butt out."

"Alison, honey. Don't be pissed. We only want you to be happy," Leah said, switching to her conciliatory voice.

Alison wasn't having it. "Leah, you're just jealous 'cause you have the hots for me and I won't give you the time of day. You need to pay attention to Angie. And Angie, I don't know what your problem is, but you can get over it. I don't need y'all trying to tell me what to do. I had enough of that with my mom and my ex-husband to last me the rest of my days. I'll make up my own mind, and I don't need y'all's advice."

She turned and walked away, and I followed her after glaring at the two shocked lesbians. Those two surely deserved that tongue-lashing.

I went to Alison and put my arm around her and asked her, "You okay?"

Between sniffs, she said, "I'll be okay once this damn car trip is over with and I get away from those two."

"What'd they say that got you all riled up?" I was starting to sound like a Southerner myself, and that pleased me.

"Oh, never mind. I'll tell you later. Let's just go."

Leah and Angie had gotten back in their car and were staring straight ahead. Alison and I slid into the backseat, I repositioned my guitar and pulled Alison close in spite of the increasing heat, and none of us said another word for the next hour.

When they dropped us off at Alison's house, I thanked them for the ride, and Alison did as well, but nothing else was said. They drove off, and we were finally alone again.

Alison unlocked the door of her nice-looking ranch house on the outskirts of Atlanta.

Suburbs give me the willies. It's not just because I'm out of place as a lesbian. When I was a teenager, we would visit my cousins outside of Trenton, and I hated their suburb. It was the sameness, the lack of trees, I suppose. I was lucky to live in an older area of Pittsburgh where the trees were big and the homes older. Now that I was a confirmed urbanite, I hated suburbs even more, and not just for their tacky, over-modern, cookie-cutter houses but for the closed-minded attitudes I attributed to their residents. Nevertheless, this was Alison's home, and I could manage to cope for a few days.

"So what's up? Do you have to work tomorrow?" I asked.

Alison grinned. "Oh. I took the rest of the week off. I figured I'd need time to recover from the festival. Recover from what, I wasn't sure, but it's lucky I did. All that sex really wore me out."

I laughed and kissed her. "There's more where that came from."

"We'll get to that. First, I don't have a bit of food in this house. We have to go shopping. She patted my cheek and lowered her eyelids seductively.

I followed her into the kitchen, looking around at everything as though it held the key to Alison's personality and somehow to our future.

"Is this your house? I mean do you own it?" I asked.

"Well. My ex-husband and I did, and I kept it in the divorce."

"Oh. Wow." Home ownership seemed very adult. I also wondered if Alison would want to sell it and leave Atlanta. I couldn't picture living in an Atlanta suburb, but I was getting way ahead of myself.

We went to the grocery store, and in spite of my unease with suburbia, I didn't feel at all weird to be grocery shopping with Alison.

We seemed to have reached an unspoken agreement to not start talking about anything about us until later. We pushed what Alison called a buggy and I called a shopping cart through the aisles of a store called, for some reason, a Piggly Wiggly. Performing this mundane activity together had a soothing effect on me.

While we shopped, Alison told me what had happened when I was making my phone call from the gas-station convenience store.

"Practically the second you left, they both started in with stuff like, 'Are you sure you know what you're doing? She's really not the one. She's gonna go back to Frisco, and you're gonna be left high and dry. Blah, blah, blah.' I said, 'Y'all are being negative because you think she's different and not a Southerner. How do you know she's not the "one"? You don't know a thing about her, so what makes you so sure?' They said, 'It doesn't take a genius to guess how this is going to end. You're just starry-eyed.'"

I couldn't think of what to say that would be constructive so I just nodded.

I was with Alison in the physical sense, in the same space and sexually, but we were still very much strangers. We'd agreed we wanted to spend more time together, but beyond that, I didn't know what we were after and, most important, what she wanted in the way of a future with me. I understood that Alison's life had rendered her extremely closemouthed and protective of her emotions, and I would have to wait, but as usual, I couldn't help but fret.

We brought the groceries home and cooked dinner, and in honor of having spent the previous ten days eating no animal protein but chicken, Alison grilled steaks.

She looked perfect standing in front of her grill in an apron, tongs in one hand, beer in the other.

"It's lucky you're not a vegetarian. I wouldn't be able put up with that nonsense," she drawled.

I sat at the picnic table, my own beer in hand, watching and admiring Alison. I admit I was picturing her naked.

She must have picked up on that because she cocked an eyebrow at me. "I know what you're thinking, Ellie. I can read your mind."

It was clear she was using the wrong name to tease me and exert a little control. I didn't mind, really. Coming from her it didn't bug me.

"How could I not?" I asked, innocently.

"I don't mind." She was looking at the steaks as they cooked, but she smiled to herself. "Except we got a whole lot more talking to do. That other stuff's got to take a backseat."

"That other stuff" was such a charmingly Southern way to put it.

"Yep," I said. "But I enjoy thinking about you. And us."

"Us," she repeated. "That's a nice word."

As we sat down to eat, I asked, "I understand why Leah's not fond of me, but why does Angie have a bug up her butt about you and me?" I'd heard some Dixie girls use that phrase and was delighted to be able to say it.

Alison laughed, but then she sighed as she chewed and swallowed, taking her time.

"She doesn't know you. You're not a Southerner. You're from San Francisco. She's protective of me. A little overprotective. I'll say one thing. Leah's crush on me sure never made a difference to her. She knows Leah's kind of a ninny. She thinks you'll end up breaking my heart, or you could whisk me away forever. She doesn't want either of those things to happen."

"Well, I suppose I get the protective part, but I'm not concerned with what they think as much as what *you* think, and you were really pissed off this morning when we stopped for me to make my phone call."

Alison took a gulp of beer and set her bottle down with a *thunk*. "People have been controlling me my whole life. First my mother, and then my ex-husband. I'm not going to put up with that anymore, not even from people who wish me well like Angie and Leah. It's not that I don't appreciate their concern, but I have to make up my own damn mind. I like it that you let me do that. You don't push me. You just kind of drew me along slowly, letting me come to my own decision. I sure appreciate that, honey." She took my hand across the picnic table.

"I hope I'm not going to break your heart. I'm going to do the very best I can not to," I whispered, my voice unsteady.

Alison put her other hand over our clasped hands. Just that touch nearly undid me, but I tried a weak smile.

Alison said, "Tell me more about you. I feel like I've told you lots about me, but I know almost nothing about you and all those girlfriends you mentioned."

I wanted to, but I was scared that more detail about my many failed relationships would scare her and ultimately discourage her from taking a chance with me. But I couldn't withhold information. What the hell. She had her baggage and I had mine.

I took a breath. "Well, I end up getting involved with the wrong women. I sleep with someone and that's pretty much that. I'm nice to them, but they tell me there's something missing in my psyche, and they eventually get tired of trying to get close to me and give up. We never part on bad terms, but they all say some version of the same thing."

"Huh. That doesn't sound good."

"No. I agree. It doesn't, but look, here's the thing. It's different with you. Way different."

"Oh? Tell me."

"I've made up my mind that you're the woman I want. I'm positively absolutely affirming I want to be with you. That's new for me. With the others, I just went along for the ride and tried to not act like an asshole, but that wasn't enough."

Alison gazed back at me with deep interest. "After everything I've told you, you still want me."

"One hundred percent."

Alison grinned. "You remember I told you I thought you were tough until we had that little girl with the seizure?"

I nodded for her to keep talking.

"Well, that gave me a different view of you, but you know what really convinced me that I didn't need to be intimidated by you?"

"What?"

"When you got so upset that those little teenagers, Robbie and Millie, didn't trust you."

"I wasn't upset," I said.

"Sure you were, honey, and that's what finally convinced me I could tell you the truth."

I just looked at her, flummoxed.

"It about killed you that the girls couldn't trust you. I saw it in your face and the way you got irritated with me. So I was still scared to tell you the truth, but when you said I could trust you, I knew I could. Nothing is more important to you than feeling like people can trust you."

I didn't know what to say. Alison's insight was amazing.

Because it felt like the right moment, I said, "Allie, will you move to San Francisco to be with me?"

She stiffened and didn't respond.

"I'm pretty sure you could get a job. There are a lot of hospitals in SF. Big ones."

"Oh, I'm not worried about that. My job is portable, for sure. It's other stuff."

More of that "other stuff"? Maybe this was *other* "other stuff"?

"Like what?" I didn't really mean to sound challenging, but I did.

"Like how the heck you and me could ever last. I'm not sure I can handle being in a relationship with *anyone*, but with you? Yikes. Just 'cause you make my knees buckle when you look at me doesn't mean it's love."

"I thought you said you love me?" I was genuinely alarmed.

"I do, but really, Lane. I'm not sure now's the time. I mean, is it too soon?"

I was getting angry, and I didn't want to be. After Alison's speech about making up her own mind, I didn't want to get pushy. And mostly her ambivalence was triggering my own. I wanted to project certainty of our future success, but to do that I needed her to be there too, and she wasn't.

I took a deep breath. "I only know how it feels to me, Allie."

"That's the problem. I still don't know if I can trust my judgment even after I made that big speech to Angie and Leah about making up my own mind. I trust you, but I'm not sure I trust myself.

That was a very good question but one I couldn't answer for her.

She said, "How do you know we're right for each other? The last few days have been great and all." She raised her eyebrows to let me know she was thinking about sex again. "But we have a lot of history, and it's not all good. Mostly I don't know what's going to happen. I've never been in love, Lane. The only people who said they loved me—my mom and my ex—sure had funny ways of showing it."

"I'm not like them."

"I know you're not. You're wonderful, and I'm sure you care about me. I know this in my mind, but I don't think my heart has quite caught up. I'm scared." She put down her tongs on the little table hanging off the side of the grill and started to cry. "I don't want you to leave, but you can't stay. I don't want to make promises I can't keep, but I know you need some sort of promise from me." She sobbed harder.

I put my arms around her and patted her back. When she calmed a bit, I got her to look me in the eye. "Alison, love. I don't know what to say about you, but as for me, I'm scared. If you decide to be with me and rip your life apart and move to San Francisco, I have no idea what'll happen. At this minute, I'm sure I could love you and make you happy. But I can't predict what will happen next year or two years from now. I don't have a great track record with women. I can only say I love you with all my heart and want to be with for the rest of my life.. I don't think I've ever said that to any other woman I've been with. I think we belong together. I think we had to be separated for a while for me to understand that fact. Coming back into each other's lives was meant to be. I take that as a sign."

During this long speech, Alison just looked at me wide-eyed. When I finally stopped talking, she kept right on looking at me. The silence went on for so long, I grew more concerned. As I was about to say something, she spoke up.

"You're pretty darn persuasive. You know, when I was talking to that counselor all about my mother and my ex-husband, she listened to me for a long time." Alison drew out the word "long." "And she finally said that holding on to the past keeps us from fully embracing the present, and that's different from having memories."

I waited for her to say more, but all she said was, "Let's eat these steaks, and then I really, really want to make love with you."

"That sounds great."

I have to say, though I miss the music festival once it's over, modern civilization has its benefits, and one huge upside is sleeping in a comfortable bed. It may have amused us to start our physical coupling on cheap, vinyl-covered mattresses on the floor of a tiny room, but when Alison and I climbed into her queen-sized bed between soft, clean sheets, we groaned a simultaneous sigh of relief.

I pulled her close and said into her ear, "Listen."

She kissed my cheek and then my neck. "Listen to what?"

"That's my point, nothing. No radio calls, no interruptions. No overheard conversations. No Leah or Angie. We're alone, fully alone."

Alison giggled and it tickled me. "Right. It's quiet."

"And this bed feels great. I don't miss sleeping and doing other stuff in a flannel sleeping bag."

"Yeah. Now that you mention it, there's that other stuff. Again." Alison wound herself around me. There was a big fan in the window, busy sucking out the hot air so the temperature of her bedroom was comfortable. We were both clean and didn't smell like garlic or sweat. Our smooth bodies slid over each other and the fresh sheets with the faintest whispers of sound. And when we warmed up and threw off the top sheet, Alison sat on me and looked at me as she moved back and forth.

"The best part is if I scream, there's no one around to hear."

I gripped her hips, then squeezed her thighs. "I'd like to hear that. Get on your knees, love."

I reached between her legs and a stuck my fingers in her, and she was soft and slippery. Her vocal response was a moan that soon turned into a very satisfying full-throated scream when she orgasmed.

The next day and a half was lovely. She showed me some of her favorite parts of Atlanta, which seemed mostly to do with the Civil War.

Mostly, though, we just lived together in the emotional sense. All talk about the future stopped. I struggled to keep silent, but I somehow knew I had to just wait for Alison to tell me what was on her mind.

On Tuesday evening, she disappeared into a spare room in her house, requesting I give her some time and space, and I stayed in the living room with the TV. After the festival, TV was still a strange sort of novelty, along with lots of other ordinary accoutrements of modern life, like supermarkets and straight people.

After a while, Alison returned to the living room with a couple of photo albums in hand.

"Found 'em," she said. "Here. Have a look." And we sat close together on the couch and opened the photo albums. There we were as campers ages twelve to sixteen, and then the pictures from our last summer, starting with the group photo of all the counselors taken at the beginning of the summer. We sat side by side, smiling. I detected an undercurrent of sadness in Alison's grin and remembered very well how I'd felt that June. I'd arrived at camp deeply and hopelessly in love with her and understanding why, not sure where it would go or what we would do.

"We were so young and so clueless," I said, touching first my face, then hers. I had no idea what I had done with my copy of this photograph. I hadn't seen it in many years. "I'm glad I'm looking at this picture with you. Otherwise it would be too painful to remember. I think I tried to forget about you. If it wasn't for that idiotic Elvis Costello song, I might have. And, of course, running into you again." I spoke lightly, but I think Alison sensed the sadness underneath.

She moved closer to me and touched my cheek to make me raise my head and make eye contact. "I'm glad we've met again. I truly am, even if I didn't act right at first." She paused. "Even though I thought it would be you, it was still a shock."

"I must have brought back some pretty bad memories."

"Yep, you sure did, but I don't hold that against you." She laughed shortly. "I was living with a lot of shit clogging up my mind. It was good you made me get rid of it."

I didn't know what to say. I just picked up her hand and kissed it. Of course, that led to more kissing and then to lovemaking. At least when we were engaged in doing that, my psyche would stop haranguing me about our future. Sex with anyone new is always a pleasurable novelty, and it was with Alison. Yet it somehow felt also familiar and comfortable. Besides those obvious benefits, it also served to keep me from talking too much.

❖

On my last day there, we woke up and had brunch before leaving for the airport. I needed to be home at a reasonable hour and able to return to work in good shape the next day.

We sat at her kitchen table and sipped coffee. I had sternly willed myself to not ask any questions, not drop any hints, not even look at her funny. I had said what I wanted to say. It was up to Alison.

She was very quiet and didn't interact with me much. Finally she reached for my hand. "Okay. Let's do it. You'll need to give me some time to find a job. I won't move anywhere without one. That'd just be about as stupid as all get-out."

I was dumbfounded. "Um. So…you…eh…it's…"

"You're so damn adorable when you don't know what to say. You ought to try keeping quiet more often."

Then I laughed. That was only too true, I guess, when it came to Alison. My ex-girlfriends would have been astonished to hear it though.

"That's terrific. Can I ask you what helped you make up your mind?"

"Lots of things. When we first got to the festival and you were there, I had a hard time absorbing it all and seeing you as real. Then I felt awful because of what happened, and I didn't want to be around you or talk to you."

"I know," I said, sadly. "That was hard for me. I'd already forgiven you, but you didn't know it."

"Then you apologized to me, when it was actually me who had to apologize to you. That screwed me up even more. Then I did apologize, but it didn't seem to change me any because I didn't tell you the whole story. Meanwhile, there we were at the festival, and though I'd hung out with Leah and Ange and a few other people, up to that point I didn't quite grasp what it was really about to be a lesbian and with other lesbians. And you were a big part of that."

I had to laugh at that.

"And I thought, oh, this is like paradise, and then we had the whole mess with Ace and Bridget, and no, it's not paradise and it's not perfect." She looked very sad for a minute.

"But somehow that was still okay. I don't know how it was okay, but it was. When I had to look at those two, I thought about my ex-husband, and then I thought, I don't have to put up with that shit any more. Ever again. And you…"

She fixed me with her limpid blue eyes. I don't think I'd ever had a woman look at me like that.

"You were who you were when we were younger, but you were also someone different, older, sure of herself."

"Except when it came to you," I reminded her.

"Yes, but that made it more real, more believable. You said you loved me, and I believed it. Right before the full-moon night, I knew I was going to go to bed with you."

"You did?" Sheesh. She was an expert at keeping herself to herself. "You were sure of yourself. I'm surprised to hear you say that."

Alison tilted her head. "I'm not a virgin, y'know."

I was embarrassed that I had thought of her in just those terms.

She shrugged, nonchalantly. "Besides, Angie and Leah gave me that old book."

I laughed. "Well, then."

Alison grinned evilly. "So I knew I could handle the basics."

"Yeah. You handled them and me fine."

"Yup. The full moon just kind of helped it along. It felt right."

Alison's phone rang and she raised her eyebrows, asking me it was okay if she answered. I nodded.

"Oh. Hi, Angie." Her eyes wide, she stared at me.

Then there were a lot of head nods and "uh-huhs" for a few minutes. She said, "Okay then. I'll see you on the weekend. Bye." And she clicked the phone off and slapped it on the table.

"Well, what do you know? They thought about our little old car ride home and rethought their crappy attitudes and called to wish us the best. They want me to come over for supper on Saturday."

"Oh, wow. That's great."

"Yeah. I guess." Alison looked thoughtful.

"Hey, that was another interruption for us. Fit rights into the pattern." I laughed, but Alison didn't.

She asked, "Where were we?"

"Talking about the full moon."

"Oh, yeah. Lost my train of thought. But after that there was the question of what next? What now? That was what stumped me so bad. I could say to myself, 'Well, we just met. We don't even know each other.' But that wasn't true."

I whispered, "No, it wasn't true at all. We do *know* each other."

She took my hands. "Yes. We knew each other then and got to know each other again. I thought and thought and thought. What the heck did I have to keep me here in Atlanta? Why would I stay? My answer was, nothing and no reason. But I have someone who loves me, who's always loved me, standing there and saying, 'Come with me.'"

I could hardly speak, and I started to cry. I hardly ever cry. "Yes." I was so happy and overwhelmed I could barely choke it out. "Alison, I thought our story had ended, but then came the festival, and surprisingly it hadn't. I didn't know at first, but now I know I want our story to go on forever." I had to stop talking because I was crying too hard.

"Hey, look at you, bawling your eyes out like some little girl. Come here, honey." She opened her arms and we embraced.

After I calmed myself down somewhat, I asked Alison what she would say to Leah and Angie.

"Oh, first I'll tell them I forgive them for how they tried to get me away from you. 'Cause I do understand where they were coming from, but then I'm going to have to tell them I'm moving to San Francisco, and I don't know how that'll go over, but what the heck."

I hugged her. "It'll be fine."

❖

On the flight back to San Francisco, I couldn't sleep, but this time it wasn't from being anxious. It was because I was happy. Alison would be coming to visit in a few weeks and start her job search. Neither of us expected it would take long. I was already planning everything we would do, starting with the gay-day parade at the end of June. I was certain the medical staff at the parade would be happy to have her as a volunteer.

Mostly I was trying to absorb the reality of what had just happened to me. I reviewed the progression of events from reading Alison's name on the list that Arden had sent all the way up to our good-bye kiss a few hours earlier. It couldn't possibly be real, but it was. It was like a crazy made-for-TV movie, possibly shown on the Lifetime channel, if Lifetime ever showed any gay-themed movies, which they didn't as far as I knew.

For sure we can't change the past. So what? Maybe all we need to do is learn to transcend it. Take it for it's worth and move on. I remembered what Alison's counselor had told her. That was why I had had to let my memories of Alison go, for my own sanity. I was sure I would never see her again, but what did I know? Nothing, apparently.

It was an improbable a tale as anything I'd ever heard or read. Too bad we'd likely never have any kids to tell it to, but who knows? I figured I ought not to rule anything out for my future. My future with Alison.

THE END

About the Author

Kathleen Knowles grew up in Pittsburgh, Pennsylvania, but has lived in San Francisco for more than thirty years. She finds the city's combination of history, natural beauty, and multicultural diversity inspiring and endlessly fascinating. Her first novel, *Awake Unto Me*, won the Golden Crown Literary Society award for best historical romance novel of 2012.

She lives with her spouse and their three pets atop one of San Francisco's many hills. When not writing, she works as a health and safety specialist at the University of California, San Francisco.

Books Available from Bold Strokes Books

Alias by Cari Hunter. A car crash leaves a woman with no memory and no identity. Together with Detective Bronwen Pryce, she fights to uncover a truth that might just kill them both. (978-1-63555-221-8)

Death in Time by Robyn Nyx. Working in the past is hell on your future. (978-1-63555-053-5)

Hers to Protect by Nicole Disney. High school sweethearts Kaia and Adrienne will have to see past their differences and survive the vengeance of a brutal gang if they want to be together. (978-1-63555-229-4)

Of Echoes Born by 'Nathan Burgoine. A collection of queer fantasy short stories set in Canada from Lambda Literary Award finalist 'Nathan Burgoine. (978-1-63555-096-2)

Perfect Little Worlds by Clifford Mae Henderson. Lucy can't hold the secret any longer. Twenty-six years ago, her sister did the unthinkable. (978-1-63555-164-8)

Room Service by Fiona Riley. Interior designer Olivia likes stability, but when work brings footloose Savannah into her world and into a new city every month, Olivia must decide if what makes her comfortable is what makes her happy. (978-1-63555-120-4)

Sparks Like Ours by Melissa Brayden. Professional surfers Gia Malone and Elle Britton can't deny their chemistry on and off the beach. But only one can win... (978-1-63555-016-0)

Take My Hand by Missouri Vaun. River Hemsworth arrives in Georgia intent on escaping quickly, but when she crashes her Mercedes into the Clip 'n Curl, sexy Clay Cahill ends up rescuing more than her car. (978-1-63555-104-4)

The Last Time I Saw Her by Kathleen Knowles. Lane Hudson only has twelve days to win back Alison's heart. That is if she can gather the courage to try. (978-1-63555-067-2)

Wayworn Lovers by Gun Brooke. Will agoraphobic composer Giselle Bonnaire and Tierney Edwards, a wandering soul who can't remain in one place for long, trust in the passionate love destiny hands them? (978-1-62639-995-2)

Breakthrough by Kris Bryant. Falling for a sexy ranger is one thing, but is the possibility of love worth giving up the career Kennedy Wells has always dreamed of? (978-1-63555-179-2)

Certain Requirements by Elinor Zimmerman. Phoenix has always kept her love of kinky submission strictly behind the bedroom door and inside the bounds of romantic relationships, until she meets Kris Andersen. (978-1-63555-195-2)

Dark Euphoria by Ronica Black. When a high-profile case drops in Detective Maria Diaz's lap, she forges ahead only to discover this case, and her main suspect, aren't like any other. (978-1-63555-141-9)

Fore Play by Julie Cannon. Executive Leigh Marshall falls hard for Peyton Broader, her golf pro…and an ex-con. Will she risk sabotaging her career for love? (978-1-63555-102-0)

Love Came Calling by CA Popovich. Can a romantic looking for a long-term, committed relationship and a jaded cynic too busy for love conquer life's struggles and find their way to what matters most? (978-1-63555-205-8)

Outside the Law by Carsen Taite. Former sweethearts Tanner Cohen and Sydney Braswell must work together on a federal task force to see justice served, but will they choose to embrace their second chance at love? (978-1-63555-039-9)

The Princess Deception by Nell Stark. When journalist Missy Duke realizes Prince Sebastian is really his twin sister Viola in disguise, she plays along, but when sparks flare between them, will the double deception doom their fairy-tale romance? (978-1-62639-979-2)

The Smell of Rain by Cameron MacElvee. Reyha Arslan, a wise and elegant woman with a tragic past, shows Chrys that there's still beauty to embrace and reason to hope despite the world's cruelty. (978-1-63555-166-2)

The Talebearer by Sheri Lewis Wohl. Liz's visions show her the faces of the lost and the killers who took their lives. As one by one, the murdered are found, a stranger works to stop Liz before the serial killer is brought to justice. (978-1-635550-126-6)

White Wings Weeping by Lesley Davis. The world is full of discord and hatred, but how much of it is just human nature when an evil with sinister intent is invading people's hearts? (978-1-63555-191-4)

A Call Away by KC Richardson. Can a businesswoman from a big city find the answers she's looking for, and possibly love, on a small-town farm? (978-1-63555-025-2)

Berlin Hungers by Justine Saracen. Can the love between an RAF woman and the wife of a Luftwaffe pilot, former enemies, survive in besieged Berlin during the aftermath of World War II? (978-1-63555-116-7)

Blend by Georgia Beers. Lindsay and Piper are like night and day. Working together won't be easy, but not falling in love might prove the hardest job of all. (978-1-63555-189-1)

Hunger for You by Jenny Frame. Principe of an ancient vampire clan Byron Debrek must save her one true love from falling into the hands of her enemies and into the middle of a vampire war. (978-1-63555-168-6)

Mercy by Michelle Larkin. FBI Special Agent Mercy Parker and psychic ex-profiler Piper Vasey learn to love again as they race to stop a man with supernatural gifts who's bent on annihilating humankind. (978-1-63555-202-7)

Pride and Porters by Charlotte Greene. Will pride and prejudice prevent these modern-day lovers from living happily ever after? (978-1-63555-158-7)

Rocks and Stars by Sam Ledel. Kyle's struggle to own who she is and what she really wants may end up landing her on the bench and without the woman of her dreams. (978-1-63555-156-3)

The Boss of Her: Office Romance Novellas by Julie Cannon, Aurora Rey, and M. Ullrich. Going to work never felt so good. Three office romance novellas from talented writers Julie Cannon, Aurora Rey, and M. Ullrich. (978-1-63555-145-7)

The Deep End by Ellie Hart. When family ties become entangled in murder and deception, it's time to find a way out... (978-1-63555-288-1)

A Country Girl's Heart by Dena Blake. When Kat Jackson gets a second chance at love, following her heart will prove the hardest decision of all. (978-1-63555-134-1)

Dangerous Waters by Radclyffe. Life, death, and war on the home front. Two women join forces against a powerful opponent, nature itself. (978-1-63555-233-1)

Fury's Death by Brey Willows. When all we hold sacred fails, who will be there to save us? (978-1-63555-063-4)

It's Not a Date by Heather Blackmore. Kade's desire to keep things with Jen on a professional level is in Jen's best interest. Yet what's in Kade's best interest...is Jen. (978-1-63555-149-5)

Killer Winter by Kay Bigelow. Just when she thought things could get no worse, homicide Lieutenant Leah Samuels learns the woman she loves has betrayed her in devastating ways. (978-1-63555-177-8)

Score by MJ Williamz. Will an addiction to pain pills destroy Ronda's chance with the woman she loves or will she come out on top and score a happily ever after? (978-1-62639-807-8)

Spring's Wake by Aurora Rey. When wanderer Willa Lange falls for Provincetown B&B owner Nora Calhoun, will past hurts and a fifteen-year age gap keep them from finding love? (978-1-63555-035-1)

The Northwoods by Jane Hoppen. When Evelyn Bauer, disguised as her dead husband, George, travels to a Northwoods logging camp to work, she and the camp cook Sarah Bell forge a friendship fraught with both tenderness and turmoil. (978-1-63555-143-3)

Truth or Dare by C. Spencer. For a group of six lesbian friends, life changes course after one long snow-filled weekend. (978-1-63555-148-8)

A Heart to Call Home by Jeannie Levig. When Jessie Weldon returns to her hometown after thirty years, can she and her childhood crush Dakota Scott heal the tragic past that links them? (978-1-63555-059-7)

Children of the Healer by Barbara Ann Wright. Life becomes desperate for ex-soldier Cordelia Ross when the indigenous aliens of her planet are drawn into a civil war and old enemies linger in the shadows. Book Three of the Godfall Series. (978-1-63555-031-3)

Hearts Like Hers by Melissa Brayden. Coffee shop owner Autumn Primm is ready to cut loose and live a little, but is the baggage that comes with out-of-towner Kate Carpenter too heavy for anything long term? (978-1-63555-014-6)

Love at Cooper's Creek by Missouri Vaun. Shaw Daily flees corporate life to find solace in the rural Blue Ridge Mountains, but escapism eludes her when her attentions are captured by small town beauty Kate Elkins. (978-1-62639-960-0)

Somewhere Over Lorain Road by Bud Gundy. Over forty years after murder allegations shattered the Esker family, can Don Esker find the true killer and clear his dying father's name? (978-1-63555-124-2)

Twice in a Lifetime by PJ Trebelhorn. Detective Callie Burke can't deny the growing attraction to her late friend's widow, Taylor Fletcher, who also happens to own the bar where Callie's sister works. (978-1-63555-033-7)

Undiscovered Affinity by Jane Hardee. Will a no strings attached affair be enough to break Olivia's control and convince Cardic that love does exist? (978-1-63555-061-0)